Mitch and the Governor

by Kathleen Willett

Chapter 1

"Here's to the best place on earth!" Marge stated without argument. As toasts go, it wasn't exactly Hemingwayesque. But then again, Marge wasn't Hemingway. Everyone in the room raised their glass to toast Marge. She had planned the biggest celebration yet to unveil the grand reopening of The Lucky U, with a little help from Mitch and Trish, of course.

"To the best place on earth," most repeated after her. Mitch just stood and watched. It was a sight to see and share, but there was no one beside her, which put a damper on the occasion.

It had been quite a couple of months, not only for Marge, Mitch and Trish, but also the state of Colorado in general. The citizens of Colorado were getting used to, if not altogether comfortable with, the idea that their newly elected governor, Rebecca Louise Fairbanks, had come out of the closet. Not in a small way. Not even in a medium way. But rather, in a grand way. In a "let's all get on some national news show and talk it to death" way. Add to that the idea that the governor had fallen deeply in love with one of the richest lesbians in the entire state, Mitch Tanner, and you had the makings of a six-month news-a-thon about their lives.

Mitch just sort of shrugged off the entire deal. Here she was, celebrating with her friends at their favorite hangout, The Lucky U. It started out as a small, intimate lesbian bar, and was now on the verge of transforming into a landmark in its own right. And there were really only two things to take credit for the occasion. One was the gambling fever that had caught Colorado in its wake. Lottery winners may come and go, but Mitch had won a major jackpot and through what she could only fathom as financial sorcery, her money manager had doubled her wealth almost instantly. The second, and perhaps more sinister reason was a sniveling little swindler named Lisa. In exchange for Mitch borrowing Marge's family ranch in Texas for a little chicanery to fool Lisa, Mitch had agreed to pay for the refurbishing of the Lucky U. So it was rather a combination of good and bad luck that had led to the moment. Mitch just wished that Rebecca had been there to witness the fun.

Being governor had both its perks and demands. Rebecca couldn't always be at every little grand opening celebration. Mitch had understood. Mitch's best quality was her deep understanding of human nature. The governor's handlers had had their hands full as it was, trying their best to smooth over the ongoing controversy surrounding the lesbian governor's activities. Going to a lesbian bar wasn't high on their list of must-do events. Dinner out was a major event, and it was during one of their recent dinners out that Mitch had been shot. She was recovering. Somewhat. Her thigh wound had healed. Her elbow was another matter. But she didn't want to talk about that today and instead went over to Trish after the toasting was complete to catch up on the latest.

Trish and Mitch had been friends for life, it seemed. Trish had been wealthy long before Mitch tried her hand at it, but it never seemed to matter who had money. Trish taught Mitch to dance. Mitch taught Trish to make margaritas. It was a friendship like no other. So now that Trish hadn't said a word about what was going on between herself and Judy, Mitch cornered Trish in a quiet booth and began the third degree.

"Where's Judy?"
"In Aspen."
"How is she?"
"Still mourning the loss of Lisa."
Mitch nodded. Lisa, the sniveling swindler had supposedly taken Judy for a cool two million dollars. What Lisa didn't know was that it was really Mitch's cool two million she had stolen. Added to that was Mitch's first bundle of money, a modest few thousand dollars that was the sum and total of Mitch's entire life savings, that Lisa had taken in a previous scheme before Mitch had won the lottery. It was all pretty complicated indeed. The upshot of the whole deal was that Judy, who had been totally enamored with Lisa, was still in love with her long after the grand theft larceny. Mitch understood this all too well, due

to that previously-mentioned deep understanding of people, and her own stubborn crush on Lisa.

"She'll get over Lisa."

"Look how long it took you."

Mitch nodded. Mitch knew that she would still be head over heels for the swindler if it hadn't been for Rebecca. In many ways, Rebecca saved Mitch from herself, from her overly romanticized, idealistic view of people. And all Rebecca had really done to make this miraculous transformation occur was stand still for the deep and abiding love that Mitch felt for her. Stand still was a relative term. Lie still might have been more apt. But then again, Rebecca wasn't so very good at lying still either. What a woman, what a sex partner, what a wonderfully creative, inventive. . .

"Hey, are you still in there, or did the aliens abduct your brain?" Trish brought Mitch back to the moment.

"Huh?"

"You're thinking about the governor, aren't you?" Trish wagged her finger. "You could tell?"

"You had that silly, stupid grin on your face again. Where is she anyway?"

"Her public relations people wouldn't let her come out and play today."

"Well of course not. They think you're common lesbian trash."

"And what do you think, Trish."

"Hell, Honey, I *know* you're common lesbian trash."

They both laughed. It was better than taking all too seriously the quandary that being lesbian had placed Rebecca squarely in the middle of. Gone were the days when she would be invited to a school or a church. Gone were the invitations to women and parent organizations. Gone were the days, also apparently, where she could go and enjoy a day with her partner in the most notable lesbian bar in west Denver.

"We were talking about Judy," reminded Mitch.

"She's in Aspen."

"She wouldn't come down?"

3

"It's like she's stuck in a feedback loop. She can't go anywhere or do anything without being reminded of Lisa, and she won't even try to get away."

"I think she's trying to reclaim her territory from Lisa. It can be tough. It's like, well, like going into a bar after you've stopped drinking. It takes a while, but you feel like you have to conquer the old familiar places again."

"She stayed in bed for a week after Lisa took off. Wouldn't even accept much food, let alone a hug."

Mitch remembered. They had left Judy in Trish's loving care and after a week, the novelty had worn off. Trish had tried to help Judy heal, but it just wasn't working. Trish normally had the patience of Job, but even with no Lisa in the middle of things to distract Judy, Trish had run out of ideas. She finally left Judy to sulk in private. Trish had resumed her real estate business, and sales were great. It kept her going. That, and the Lucky U crowd. A beautiful young woman came over to the booth, wondering if Trish wanted to dance.

"Go for it," Mitch intoned quietly.

"I think I will." If the sweet thing didn't know how to dance, she couldn't have been in better hands.

Marge came over and sat in the seat freshly vacated by Trish.

"How you feeling, gimpy?" Marge asked, not unkindly. It was Marge's way, tackle the problem head on.

"Gimpy is when you can't walk," Mitch answered.

"So? You were gimpy for a while."

"Now what am I?" Mitch asked, knowing that Marge was just doing her usual checkup on the elbow. It was a mangled mess, in case anyone really wanted to know. The nut case had shot it up good, and now, even though Mitch was going through therapy, it was still obvious that she would never, as she told the press, play the violin again.

"You're the best friend an old bartender could ever ask for," Marge stated out of the blue.

For a moment, Mitch didn't know how to respond. Marge took advantage of the two-second delay. "The place looks good." Marge was referring to the renovations, paid for by Mitch. The Lucky

U looked a whole lot better than just good. It was like one of those TV reality shows had descended on the place and transformed it from a dingy bar and lunchroom into a fashionable and trendy hot spot on the west side of town. This took some doing. When they had first started talking about the idea of redoing the place, items like new flooring and booths and bathrooms and swag lamps had all been mentioned. And that was within the first two minutes of observation. It was, in reality, an entire reclamation project. They would've probably saved money by tearing the whole place down and starting all over again, but Mitch honestly didn't think that Marge could survive that kind of trauma. When they stripped off the tile flooring, it was apparent that the wood floor underneath had been damaged by termites. Customers hadn't been the only ones feasting at The Lucky U. Then there was the matter of the walls being damaged by years of wear and tear. The wiring was out of compliance and there were no fire walls to speak of, and not the kind you have on computers. It was a good thing that there had been no true emergencies in the kitchen. The whole place would've gone up in smoke in a matter of minutes.

So, after doing hundreds of thousands of dollar worth of basic repairs, only then did Marge begin to get enthused about the possibilities of redecorating her place of business. For a while, her enthusiasm had been tempered by the fact that she was spending Mitch's money. It took some doing to convince Marge that the sky was the limit. Almost. It made sense to all concerned that good quality booths be installed, but Mitch drew the line at gold-plated toilet seats. When the redesign was complete, the U had a brand new, high tech bar. It was easy to clean and efficient to work behind. All glassware was cleaned and sterilized in the kitchen. No more dishpan treatment behind the bar. All ice was protected from stray shards of broken glass by covered coolers and the beer coolers were now waist high so that whoever was filling orders could do so with minimal bending and lifting. Even the flooring had been replaced with leg-friendly materials. Every improvement was done in the spirit of making the restaurant easier for Marge to operate. The effect was not lost on her, but she was always shy about expressing her true gratitude. Still, she had come over to sit with Mitch when there were so many other things she could be doing.

"You're alone. Where's your woman?"

"My woman," Mitch used her best Texas drawl, "is prolly in a meetin."

"Well, she should keep better track of you. Somebody better tell her straight out that you're still one of the best lookin, richest lesbians this side of Denver and if she ain't careful, you'll be snatched out from under her like there's no tellin." "That would be quite a feat."

"Why? You on top most nights?"

"You're feeling kinda frisky since you've been on that new medication, aren't you?"

Mitch wasn't the only one who had been back and forth to the doctor's offices a few times. Marge had gone in for a long overdue checkup since their last Texas adventure, and seemed to be feeling as fit as the proverbial fiddle.

"I think it's the estrogen. I'm feelin ten years younger."

"Pretty soon, you'll be feeling like a twenty-one year old."

"You go find a twenty-one year old. Let me know how she feels." With that, the reigning comedian of the U left Mitch alone. Mitch had a better idea. She'd go and try to find her forty-five year old and see how she felt. Mitch kissed Trish goodbye right in the middle of the dance floor and took off for the governor's mansion. She had finally gotten a chance to move in formally. The occasion was marked not by any big wing ding party, but rather just a stunningly terrific night of sex. Then again, what sex with Rebecca wasn't stunningly terrific? Before Mitch and Rebecca had made things official, but soon after they began their affair, person or persons unknown had vandalized, ransacked and torched the mansion. Rebecca and Mitch had spent time in Mitch's five room shack, her home in the woods as she called it. A survivalist would have thought it just about the right size, but Mitch and Rebecca had spent many fulfilling minutes there. But convenient it wasn't. Soon after repairs were complete, they were back at the mansion. The press, local, national and international, had grown weary of photographing her entrances and exits, and now Mitch went in the front door without making the ten o'clock news. Ta da!

"Honey, I'm home."

"She's unavailable," the guard replied.

The staff and security hated Mitch. They made no bones about it. She had corrupted their fair-haired girl, their great conservative hope for the future.

"Tell her I'm up in bed."

"Tell her yourself."

"Okay."

Mitch went to the room that Rebecca claimed for her office space. As usual, she was deep in reading. Being governor required many hours of study and rumination.

"Hey, gorgeous."

"Hey yourself. You're home early."

"I couldn't stay away from you."

"I know. Isn't it great."

What Rebecca lacked in experience, she more than made up for in ego and enthusiasm. Once Rebecca discovered that she was lesbian, it was as if she was determined to be the best lesbian on the planet. It wasn't exactly a burden for Mitch to bear, but she had been missing out on sleep. "Everybody says hi."

"Hi, back."

"They all wonder when you're coming by for a visit."

"Soon."

"You gonna read all night?"

"You got a better idea?" "Oh, sweetie! I'm full of ideas."

Rebecca laughed, a sound that still shook Mitch clear to her bones. "I'm black and blue, you know."

"Was I that rough last night?" Rebecca looked a little concerned. "No, I just keep pinching myself to see if this is a dream. You, me, us."

"Come here."

"You come here."

Rebecca stood up and stretched. "I could use a break."

"You're lucky break is here."

They went arm in arm upstairs, to the consternation of the staff.

Chapter 2

Mitch was opening the Lucky U just like how Marge had showed her. Since the grand-reopening party celebrating the refurbishing of the U, business had started to pick up. Always known as a versatile restaurant during the daylight hours, it became even more so now. Although it was still gay in nature, the crowd during the day had become more stratified. It wasn't unusual to find mothers with babies in strollers lunching alongside gay guys. Even straight dinner customers were comfortable in the place, although they were still outnumbered by the lesbian crowd that had made their home here for years. For a while, Mitch had figured that people were there just to see her. Not that her ego had gone over the edge, but she knew that she was a "curiosity." People came to see the woman who slept with the governor. There were two sides to this story, and Mitch saw both. Lesbians and gay guys came to see who had managed to "recruit" the right winged politician. Recruit was such a strange word, one that Mitch had rallied against for years. But, like the word "gay", it had survived through its metamorphosis and was now stuck somewhere in the lexicon that catalogues all slang. Gay didn't necessarily mean happy anymore, and recruit wasn't something limited to the armed services. Once in a while, straight customers came to gawk at that "awful lesbian" who had literally destroyed the career of the best governor in the nation. They couldn't fathom the fact that things were mutual. Perhaps Mitch had ruined Rebecca's political career, but Rebecca had ruined Mitch's anonymity. How many other people get gawked at just for who they're sleeping with? Mitch finally just capitulated to the situation and served everyone equally, and when things got too intense behind the bar, she hid out in the kitchen.

And speaking of the kitchen, Mitch had begged, cajoled, pleaded, and finally convinced Marge to hire some chef help. Compromises were forged in the deal so that now, not only could you get a good greasy cheeseburger, but also a meal of nutritional value. Until all the bumps were worked out, Mitch was working two full days in each twentyfour hour stretch. It was worth it since this allowed Marge to take it a little easy. Although she had tried to keep up her good spirits, her medical work-up had revealed a couple of potentially serious problems, which she wasn't prone to discuss in detail. It was okay for her to butt into Mitch's life, but the door didn't always swing both ways. Hence, Mitch came to the rescue on days when Marge needed to rest and relax.

The day started out with great promise. All the kitchen staff was present and healthy. Food was delivered, from produce to pie. Floors were mopped and glossed to a high shine. God was in her heaven and Mitch was behind the bar, taking inventory. Mitch had filled the beer coolers to the max, rotating stock to keep everything fresh, and was checking the hard liquor inventory when she heard the back door open and close. With all the personnel accounted for except Marge, Mitch was only mildly curious about the early morning visitor. She didn't even look up until the caller was perched on a bar stool.

"Sorry, we're not open yet," Mitch intoned the usual greeting.

"It's a bit early for me as well," she replied, now turning to face Mitch.

The bottle of scotch that Mitch was holding slipped from her grasp. Even with the baseball hat, shorter hair and drab T-shirt, Mitch still recognized the woman. The eyes, the lips, the voice. They sent an unstoppable shiver through Mitch as she felt scotch dribble onto her shoe.

"Lisa?"

"You recognize me! How flattering. I tried to come incognito."

"It's really you?"

"Well, it's not my twin sister!"

"You have a twin sister?"

"No, silly! God, Mitch, you can be so dense sometimes. Give me a glass of wine."

In spite of the early hour, Mitch complied, as if she still, even after all that had happened between them, couldn't refuse this woman any request.

"Join me?"

"No thanks. I have a business to run."

Mitch inhaled. Twice. Then, she tried to busy herself with other tasks. She picked up the bottle of scotch that had leaked all over her shoe and put it back on the shelf. Her mind was going off like firecrackers, asking a dozen mental questions. Her hands worked at other things. Her mind still crackled with confusion.

"Aren't you going to ask me why I'm here?"

"Why would I?"

"Because you still care."

"No, I don't."

"Then why did you just make a pot of coffee without putting any coffee in the basket?"

Mitch watched the clear water draining out of the basket.

"I'm making hot water for tea."

"You don't have any tea out here."

"Damn you, Lisa, why did you come back!" Mitch snapped, suddenly tired of the banter.

"I thought you'd never ask. I brought you something!" With that announcement, Lisa plopped a big bag on the bar.

"What's that?"

"Open it and see for yourself."

Against her better judgment, Mitch opened the bag and peered in. Bundles of hundred dollar bills met her cursory glance. "What's this?" Mitch acted dumb.

"It's your two million dollars. Actually, it's not quite two million. That's what I'm here to talk about."

"What two million dollars?" Mitch was still going for the Oscar.

"Oh, please. I had the scam figured out from the minute Trish, the real estate agent turned lawyer showed up on Judy's doorstep!" This brought Mitch's actions to a complete halt. Damn! She looked at the clock. It was a little after nine.

"Take this bag of cash and go sit over there in that booth."

"What are you going to do?"

"I'm going to make some real coffee. I'll be over in a minute." "Got something for breakfast? I'm starved."

"Gee, let me check," Mitch had tried to sound sarcastic. It didn't come out sounding that way. It came out sounding more like, "Your wish is my command," just like the good ole days.

Mitch reset the coffee and then went to the kitchen. Everyone was busy with their own routine and virtually ignored Mitch as she reheated leftover quiche and warmed some homemade yeast rolls.

Taking all of this and some apricot jam out on a tray, she set a place for both of them as Lisa drained her wine glass.

"Coffee, now?"

"Sure, thanks."

Lisa dove into the food without waiting for Mitch to return with cream and sugar. Mitch allowed the gorgeous urchin to eat without interrogation. She did so, hungrily.

"This is beginning to feel like my last meal before the execution."

"You seemed hungry," Mitch said as she picked at one of the rolls.

"I'm on a budget." "Denver on two million?"

"I wanted to bring back as much of your money as I could manage. I've been on a bus for three days."

"You're been traveling on a bus for three days with two million dollars?"

"Yeah."

"How did you sleep?"

"Not very well, and it isn't the full two million. I already told you that. You need to start taking something for your memory. Maybe some gingko."

"You've been gone for a couple of months. I just assumed that a lot of the two million is missing."

"Not as much as you might think. I came across your note quickly."

"My note?"

"You don't think for one minute that I thought it was Judy's note, did you? The woman doesn't have a poetic bone in her body!" "Why don't you just start from the beginning and tell me the whole story," Mitch asked. It sounded like more of a challenge and the tone wasn't lost on Lisa.

"Start from the very beginning where I took your first forty thousand?"

Any other woman would have tossed Lisa out after a comment like that. Mitch just corrected her, "$42,851.32."

"Yeah, that," Lisa nodded and then drank her coffee down. "You want some more coffee?" Mitch couldn't help it. She wondered if she would always be this hopeless.

"Sure. You got any pie?"

"Cherry."

"Yum. My favorite. You have vanilla ice cream, too?"

"You want it ala mode?"

"And warm if it isn't too much trouble."

"No trouble at all." Still no sarcasm.

Mitch disappeared into the kitchen and returned in a couple of minutes with heaven on a plate. Warm, gooey cherry pie dribbling with melting ice cream.

"Just start from where you recognized Trish."

"Oh, sure, when Trish showed up, I knew I had seen her somewhere before. Took me about ten minutes to come up with her real identity. She was a friend of yours."

"Still is. But that alone wouldn't tip you off. Trish could've very easily gotten a law degree."

"Yeah, she's one smart woman. That's why I had to call the bluff. Texas was so great! I'm going back there one of these days."

"You went along with the sting on purpose?"

"Sure. Marge was a great pretend widow. And that dead Uncle Clyde stuff was a hoot!"

"You knew I'd won the lottery."

"I watch the news. I keep track of this stuff. I know I look and act the dumb blond part, but I'm smart."

"I realize that."

"How did you talk the governor into driving you and Trish and Judy around Aspen?"

"You didn't miss a trick."

"And tell the governor's daughter to keep her day job because she sucks big time as a domestic."

"Are you about finished?"

"I want to know how the governor is in bed, how your elbow is and what's it like to be rich?"

"Fine, fine and fine," Mitch snapped the answers out, cutting each off to fend for themselves. "Oh, so serious. So angry."

"Not angry. Just tired. Tired of playing games with you. Why don't you please just take your bag of money and leave and never come back."

"No can do. Remember? Your note?"

"My note."

"You told me to find something more important than money. So that's what I'm going to do. My first step is to return this money, and to find a way to repay my other debt to you. They call it retribution or something like that on the talk shows. Like, if you've been an alcoholic or something."

"All the money? You're going to return all the money? The two million plus the other thousands?"

"All of it. The two million plus that $ 42,851.32 you keep jabbering about. I figured I'd come and work for you until I repaid everything. If I work here at the Lucky U for tips, sleep in a shelter, and cut back on sweets, I could pay you back in four or five years."

"You want to work here?"

"Minimum wage too. Wouldn't want to break any labor laws."

"The shelter won't take you. There are too many mothers with children on the list as it is."

"I'll sleep here. Isn't there an office or storeroom?"

"So all you want is minimum wage, tips, room and board?"

"I'll buy all my meals from you, full price."

"What's the catch?"

"No catch. You've finally convinced me that redemption is more important than anything. I need to make right the wrongs I've done to you."

"You're serious?"

"I'll start by cleaning the bathrooms."

"I did that."

"Okay, I'll scrub the floor."

"I did that."

"Tell me what you need."

"I need to restock the liquor."

"I'll help."

"Before you do anything, follow me."

Mitch gathered up the bag of cash and without even bothering to count it, took it into the office with Lisa in tow. She put the bag in a locked file drawer and gave the key to Lisa.

"What are you doing?"

"Anytime you change your mind, get fed up with our arrangement, take the money and leave town. Just don't ever show back up again. You understand?"

"I understand."

"So don't just stand there. Get to work."

"Yes, Ma'am."

They worked side by side the rest of the morning. Lisa began her career as a bar rat by cleaning up her own dishes, carting cases of liquor out for Mitch to count and picking up trash in the parking lot. She was given the lowly designation of waitstaff-in-training during the lunch hour and meekly followed the experts around. She bussed tables, restocked the bar with clean glasses and mopped up spilled beer until Mitch found her pale and shaking on a stepstool in the kitchen around about three o'clock in the afternoon. "You okay?" Mitch asked with a proper if reserved amount of compassion.

"Just needed a breather."

"Come on."

"What? Where?"

"To the doctor."

Mitch checked out with Marge, who was present if not too perky. Mitch steered Lisa to her Subaru and loaded her in the passenger seat. As she warmed the car, she phoned her doctor, who told her to bring Lisa by the office. After helping Lisa into the office and settling her on one of the examination tables, Mitch went out and started up the paperwork. She knew some of the vital information. Birth date. It brought back a feeling of heartbreak. There had been a birthday celebration. It had been very special. Age? Too young to be so larcenous. Mitch didn't know the insurance information and wasn't in the mood to continue anyway. Mitch would pay for this in cash, as usual.

The doctor came out after an hour and sat next to Mitch. "Sorry it took so long. I had to fit her in between appointments. She'll be okay. A few nagging health problems here and there. Nothing a better diet, a round of antibiotics, some vitamins and rest won't cure."

"How much rest?"

"A couple of days. She's been drinking too much, and not eating right. If her blood work shows anything else, we'll get in touch." Not eating right for Lisa was usually one skipped meal, Mitch mused to herself. Out loud, she said, "Thanks. I'll get her prescription filled. Anything else I can do?"

"Fresh fruit and home cooking."

Lisa came out about five minutes later, looking a little better. Resting for a while had improved her color and she was steadier on her feet even though she was a pint low on blood.

"Let's go."

"Back to work?" she said with a lot less enthusiasm than her morning attitude.

"No." Mitch sounded a lot more cross than she actually was.

Mitch stopped long enough to get the medication, a quick few minutes, and then drove Lisa to her home in the woods. It wasn't the Ritz. It would have to do. Although the refrigerator was woefully short on fresh produce, the place had a great bed. Mitch guided Lisa to it and told her to undress. She gave her a spare pair of pajamas and as Lisa was getting more comfortable, Mitch called and ordered pizza and salad for four from her favorite pizza outlet. Forty minutes later, Lisa was once again filling up on her favorite foods while Mitch looked on.

"Got a beer?"

"No more booze. Doctor's orders. Here, stuff one of these antibiotics down with your next mouthful of pizza."

"It would go down better with a beer."

"No! I'll make some orange juice." Mitch remembered the stock of juice in the freezer.

"Any more pepperoni?"

"Eat the veggie pizza first. And finish your salad."

"Okay. But next time, please don't order pineapple. Yuck."

"When you finish your dinner, go to sleep. I'll check up on you tomorrow."

"Where are you going?" she sounded truly disappointed.

"Somebody's got to go back to work."

As Mitch was halfway out the door, she thought she heard Lisa say "Thanks."

She left, not even knowing how to answer. The third degree was waiting for her when she got back to the U, in the form of Marge.

"Who's that new employee?"

"Just a kid who needs a job."

"A kid named Lisa?"

"Can't get much past you."

"You're still trying?"

"Not really. Lisa showed up with most of the money. She wants to work off her debt. I thought I'd humor her." "She's back to try to get the other 20-plus million."

"Yeah, but what she doesn't know is that I've put all of my money in a blind trust. I can't even find out where my money is anymore." Marge nodded. Since Mitch had begun living with Rebecca, she had put her request in the hands of her financial advisor to place her investments where they would be embarrassment free to Rebecca's political career. Many people involved in politics did so to avoid conflict of interest. Besides, coming back to the moment, Mitch didn't honestly believe that Lisa had one more swindle in her. As far as Mitch was concerned, money was the least of her problems with Lisa. Nope, the real problems had names like Judy and Trish and Rebecca. Rebecca! Oh Damn!

"Marge, I promised Rebecca that I'd have dinner with her." "I thought you had. You smell like pepperoni. I caught the first whiff of you ten, maybe fifteen feet away."

"Got any mouthwash?" Mitch asked, realizing that the two bites she had managed to cram down would follow her around for the rest of the evening.

"In the office."

Mitch rinsed and took off, promising Marge to be back to close up for the night. She drove across town to the governor's mansion. Lady luck was on Mitch's side for once and she scooted in just under the dinner bell. Any later and the staff got prissy, like they needed an excuse where Mitch was concerned.

"Hello, Dear," Rebecca offered a cheek to kiss. The staff couldn't stomach much else.

"Hi, Honey. Am I in time for dinner?"

It all sounded so like Ozzie and Harriett. Nelson. Sheesh.

"Yes, Sweetie. What's that smell?"

"What smell?"

"Is pizza the special at the U?"

"We had some on hand. I was heating some up for Marge."

"You have to go back tonight?"

"I promised to close."

"Darn, I don't have any meetings tonight."

"That works out. I'm all yours from six to midnight."

"I thought you were mine forever."

"I am," Mitch smiled, "just on a tight schedule."

"It doesn't need to be that way. You don't need to work." "And you don't need to be governor," Mitch answered abruptly. Where was this tone of voice when Lisa asked for breakfast, cherry pie ala mode, and pepperoni pizza with a beer chaser? Mitch wondered to herself.

"Good point. Except you're the millionaire. I'd still have to work at something."

"My millions aren't enough for you?" Mitch asked, trying hard to swallow the sarcasm that was coming out way too late for the benefit of Lisa.

"There's nothing formal about that and you know it." Mitch had wondered when they were going to get around to this conversation. Their affair had been precipitous, the planning had lagged behind. Sometimes considerably.

"Do you want something formal?" Mitch asked in a now-reassuringly neutral tone, relieved to hear the softer tone in her voice. Rebecca didn't answer. Obviously she hadn't planned for this discussion at this precise moment. Mitch waited patiently for a response.

"I haven't thought it through."

"Are you really hungry?"

"Not really."

"Then let's go upstairs and talk some more. Naked. In bed."

"Sounds like a great idea."

Mitch collected a chilled bottle of wine and a couple of glasses while Rebecca got a head start. The governor took time for a shower to refresh after a long day of meetings. Mitch was well into her second glass of wine by the time Rebecca stretched out beside her in an emerald green silk robe. It offset the blush that managed to crop up at the most unexpected times.

"You're having a bad day, aren't you?" Rebecca queried, noting the nearly half empty bottle of wine.

"I've had better."

"Did I make it worse?"

"I'm going to call Dan tomorrow." Dan was Mitch's genius financial advisor.

"Don't do anything rash."

"It's time Rebecca." Mitch pulled the glowingly beautiful woman toward her. "It's time I made things more formal. I'm going to have Dan transfer half of my money to you."

"I'm not sure that's wise."

"I'm sure it is. I owe you that much since I've practically ruined your political career."

"I'm still in office, and besides, I was thinking more along the lines of the wisdom of that significant of a financial transaction."

"You're the best damn governor this state could hope for and they can just allow you to be wealthy." "You really need to go back in tonight?"

"I promised Marge."

"I have a great idea. Let's make love, eat dinner and then I'll go in and hang out while you close up. I've been wanting to talk to Marge anyway. Check up on her health."

"Oh, gosh," Mitch was thinking fast. If Marge blabbed about Lisa, there would be a lot of explaining to do. "I don't know?" "You don't want me to go in?" Rebecca asked. Probed would have been a better description. Mitch wished she had thought more about the predicament. Should she tell the whole story about Lisa's return? For all she knew, Lisa would change her mind, gather up the bag of cash and, poof, be gone before any explanation would be needed.

"You're angry about the remark I made about your working?" Rebecca began to guess at the reason behind Mitch's frown.

"No. I'm okay with that. Sometimes I wonder why I work myself. Maybe Marge would close for me tonight, after all."

"Is there something you don't want me to know about? Some secret at the U?"

"I've been trying to get you to come in for a month!" Mitch retorted, still stalling for time. It was hard for her to debate and think at the same time.

"You're dying?" Rebecca started up with ridiculous guesses, apparently to lighten the mood. It wasn't working. Who kids around about death anyway? "Everyone's dying, Rebecca."

"You're sick?"

"You want to go to the U? Let's go."

"Is there any pizza left."

Mitch exhaled slowly. There was just no way out of this tangled web.

"There never was any pizza at the U. Congratulations, you caught me in a lie."

"You're lying? About pizza?" Rebecca sounded truly puzzled.

"Yeah."

"Are you sure you're not sick?"

"Is honesty always the best policy in any relationship?"

"Yes."

"Okay then, here's the truth. Lisa is back."

"Lisa, as in your old girlfriend the swindler?"

"Right. She's back."

"Back how?"

"She showed up at the U bright and early this morning."

"What did you do? Call the police?"

"No. I cooked breakfast for her, perked coffee, twice. Don't ask. Gave her a job."

"Are you out of your mind?"

Rebecca pulled away from Mitch. This didn't bode well for the lovemaking plans that had been laid, so to speak.

"Then, she nearly passed out in the kitchen so I took her to the doctor, bought her a pepperoni pizza and put her to bed in my house in the woods."

19

Rebecca seemed to be trying to formulate a lengthy response. The only thing that came out was, "Screw you!" The door slamming happened in the blink of an eye and Mitch found herself alone in bed with a chilly bottle of wine.

"That went better than I expected," Mitch breathed and then got up and showered for work. She stopped in to check out with hurricane Rebecca, who had blown back into her office to bury her feelings in her work.

"I absolutely respect your anger in this matter. I'm the scum of the earth," Mitch said from the doorway.

"Go to hell!"

"I'm heading there now. I'll be home about three. If you want to drop by, well, whatever. Oh, hey, I forgot to mention that Lisa brought back most of the two million, so that's like, another million for you."

No response. That was good. Rebecca was running out of invectives. She probably didn't know many more, having been raised in a holy household. Of course, as a child, Mitch had never even heard the words damn and hell until her parents took her to church. Oh well. Things would be okay, like maybe in time for the next ice age.

Mitch didn't realize how truly upset she was about Rebecca's reaction until Marge noted for the record her reticence. There hadn't been the usual friendly badinage that often marked their late night hours at the U, and even the customers were noticing the quietude. All two of them. Marge was more than ready to shoo Mitch out the door when Rebecca strolled in.

"You take her," Marge pointed. "I'll handle the two in the booth."

It sounded like dialogue from High Noon.

Mitch poured two snifters of brandy and went over to what was now referred to as "Mitch's booth." It didn't actually have her name on it, the booth that is. But everyone knew, especially Rebecca. They had met when Rebecca came in unannounced months ago to warn Mitch to stay away from her daughter, Mary. Suffice it to say, there was only one Fairbanks woman that Mitch had been interested in, and it wasn't the daughter.

"Is brandy okay?" Mitch asked.

"What flavor?"

"Apricot."

"Sure. That's fine. Thanks."

Mitch looked at Rebecca and smiled. No, grinned was more like it.

"What?" Rebecca asked, pointedly.

"I was just thinking that it isn't every day that the woman whom I adore tells me to go to hell."

"I didn't mean anything I said."

"I know."

"I'm sorry."

"Oh, don't go apologizing. God knows I deserved it."

"No, you didn't. I just have this new blind spot where old girlfriends are concerned." "She's not so old."

"That's part of the problem, I guess."

"I see. You have a problem with the fact that she's young and blond and nubile and-"

"That's about the size of it, yes," Rebecca interrupted, giving the distinct impression that one more word about Lisa would be an unfortunate choice.

"You want another?" Mitch pointed to Rebecca's empty glass. The brandy had gone down like fruit punch.

"Nope. I want to take you home and make love to you." This relatively new side of Rebecca made Mitch blush. "Finally!" Rebecca said triumphantly. "You blushed."

"So!"

"You've been making me blush since day one! Finally, I get you back."

"If you'd told me the first time we met that you wanted to make love to me, I would've blushed then, too." "Too bad I didn't think of it sooner."

"All I had to say to you to get you to blush back then was how beautiful your eyes were. And still are, for that matter."

"Let's go home."

Mitch followed Rebecca back to the mansion and they made love like a couple of sex-starved teenagers. Rebecca, who had been experimenting with her sexual assertiveness, was in a rough and tumble mood. Of course, she was never really rough, just dang blasted in a hurry some days, and the tumble part only encompassed about as much tumbling as the usual forty-five year old could manage. But then again, Rebecca had kept herself in shape. Mitch was breathing heavily after the exertion. "Are you sure you've had enough orgasms?"

"I'll try again in an hour."

Mitch laughed and then turned serious. "I love it how you don't treat me like an invalid." "Because of your elbow?"

"Yeah."

"Will it ever be straight?"

"Probably not, but then again, neither will I."

"How could I ever treat you like an invalid when you don't think of yourself as one?"

"I'm not, really. One bad elbow hardly qualifies for invalid status." Rebecca stroked Mitch's damaged arm lovingly.

"What are you, if you're not an invalid?"

"I'm the lucky person who's in love with the most beautiful governor in the world." "The universe."

"Huh?"

"The most beautiful governor in the universe."

"I stand corrected!"

"And don't forget it."

"I'll have it tattooed on my butt on my next day off."

"That should be about 2013."

"Sounds about right."

"What time do you have to go in tomorrow?"

"What time do *you* have to go in tomorrow?"

"I asked first."

"I knew I heard it somewhere."

"What time?" Rebecca pushed for an answer.

"Maybe nine?"

"My first meeting is at ten."

"Nine forty-five, then."

"I love you."

"I love you back."

"I want to sleep in your arms, and make love in the morning."

"Snuggle up and sleep fast."

Mitch was up and out by nine-thirty after Rebecca got stuck on a phone call. When was the last time *you* tried to French kiss a governor who was talking long distance to a fellow governor. Okay, it was a tough question. Mitch thought about it all the way to her house, which made her want to turn around and go back, but it was time for work on both their parts. Mitch had planned to simply peek in on a sleeping Lisa and instead was nearly bowled over by her as she came full speed out of the bedroom. She was clean, fluffy and fully dressed.

"I'm ready for work!"

"I don't *think* so."

"Sure I am. I showered and shaved. *You* need new razor blades. My legs aren't going to be the same for *days*!"

"You need some clothes that fit. Where is your stuff, anyway?"

"My stuff?"

"Your luggage, your clothes?"

"I sold it all at a second hand store. I needed the cash to bring back to you."

"And so all you have now are the filthy things you had on your back yesterday and anything you helped yourself to in my closet?" "I borrowed a T-shirt. Big whoop. My jeans aren't too bad, yet. Are they? I smelled them and they smell okay to me."

"You're going to stay home and rest anyway, so it really doesn't matter."

"I'm going to work. I feel fine. I'm rested and ready for breakfast. The doctor did say I should eat more fruit. Got any more of that cherry pie at the bar?" This stymied Mitch. She hadn't thought about breakfast for her guest. Her young, energetic, smiling indentured servant.

"Come on, then," Mitch grumbled. The "damn it" she added on was silent.

They climbed into Mitch's car and got to work in time to grab a quick bite between chores. Between leaving early the night before and sleeping in today, Mitch was behind before she even got started. Vegetarian lasagna was the special of the day and Mitch made sure Lisa ate two helpings during her break. Things were going along beautifully until the lunch crowd brought Trish for company. Mitch

23

heard the trouble before she saw the action and by the time she got out of the kitchen, Marge was standing between Trish and Lisa, each poised to defend themselves.

"What the hell is she doing here!" Trish demanded loudly.

"Sit down and I'll explain everything."

"Get her out of my sight!"

Mitch pulled Lisa from the bar to the kitchen and handed her the key to her car. "Go somewhere."

"Grocery shopping?"

"Sure."

"I don't have any money."

Mitch felt the muscles in her neck tighten. If she wasn't careful, she was going to have a migraine by the end of the day. She pulled out her wallet and handed two twenties to Lisa.

"This isn't going to be enough. When was the last time you went to the grocery store anyway. The prices are nuts and besides, razor blades aren't cheap."

Mitch held up a ten. "That's fifty total. Make it do, for now."

"Okay. When should I come back?"

"Go back to my house when you get done shopping."

"How will you get home?"

"I'll improvise."

"I'll need the house key."

Mitch handed her the whole damn key ring. Just the thought of this tightened her neck even more.

Trish had observed all of this from the booth she was still shaking in when Mitch sat down to explain. She waited for everyone else to return to their own business before launching into a preemptive statement. "It's a long story." "What the hell is going on!" Recounting the same story twice in twenty-four hours didn't seem to make the task any easier. It would neither abridge nor lengthen much, but it still had the same stunning effect.

"She brought back the money my ass!" Trish huffed.

"You want to see it?" Mitch countered, calmly but firmly, ready to honor the dare.

"No. I'm just glad that Judy's still in Aspen."

"Me, too, I think."

"Are you going to tell Rebecca?" Trish asked.

"I already did."

"What happened?"

The question confounded Mitch. So many things had happened. Foul language. Doors slamming. Utter silence. Soul searching. Great sex.

"Was she okay with it?" Trish inquired, noticing the long silence that had ensued.

"Eventually," Mitch nodded.

"How eventually?"

"About five hours eventually."

"Five hours isn't too bad."

"I guess not. I mean, it could have been five days, or five weeks."

"Which is probably the length of time it will take Lisa to get fed up and leave. I can't believe you're still leaving the money within her grasp."

"The two million offer still stands. You should hope she'll run. It will keep her out of your way."

"With Judy? There's no problem there. Judy won't even leave Aspen, let alone wander down here."

"I wouldn't be too sure."

"Why?"

"Because either Judy or her twin sister just walked through the front door."

"This is no time to start kidding around," Trish admonished as Judy walked up to the booth. She had spotted Mitch soon after coming in, and made the logical inference that wherever Mitch was, Trish couldn't be far behind. When Trish looked up, the only thing she could think of to say was, "Oh, my god."

"Hello, Trish. Hi, Mitch."

"Hi, Judy, welcome to the Lucky U," Mitch said as she rose. It took Judy's attention away from the gawking Trish, who repeated, "Omigod," again and turned a ghastly shade of white. Good thing she was in a bar. If she was in a hospital, she'd be wearing a toe tag by now. Mitch realized the magnitude of the problem and blathered on and on to Judy about things inconsequential until Trish could get a little steadier. Mitch steered Judy into her seat at the booth, admonished Trish to drink up and then set forth to refill Trish's drink and fetch one for Judy as well. Good wine, and plenty of it would warm Trish's clammy complexion. Then she announced that vegetable lasagna was not only the special of the day but was on the house as well and that the official taste tester of the place had given it two thumbs up. Mitch had been thinking about Lisa when she said it, and when Judy asked who the taste tester was, Mitch only paused a second or two before declaring herself as the guilty party.

"It's great, you'll like it."

"I trust your judgment."

"At least one person does," Mitch sighed and then left them alone to pursue their next topic of conversation. Other people needed Mitch's attention, two waitstaff had called in sick and they were short on help. She placed the order for Trish and Judy and then bussed tables and refilled water glasses with new-found ease and grace. When Mitch was putting herself through school, she had waited tables for extra money. Now, she did it for lack of anything better to do. She kept telling herself she was helping out Marge, but it was turning into more of a hobby than anything else. And hobbies, just like anything else, got better with practice. When she got a minute to herself, she checked back in with Marge, who was holding court behind the bar.

"You mean to tell me that we went through alla that trouble in Texas just so those two could sit there and look like two lumps on a log?"

"Bumps," Mitch said.

"Bumps?"

"Two bumps on a log."

"Not lumps?"

"You're thinking about two lumps of sugar in tea."

"I hate tea."

"Never mind. Forget I said it."

"You're as grumpy as they are. Grumpy *is* the right word, ain't it?"

"You come up with one more 'umpy' word and you got yourself a poem."

"But it'd probbly be obscene."

"Not if it was baseball season."

"Yeah, then it'd be just plain boring."

Marge always preferred football to baseball, but still agreed to let Mitch buy enough satellite equipment to show all sorts of sports. Their more athletic lesbian customers enjoyed the coverage and bought enough wine coolers to offset the investment. Of course, they still had to watch talk shows and the cooking channel from time to time. It all depended on who had control of the remote.

"So?" Marge interrupted Mitch's reverie.

"So, what?"

"So maybe I should go over there and talk some sense into the two of them?"

"Whatever you do, don't mention that Lisa has returned. Okay?"

"Sure, no problem."

Marge had a magic about her that could brighten the darkest day. Years of soothing the troubles of literally thousands of customers made her an expert at diplomacy. She had them laughing and cajoling within minutes, and Mitch breathed a sigh of relief. At least they were talking again. Marge left them to their own devices after about five minutes.

"So, how are things in Aspen," Trish asked Judy. Again. She had forgotten the answer.

"Oh, Aspeny, I guess," Judy answered. Again.

"Is the ski season winding down?"

"Not a lot, yet. The shops and slopes are still pretty crowded, but I managed to get out and about anyway."

"I'm glad."

"I know you've been worried about me," Judy ventured into uncomfortable but necessary territory. "At least, I guess I hope so. Not that I meant to worry you."

"I understand what you mean. I was concerned, but I knew you were going through a process. A painful process. A very, very painful process."

"It wasn't all that painful. It was more a case of just coming to grips with my anger and shock. Lisa really had me fooled."

"She had us all fooled," Trish had to agree, even more now with her newly-acquired knowledge.

"So, I thought it was time to come out of my cocoon and track you down."

"I'm glad. You sure didn't have to look very far. I'm either at home, at work or here."

"I came here first. This place is famous."

"More like infamous, I'd say."

"So, it's really true that Mitch and the governor are an item?"

"Absolutely."

"I tell you, when I got in the car that morning, and the governor was behind the wheel, I couldn't believe it."

"Yeah, imagine Mitch letting anyone else drive," Trish teased. Judy had the courtesy to laugh. Mitch showed up to check on dessert orders and questions.

"What's so funny over here, and do you need more wine or is it time for cheesecake and coffee?"

"We were laughing at you," Trish confessed.

"Me?" Mitch replied, not knowing quite whether to be flattered or offended.

"We were chuckling over the driving arrangements the day that Lisa took off."

"You mean, our fearless governor."

"Right."

Mitch checked their wine supply. There wasn't much left. These two would've laughed listening to each other read the residential section of the phone book. It was a welcome change from the earlier awkwardness. Now, however, it was Mitch's solemn duty as a bartender/manager to sober them up. More food and some strong coffee would do the trick, and after she filled the order, she left them to chat some more.

"How long are you staying in town?" Trish ventured the question. "I reserved a room for a couple of nights."

"I have a spare bed at my place," Trish offered. "You're more than welcome."

"I appreciate the hospitality, but I think I'll keep my room."

A second or two of silence engulfed them.

"I'm still working things out," Judy explained.

"I know. It's okay. I just wanted to spare you the expense."

"Thanks. I'm not broke, though. Remember, it was Mitch's two million, not mine."

"I remember it well," Trish nodded, trying to formulate a plan to keep Lisa and Judy apart for two entire days. "So, where are you staying?" Trish asked with a lilt in her voice, trying to sound unconcerned but friendly.

"Somewhere downtown. A real honest-to-goodness hotel with room service. The Brownstone."

"Right in the middle of the city?" Trish declared it in the form of a question.

"I needed a change. I live the quite country life all the time. I thought a little hustle and bustle would do me good." "It's close to my office. You should come for a tour."

"That sounds lovely."

By the time they had indulged in or sobered up on, depending on how you looked at it, double helpings of cheesecake, they had the entire next day planned. Trish could relax now. One day planned, just one more day to worry about. What could possibly go wrong?

After the coast was clear, which was Marge's way of saying that after Trish and Judy were gone, she wanted to have a short serious conversation with Mitch. In the office. It was either time to reassure the creditors that the checks were in the mail, or pay the employees. Mitch had gotten used to these meetings, and was slowly but surely learning the ins and outs of the business.

"I want you to do something."

"Okay, what."

"You take Lisa out and get her something nice and classy to wear." "She does need some new clothes," Mitch agreed. "She needs to look like a classy bartender." "A bartender?" Mitch asked.

"Yeah."

"But she's a dishwasher."

"She's a bartender now. Dress her like one."

"She got a promotion."

"You think workin behind the bar is a promotion?"

"I guess not, but what's with the change?"

"Don't you see it? Of course you don't. You're still too busy doin it." "Doing what?" Mitch furrowed her brow.

"You, and everybody else, is watching every move she makes. She's like a magnet. People can't keep their eyes offa her. She'd be great for business as a bartender. Pick something classy. I don't want her hiney or boobs bouncing around. I just want her to look nice and neat and…."

"Classy."

"That's the word I'm lookin for."

"And when should I do this?"

"Take tomorrow off."

"Okay."

"You look like I just fired you. What's with the unhappy face?"

"I'm not unhappy. I just need to figure out how to explain this at home."

"You have to explain everything at home?"

"Just little things like why I'm taking my old girlfriend classy clothes shopping. Why don't you take her out?"

"I'm too old."

"No, you're not."

"I'm too old for this."

"You're too old to go out and buy a white shirt and a pair of black slacks."

"Take the money outa the register."

"I'll bring back the receipts."

"I want her ready to tend bar tomorrow, by four."

"What if she can't mix drinks?"

"I'll teach her everything I know, just like how I'm teachin you the business side of the business."

"Is there anything you want to tell me, Marge?" Mitch asked suddenly but subtly.

"If you buy her a vest, make it shimmery."

"Shimmery?"

"The clerk will know."

Mitch nodded sagely. Marge hadn't been shopping in a while or she would know that clerks nowadays not only didn't know much but were impossible to find except around the Christmas season. The new idea in retailing was that the customer wanted to be left alone to make decisions. If Mitch wanted to be left alone, she'd go to the Grand Canyon and ride a mule down to the bottom. When she shopped, she enjoyed help. She admitted she needed it. She was shopping challenged, deemed so by Trish, and practically knighted with the title.

"Okay, I'll do this for you, but you owe me, Marge."

"Yeah, I know."

Mitch arranged to go home via taxi and was relieved to see her car in the dirt driveway. At least Lisa hadn't gone on a joyride to Vegas. Probably didn't have enough gas, or cash for that matter. Mitch found herself scrounging through her own pockets for cab fare and managed to count out a decent tip. So what if it was in quarters. They spent. The cab driver scowled. Apparently, he didn't know Mitch from Adam and assumed he had just dispatched Ma Kettle to the Kettle Farm. His tires kicked up dirt and gravel as he shot out of sight. Mitch girded herself for her next meeting with Lisa. Every encounter seemed to require an iron stomach.

Lisa was humming quietly to herself as she stirred something on the stove. It smelled heavenly and brought Mitch to the sudden realization that she hadn't eaten since breakfast.

"Oh, hi there. I cooked. Is that okay?"

"Why wouldn't it be?"

"Maybe because I haven't done anything right yet?" Lisa answered back so tartly that a lemon would have suffered from an inferiority complex by comparison.

"You can cut the 'oh poor me' attitude."

"It isn't an attitude. It's a fact."

"If it's a fact, it's a well-deserved fact."

"What's that supposed to mean!"

Lisa stopped stirring in order to engage more fully into the argument. Maybe she had stopped stirring the dinner, but Mitch's stomach was doing pirouettes. God, she hated this.

"It means," Mitch said as she picked up her key ring from the kitchen table, "that you can't expect sudden forgiveness. Particularly when you crush people's hopes and dreams."

"I brought the money back."

"That doesn't even begin to undo the damage. What part of that don't you understand yet?" "I don't know what else to do."

"We have to go shopping tomorrow."

"I already got razor blades."

"We're going clothes shopping for you."

Maybe it was just Mitch's imagination, but Lisa seemed to brighten up considerably. She tried and failed to keep the sheer glee out of her voice as she quizzed, "Clothes shopping will help me make up for my wrongdoing?"

"No. But it will give me back my wardrobe," Mitch countered.

"You want me to start now?"

"Shopping?"

"No. I meant, do you want me to start giving you back your wardrobe? Like, right now?"

It took only a split second for it to dawn on Mitch that Lisa could still take off a T-shirt with the same smoldering sensuality that used to drive Mitch to the brink of passion. Before Lisa could even say another word, Mitch was on her way out the door.

"Aren't you going to stay and have something to eat?" Lisa called out from the doorway.

"Sorry. Gotta go. Tomorrow. Shopping." Mitch said as she left without looking back.

One down, one to go. Mitch felt her stomach loosen up a bit but her temples were beginning to pound. All the way to the mansion, she kept hearing over and over in her head, "stay and have something to eat" and the phrase stuck in a place in her heart that hurt just from the words.

"Damn her," Mitch muttered as she went in through the back door of the mansion and checked out the offerings in the kitchen. She remembered that Rebecca was in a meeting, so she grabbed a quick bite of a casserole that was in the oven and, after grimacing and taking a couple of swigs of ginger ale, retreated to the bedroom with a box of crackers. Rebecca found her deep into a mystery book when she wandered up about eight that evening.

"What are you doing here?"

"I'm eating crackers and fending off nausea. How was your day?"

"Better than yours, no doubt. Do you have the flu? You can't possibly be pregnant."

"I'm not pregnant and I'm pretty sure I don't have the flu either. What did the staff cook for dinner? It was awful."

"The staff didn't cook dinner."

Mitch said a mental "oh-oh" to herself. She prayed that Rebecca hadn't cooked the casserole. There's nothing like criticizing the cook to get you in big trouble.

"Really," Mitch said, trying to sound casual.

"Nobody cooked anything."

"Something was in the oven."

"I bet the staff was making something for the dogs."

"We don't own any dogs."

"I know, but one of the staff does. I gave her permission to take any leftovers she wanted and feed her pets."

"And she cooks it first?" Mitch grimaced as her stomach gave another twist. It wasn't the food so much anymore as the thought.

"I have no idea. Do you want to go to the doctor?"

"No, I just want another dose of ginger ale."

"I'm sorry I didn't warn you first. Maybe you better take tomorrow off."

Another twist of the stomach reminded Mitch about her plans for tomorrow.

"Do me a favor," Mitch asked Rebecca.

"Sure."

"Tell me about your day, and then I have something to tell you." "And I have to go first because why?" Rebecca couldn't keep the suspicion out of her voice.

"It would be easier. Maybe my nausea will subside by then."

"Okay," Rebecca agreed as she laid down next to Mitch. "I had a great meeting with the person in charge of the Advocates for the Homeless in Colorado."

"Well, it's nice to know someone in the establishment is still speaking to you."

"They are not only interested in speaking to me, but also working on the homeless situation with me, and we also talked about feeding people at Thanksgiving and Christmas."

"So early? It's only spring."

"I know, but these things take a lot of time to coordinate. Besides, we do have homeless all year round."

"Yes, we do," Mitch agreed. She had made sure that Rebecca personally bore witness to the plight of the downtrodden when she first took office. Now, however, Mitch could sense something coming. Something about the way she spoke told Mitch that there was a favor lurking somewhere in this innocent story. A big favor. Mitch just allowed Rebecca to continue. She would get around to asking sooner or later. Thankfully for Mitch's stomach, it was sooner.

"Anyway, these Thanksgiving and Christmas events are really huge efforts. But they are so important to so many people. We're talking about a lot of people."

"Why don't you let me ask Marge to lend the Lucky U as one of the participating restaurants?" Mitch asked innocently enough. "You knew I was going to flatter you until you said yes, didn't you?"

"Marge hasn't said 'yes', but she will. I'll help her financially with it."

"You could have made me squirm about asking you."

"I wouldn't do that to you." "I love you."

"I know, but you'll probably feel differently when I give you my daily news summary."

"More about Lisa?"

"Yeah. Marge promoted her."

"From what to what?"

"From restroom attendant to bartender."

"Remind me not to come in for a drink for about a year."

"That's not all the bad news."

"There's more?"

"Isn't there always more? Anyway, Marge wants me to take Lisa out tomorrow and buy her something decent to wear."

"And?"

"Isn't that bad enough?"

"That's not so bad. If what you said is true, she needed something besides your T-shirt to wear."

Mitch nodded, reminded of Lisa's offer to undress right then and there. She shivered.

"Are you sure you don't have the flu? You want me to take your temperature?"

"No. I just wanted you to be warned just in case the media follows me around, and puts the shopping spree on the five o'clock news."

"You'd think they'd have better things to do."

"Oh, I don't know. You know my fashion sense. It'll probably be pretty comical. Some ambitious soul could write it down and send it to Hollywood. Sit-coms are big this year. Shopping Disasters of the Rich and Famous coming to your television screen this fall!" Mitch waved her hands like she was Cecil B. DeMille.

"Is that all the bad news?"

"Judy showed up, but that isn't necessarily bad news."

"Judy from Aspen?"

It sounded like a royal title. It might be a royal something else before the week was over.

"Yeah, right there. First, of course, Trish and Lisa squared off at the U. That I could've sold ring side seats for."

"Okay, first Trish ran into Lisa."

"Right, I was in the kitchen, Lisa was in the bar restocking glasses and Trish came through the front door. Good thing Marge was there to step between them, or we would've had about an inch and a half on the police blotter report."

"And then Judy showed up and saw Lisa?" Rebecca asked.

"Oh no, thank goodness. I sent Lisa out for razor blades before that."

"Do you think that was smart?"

"What?"

"Sending Lisa out for razor blades?"

"I sent her shopping. The razor blades were her idea. I guess mine were all dull. My razor blades, not my ideas."

"Just how much of that dog food did you eat?" Rebecca asked, holding back what could easily become an infectious giggle.

"I saved you some," Mitch replied dryly.

"Thanks anyway. So, Lisa is out buying razor blades and?" "Judy shows up. Trish about faints dead away. And now I need to keep Judy and Lisa away from each other until Judy goes home."

"So, you're taking Lisa shopping."

"I guess."

"Why doesn't Trish just tell Judy?"

"That was my suggestion. I told her how well you took the news about Lisa showing back up."

Rebecca looked over to see if Mitch was smirking or smiling angelically. It was neither actually. Just a serious, no maybe just pensive look. Or maybe she was going to heave up dog food. It was a long look. Mitch noticed the passing of time.

"What are you looking at?"

"I haven't made up my mind, yet."

"What are the choices?"

"A liar or a damned liar," Rebecca vacillated.

"I told her it took you about five hours to forgive me. I personally think that's pretty good. Don't you?"

Rebecca didn't know how she always ended up agreeing with Mitch about these things. It confounded her. No wonder she couldn't stay angry long. Who could with such a reasonable person by their side?

"I want to ask you something."

"Uh-oh," Mitch said out loud. Inadvertently.

"What do you mean, 'uh-oh'?" Rebecca said defensively.

"Whenever you want to know about 'something,' it's usually about sex." "It is not."

"Is too."

"Is not!"

"Okay, what 'something' do you want to know about tonight?"

Rebecca rearranged herself huffily. A sign that Mitch, once again, was correct. Sort of.

"I just wanted to know why you like talking more than you like sex?"

Mitch could tell right away that this had the potential to be dangerous territory. A slippery slope to just slide right on by. Unfortunately, Rebecca was still waiting for an answer.

"I told you it was about sex."

"Not in the technical sense that you were expecting, just a simple philosophical discussion." Yeah, right, Mitch thought to herself.

"I like sex, with you," Mitch said with what conviction she could muster without sounding defensive.

"I know you like sex," Rebecca said, as if her follow up sentence was going to be, "Who wouldn't like sex with me."

"I love our sex life," Mitch went further, why she didn't know.

"Of course you do," Rebecca was agreeable. "But you really like talking, too."

"Talking to you is the highlight of my day."

"Not the sex?"

Mitch could feel that dog food lurching around in her stomach. There had to be a right answer somewhere here. Maybe if she took time out to toss up what she hadn't digested of the dog food, she could think more clearly. The stall might help as well.

"I don't mean to start an argument," Rebecca clarified. "I just wanted to talk about this."

"Imagine you wanting to talk," Mitch teased, and then glanced to see if she was in more or less trouble than before. It looked like less, and her stomach sort of rumbled to a safer place as well.

"I guess I'm not used to this," Rebecca explained.

"Used to what?"

"Talking, the way we talk."

One of the first things that had been disclosed early in their budding relationship was that Rebecca's marriage had been a little less than fulfilling in the sexual department. Actually, a lot less than fulfilling, if anyone was keeping score. That usually happened when gay people were married to straight people. It only followed logically that the conversation part of her marriage was also lacking. People who go day to day in a disintegrating marriage not only stop making love in bed, but they also usually stop talking in bed. Sometimes, they stop talking at all, except to discuss the most urgent of issues, like the house being on fire, for instance. Mitch had discovered that, soon after she and Rebecca had started their romantic relationship, the sex part had come back to Rebecca pretty quickly. What had taken time to regenerate was the communication that had also been lacking in her love life. So, slowly but surely, Mitch had worked on that aspect as well, sometimes stalling as long as possible in the lovemaking part of

37

their evenings just to hear about Rebecca's meetings or speeches or other official business. Apparently, her efforts had not gone unnoticed. Finesse wasn't always Mitch's strong suit. She couldn't be sure it was even in her deck most days.

"I just wanted you to know that I appreciate the effort," Rebecca smiled.

"It isn't an effort, really. I enjoy hearing about your day."

"You're bored out of your gourd most nights, don't kid a kidder."

"Honestly, your stories are getting more interesting."

"I try to pick one or two good ones."

"I appreciate the effort."

"So, now that I know that talking is very important to you, I want to know what's wrong." "Wrong?"

"Something's wrong."

"It is?"

"Something's bothering you."

"It's been a strange day."

"Is that all?"

"Yeah, I think so," Mitch answered as honestly as she could. She knew something was bothering her as well. She just couldn't put her finger on it. "Can I ask you something else, then?" Rebecca ventured forth again.

"This is going to be the technical question, isn't it."

"How do you always know exactly what I want?"

"Sex-wise?" Mitch asked for clarification more as a stalling tactic than anything.

"Uh-huh. How do you know?"

"Because you let me know," Mitch answered.

"I do?"

"Yes."

"How do I do that?"

"Well, we talk about stuff. Remember."

"We don't talk about everything."

"We don't?" Mitch thought back. She remembered the night they first made love, when she had made a crucial promise to Rebecca. They could talk about anything, anytime. No reservations, no hesitations.

Rebecca hadn't had the freedom as a child to ask such questions of her parents. And as an adult, she hadn't fostered the skill with her exhusband. Now, it was time.

"If I tell you how I know what you want when you want it, you'll know all my secrets. Then, there won't be any mystery."

"But I don't always do what you want."

"You don't?"

"No, I don't, and that's what I want to be able to do."

"I thought you did, do it, I think," Mitch stammered on, not able to quite get a handle on the conversation.

"I always have an orgasm, and you don't always," Rebecca explained it. Bluntly.

"I don't?"

"You don't."

"Are you sure?"

"Are you teasing me? You know how upset I get when you tease me about this stuff. You told me you'd talk about anything."

"You're right. I just really, truly haven't been keeping track of this, whatever."

"Not having an orgasm is a 'whatever' to you?"

"It's a non issue with me."

"Fine."

If the conversation had ended any more abruptly, the silence would have missed its cue. Mitch could've sworn she heard the screeching of tires. Okay, time to start over.

"Can we start over with this conversation," Mitch asked, calmly.

"Fine."

"How many orgasms have I missed?"

"A few."

"Less than five, more than five?"

"I feel like I'm on the stand."

"Less or more?"

"Less."

"Okay, so we've made love about thirty dozen times in two months. That doesn't seem like a bad percentage to me."

"Look," Rebecca turned to face Mitch, "I just don't want to be doing something or not doing something that I should be doing, or not doing. Does that make sense?"

"It makes perfect sense."

"You bring me to a climax every time."

"I've had more practice."

Mitch hadn't even breathed out the last word before the true direction of the conversation became crystal clear. How stupid could she be. Lisa had wanted to know about Rebecca. She had even gone to the extent of asking point blank how she was in bed. It was only natural that Rebecca would want to know about Lisa. In this way. Rebecca just had a lot more finesse, or sneakiness, depending on how you weigh these things.

"I guess so," Rebecca said innocently. What an actress! Why did she even bother with small potato stuff like politics when she could rule Hollywood.

"Why didn't you just ask me how sex with Lisa was?"

"Why would I want to know that?"

More angelic innocence. Mitch laughed out loud.

"You think this is funny?"

"Lisa wanted to know the same thing about you."

"So?"

"So! You and Lisa are on the same mental wavelength. I think this is pretty interesting. Why don't the two of you just sit down and talk about it? Someday. When I'm not around. Like at my funeral."

"What was she like in bed?"

Mitch stroked Rebecca's face. Mitch had forgotten one of the most important rules of discussions. Don't tell someone to ask a question if you don't have the answer ready. Mitch inhaled. At least the dog food was settling in for the night.

"When I met Lisa," Mitch started the story, as Rebecca cuddled in like it was The Three Bears, "I was a virgin."

"A real virgin?"

"A real, real virgin."

"Okay."

"And Lisa was, well, she was young and who wouldn't want to be with her. You know, deep down, Lisa is an okay person." Mitch looked over at Rebecca to see if this was going over like the proverbial lead balloon. She was listening. Intently.

"I mean, it's like, you know about those kind of people who are very moral and the upstanding pillars of their community, yet they're as mean as a snake if you cross them. Well, maybe Lisa isn't the most moral crayon in the box, but she's nice. She doesn't have a mean bone in her body. Is this making sense?"

"Yes."

"And in bed, she was just that way. Nice and patient. Never an unkind word. And believe me, she could have very easily criticized my lovemaking technique, which was pretty clumsy and novice. But, she had a gossamer touch. You want me to slow down so you can take notes?"

"Just shut up and talk."

"I really don't know what else to say?"

"Did you ever miss an orgasm, with her?"

"How do you expect me to know the answer to that? I wasn't even paying attention a month ago, let alone two years ago." "I see."

"But I'm sure I frustrated her beyond belief for the first month or so, which is something you have never done to me. I have zero complaints about our sex life."

"Zero?"

"Zero."

"You're not going to tell me how you always know what I want, are you?" Rebecca finally circled back around to her original question. "I told you, you let me know what you need and want."

"You must be doing the same for me, but I keep missing the clues."

"Don't worry about it. I read the last page. The butler did it."

"One of these days, I'm going to make you tell me your secret."

"I look forward to the duress."

Chapter 3

Mitch noted for the record that Lisa had borrowed something really nice from her closet to wear for their shopping spree. She had left so abruptly the day before that only now did Mitch notice how clean and fresh the house was. Mitch thought back to their days together while Lisa put the finishing touches on her makeup. Why was there always such an emphasis on sex when there is so much more involved in any relationship? Mitch mused the question to herself. Was their place so squeaky clean back then? Lisa had never been lazy, that was a fact. She cooked, she cleaned, in fact, she was a real neat freak now that Mitch took time to think it over. She was neat and clean about everything. Mitch closed her eyes to clear her mind, but it wasn't working, at least not in the way she'd hoped. A dozen visions teased her mind, memories of Lisa, neat and clean and ready for anything. So clean, and fresh, and ready. So very, very ready.

"I'm ready," Lisa's voice called Mitch back to reality. Her eyes jerked open.

"Okay."

"Were you asleep?"

"No, just deep in thought."

"Well, it must have been a really, really nice thought. You had a big smile on your face."

"I did not."

"How would you know, your eyes were closed."

"I was thinking about shopping."

"Since when have you enjoyed shopping?"

"Can we just go," Mitch snapped irritably,

"I'm ready when you are."

Mitch made a mental note to avoid the use of the word 'ready' for as long as possible. Ten or twenty years ought to do it. They rode in blessed quietude to the mall. Lisa, to her credit, knew when to remain silent. She also smelled wonderful. Mitch hadn't demanded an accounting or receipt to explain where the money had been spent yesterday. Obviously, she had purchased razor blades. Her legs were shaved and well represented by the skirt she borrowed. Mitch only owned one skirt to wear to banquets and funerals, functions not all that different in scope except for the dead body. Perfume had also been purchased. Obviously. It was driving Mitch to distraction. How Lisa got something that smelled so good on her with less than fifty dollars was the real mystery.

The mall was almost empty when they arrived and Mitch decided to begin the day with a coffee break. They stood in line for five minutes to buy a regular drip for Mitch and a mocha for Lisa. Lisa could still stand some extra calories. She looked a little gaunt under the bright glare of mall lighting. They found a table that didn't wobble, no easy feat, and sat facing each other. Mitch sat for a full minute and then couldn't help but ask. "What's that perfume?"
"What perfume?"
Mitch couldn't tell if Lisa was fishing or full scale trolling for compliments. Why should today be any different. Mitch could have said, "You smell nice." Instead, she said, "I thought I smelled perfume. Maybe you bought some at the grocery store?"
"At the *grocery* store! You're kidding, right?" "So, what smells?" Mitch resisted being drawn into a guessing game. "You always had a way with a compliment. I guess maybe it's the shampoo?"
"Hmm," Mitch replied. "What brand?"
"That brand where years ago the woman is using it in the TV commercial and it's like she's having an orgasm."
"What?"
"That TV commercial! You've never seen it?"
"I work."
"You have a TV."
"That doesn't mean I have time to watch it."
"You work hard. I know that."
"You're going to be doing it by four this afternoon."
"What? Having an orgasm?"
"No, working behind the bar."
"I am?"
"Marge didn't tell you?"
"Nope."
"That's why we're out here buying something decent for you to wear. I'm supposed to have you outfitted and ready to tend bar by four."

"But, I don't know anything about mixing drinks."

"This wasn't my idea."

"But you didn't fight it, obviously."

"It's Marge's bar."

Lisa had slowly sipped her mocha until it had cooled enough to drink. She did so in a few long draws and bussed the table from habit."

"I'm ready to shop."

Mitch's stomach jumped at the word "ready." There had to be another word.

"I'm supposed to get you something classy, yet conservative."

"Maybe Rebecca should've come with us. She is one classy dresser." Mitch only nodded.

"She's classy through and through, isn't she?"

"She sure is."

Mitch felt like déjà vu was making a habit of visiting every day. Now, Lisa was asking questions about Rebecca in a not-too-obvious manner. What could be more natural, Mitch pondered. Former lovers wanting the skinny on current lovers was a hobby in some circles. How easy it would've been to be cruel. Mitch weighed the temptation. Could she resist telling Lisa how superior Rebecca was, how much better in bed? Could she lie and get away with it? Probably not. Lisa had x-ray vision in these matters. Mitch stood for a second, considering her options and then said, "Let's look around."

They walked methodically through several shops, studying styles and materials. Several times Lisa held up blouses and slacks, only to see Mitch shake her head.

"Too expensive?" Lisa asked.

"Not classy enough."

It was already eleven and with still no purchases to their credit (quite literally), they clamored back into the car and were heading downtown. Once, several months back, Trish had been looking for a certain style of clothing and stumbled upon a group of shops in Downtown Denver. Navigating the traffic like an expert, Mitch surrendered the car to a valet and escorted Lisa into the first shop. It was perfect. They immediately found several items that passed the classy test. Lisa preferred blue and black silk, but Mitch insisted on crisp white tuxedo style shirts. The neck wear could be whimsical as opposed to staid, and Mitch stopped short of complimenting Lisa's selections of geometrically-patterned ties. Within half an hour, the staff of the shop had outfitted Lisa for an entire week of work. Mitch requested that one outfit be pressed so that Lisa could wear it that day. It was in a garment bag before Mitch could count her change. It hadn't been cheap, but whatever Marge wanted, Marge got. They rescued the Subaru from the valet and were loaded and ready well ahead of schedule. Lisa had become quiet. Even too quiet for Mitch.

"You okay?"

"Just a little nervous."

"You! Nervous!"

"What if I spill something?"

"You will, I promise. You just clean it up."

"But on the clothes. What if they get all stained?"

"I guess you'll go topless."

"This isn't funny!"

Mitch studied Lisa as they waited at a red light. She looked pale and upset. The honking of horns alerted Mitch that the light had turned green.

"Let's have some lunch."

"Lunch?"

"Yeah, that's the meal you sneak in between breakfast and dinner."

"Sure, okay."

Mitch didn't even have to think twice. One of her favorite places was about four blocks away. It had a touristy feel about it, but it served some of the best mud pie this side of the Mississippi. And it, too, had valet parking. A smart investment on a cool day. They were asked if they wanted to put their name on a long waiting list and after General Grant showed up, they were seated. Immediately. Mitch didn't have time for such foolishness.

When the menu arrived, Lisa studied it like she was going to take a final exam on the contents. She must have been starving.

"What looks good?" Mitch ventured into conversation.

"Besides me in silk?" Lisa responded, a little less pale.

"Besides you in silk," Mitch replied, glad to see that one thing hadn't changed over the years. Food and Lisa went together well. How she kept her figure was anyone's guess and the envy of many. Mitch remembered vaguely one way she burned calories. As the memory grew sharper, it snapped Mitch painfully out of the reverie.

"The salads look good."

"You need more than a salad!"

"Did you, like, go to college to get that mother hen degree, or is it something you can get in correspondence school?"

"Mother hen school," Mitch nodded, "I like that one. Gosh, too bad the Lucky U doesn't need a stand-up comic."

"Well, they have you, don't they."

Mitch knew better than to trade further snide remarks with Lisa. She could never keep up before. Why try now.

"I suggest a salad, some chicken, a side of rice pilaf, and mud pie for dessert." "Who's buying?"

"Who else."

"What are you having?"

"A salad."

"Big or little?"

"Chicken oriental salad."

"With honey mustard dressing."

"On the side."

"Why don't you just live dangerously and have them drizzle it all over."

Mitch was beginning to understand why Marge wanted this woman behind the bar. She could read War and Peace backwards and make it sound sensual without even half trying. They placed their orders and talked about mixed drinks until Lisa was tired of taking notes.

"There's a lot to learn," Mitch chided when Lisa's attention wandered.

"So, Marge will be there to help me out."

"It's still good to have an inkling of what you're doing."

"I'm all inkled out."

"Fine."

Salads arrived to rescue them from more quibbling. Lisa launched into her shrimp salad while Mitch spooned dressing sparingly over the

46

teriyaki chicken hiding under her greens. She had just picked up her fork to start when she noticed a familiar face coming directly at her. Oh, Dear Lord, it was Judy and Trish, and there wasn't time to duck. What were the chances of this happening? Other than the fact that both Trish and Mitch shared a mutual affinity for mud pie. "Long time, no see," Judy started right in on Lisa, not bothering to hide her anger from anyone in the restaurant. Lisa remained silent. Lucky for her. Mitch spoke up, "It's not what you think." "And *you*," Judy turned her wrath Mitch's direction. "How *dare* you make a fool out of me!"

Mitch was just barely able to voice one syllable of a rather good reply when Judy picked up Mitch's salad plate and dumped it down the front of her. The honey mustard dressing was now drizzling all right. Right between her breasts. The sensation was somewhere between gummy and sticky and Mitch squished when she breathed. The remaining salad resided on her lap and the floor. Thankfully, no one else was in the line of fire and although everyone was prepared to take cover, Judy turned on her heel and walked toward the door. Trish looked shocked and stood paralyzed with indecision.

"Obviously, you didn't tell her," Mitch put it all together in a few short seconds.

"No."

"Go after her."

"Are you going to be okay?"

"Sure. Go."

Trish left the salad fiasco to go sort things out with Judy. Now, Mitch was glad she had told Rebecca about the reappearance of Lisa when she did. A couple hours of tension sure beat the hell out of a public display, especially when it involved salad dressing.

"Well, one thing's for sure," Lisa sounded like this was going to be the philosophical statement of the millennium. Mitch patiently waited for her insight.

"Lunch is certainly on you."

"I have all the luck," Mitch replied, neither hotly nor coolly.

"Can I help?"

By that time, the restaurant manager had arrived with apologies, a mop and a brand new T-shirt with the restaurant's logo emblazoned on both front and back.

"You just keep eating. I'll go and clean up."

"Okay," Lisa chirped, happy with her assignment.

Once Mitch went into the ladies room, she gingerly pulled off her mustard-plastered shirt. Thankfully, the restroom was empty. She rinsed her blouse and toweled off her slacks. In spite of Judy's intention, her aim had been merciful. She could've, after all, dumped the meal on her head. That would have been a mess. By the time Mitch emerged from the bathroom, Lisa was well into her entrée and Mitch had been given a new chair. Lisa took two more bites, asking in-between them if Mitch wanted to stay or go due to their timetable.

"You get enough to eat?"

"Uh huh. They're packing up a nice, free dessert for both of us. Also, a new meal for you. I'll drive if you want to eat on the way."

"We need to stop by the mansion."

"The mansion?"

"The Governor's mansion. I need to get something clean for work."

"You do resemble a walking billboard," Lisa remarked about the gaudy shirt.

"Yeah," Mitch replied distractedly and she dialed Rebecca's office phone number. The cell phone was a gift she gave herself when it was important to keep Rebecca in touch about her schedule. Bringing the old girlfriend by wasn't exactly inked in on the calendar.

"Who are you calling?" Lisa asked.

"You get three guesses."

"Oh, the love of your life!"

"She deserves to be warned."

"You make me sound like an incoming warhead." "Hi, Sweetie," Mitch changed tone in mid conversation. "I'm in a meeting," Rebecca stated in her famous monotone. It meant, "I can't talk long, and this had better be good!"

"Well, I'm in a restaurant with chicken salad all down the front of me."

"How did that happen?"

"You're in a meeting," Mitch reminded in monotone that meant without saying, "You'll have to wait for this story."

Mitch continued, "I'm stopping home to change. I'm bringing Lisa with me." "Okay."

"I love you."

"Uh huh."

"Bye."

Rebecca wasn't one to be flowery on the phone, particularly with people present. It was a "Governor" kind of thing.

"Let's go."

Mitch drove in spite of Lisa's offer and they pulled into the garage by 3:15. Time was getting tight, but Mitch walked in the door like she had about thirteen hours to spare. The staff were their usual icy selves. Mitch maneuvered Lisa upstairs into the master bedroom and gave her instructions to change her clothes and then sit in one of the armchairs while Mitch took a shower.

"Okay," Lisa agreed readily. This was going too well. Mitch's stomach began to practice for a trapeze tryout. They parted company, each on a mission. If Tom Cruise were here, he'd pass on this one.

The shower felt wonderful. Once Mitch was halfway through, she was tempted to stay another six or seven hours. She knew better, the clock was ticking. Dripping wet, she stepped out of the shower and began to towel off. The knock on the door startled her.

"It's me," Rebecca announced. Loudly.

"Hi," Mitch answered back. Loudly.

"Lisa is sitting out here," Rebecca peeked in.

"Good, that's what I told her to do."

"You need your robe?"

"Got it, thanks."

"Okay. Good. Are you okay?"

"I'm really frazzled. I need to get Lisa to work by four."

"It's twenty of, now."

"I know."

"You want me to take her?"

"I can't ask you to do that. Didn't you have a meeting?"

49

"I'm done for the day. Miracle of miracles. I'll take her to work. You take your time getting ready."

"I have a better idea. Give her my car keys and let her drive herself. I'll figure out a way to get there a little later."

"Good idea."

Rebecca closed the door and Mitch finished drying. She drew out the process now that she had a little breathing space. She was a little less frantic, but not much. Her current lover and her former lover were pawing through her personal belongings, looking for car keys.

Garbed only in a robe, Mitch surveyed the bedroom. It was empty. Car keys gone, stinky gooey clothes gone, lovers past and present gone. Mitch slipped on underwear, slacks and an oxford broadcloth white shirt. It felt much, much better. Rebecca reappeared and studied the freshly attired Mitch. Was it guilt that made Mitch think that Rebecca was making a scowl.

"You're going into work right this minute?"

"Heck no. I've just taken to wearing regular clothes to bed." Four-plus hours of being with Lisa had kindled a snippiness that surprised even Mitch. It didn't seem to bother Rebecca, who was standing a few feet away, serene as usual.

"I'm sorry," Mitch said anyway, just in case.

"Like you said, it's been a bad day."

"Yeah."

Mitch walked over to Rebecca and took her gently by the hand. Without speaking, she pulled her across the room and guided her onto their bed. Offering no resistance, Rebecca, in fact, took the next step. She wrestled Mitch onto her back and straddled her securely but snugly. It was the best position Mitch had been in all day. Rebecca lowered her face until it was so close to Mitch's that she could feel the warmth. When Rebecca was in the mood to be intimate, she practically glowed. Mitch basked in the passion, patiently awaiting the kiss that she knew could stir her instantly into reckless need. Rebecca teasingly kissed Mitch lightly, on the forehead. Try as she might, Mitch couldn't alter Rebecca's aim, and remained submissive as the governor kissed her way slowly but surely down the side of Mitch's face. Her temples were throbbing. Her knees were gone for good. Every other point in-between was aching to be touched.

Then, the phone went off.

Mitch groaned. Both she and Rebecca had phones, and had found it necessary to alter their ring tones. Rebecca had opted for a simple, conservative beep-beep-beep. Mitch's sounded like a Las Vegas slot machine. It had to be cruel irony that the sound of hitting a jackpot was thwarting Mitch from doing the exact same thing with Rebecca. Damn phones anyway!

Mitch checked the number just from habit. She knew it was the U. By now, not only had Rebecca disengaged herself from Mitch's embrace, but had also handed the phone to Mitch. Lisa picked up on the first ring. "Lucky U."

"You're there already!" Mitch looked at her watch. It had been a scant ten minutes.

"I drove ninety."

"YOU DROVE NINETY!" Mitch hollered into the phone. "I only drove ninety down the highway. I obeyed the speed limits on the residential streets. Besides, that's not the problem."

"What the hell do you mean, it isn't the problem. Driving around in my car at ninety is a *big* problem!"

"The problem is Marge isn't here! That's the BIG problem."

"Marge isn't there?"

"Do we have a bad phone connection! I said MARGE ISN'T HERE! I have all these customers and no one to tell me what to do." "Is Sandy there?" Mitch asked calmly. There had to be one responsible adult on the premises.

"Yeah, sure."

"Put her on the line."

"Okay."

Mitch looked over at Rebecca while she waited for Sandy. "I'm sorry, again."

"It's okay. Work is, well, work."

Sensing that this was more than a simple problem that was going to be fixed with a mere phone call, Rebecca went off in search of Mitch's socks and shoes. Mitch would have to find a way to repay her kindness and understanding. Sandy came on the line.

"Hi, Sandy. It's Mitch."

"Right."

"I need your help."

Silence. Mitch understood full well the reason for the silent treatment. Sandy had worked off and on for a couple of months at the U. She was an excellent cocktail waitress and a hard worker. As far as Sandy was concerned, Lisa had been promoted over her. Five minutes ago. Mitch now had to fix the problem.

"How would you like to be a bartender?"

"For one night?"

"No, for keeps. Pay raise, benefits, full time."

"What is going on?"

"I'll explain it when I get there."

"What should we do in the meantime?"

"I'll be there in about twenty minutes. Here's the plan, let's keep a line open through my cell phone. I can answer questions while I drive. You know most of the drinks, anyway."

"I just don't know the fancy ones."

"Okay, I can help with those. Call me back in about five minutes. Okay?"

"Give me the number."

After exchanging vital information, Mitch hung up. She checked Rebecca's expression for consternation. It wasn't there. Its second cousin, twice removed, however, was. Disappointment.

"I'll make this up to you."

"I'll look forward to it."

Mitch nuzzled Rebecca's neck with a quick array of kisses. "Go on, get out of here while I'm still reasonable," she said sternly, but her eyes betrayed her.

"I love you."

"Love you, too. Take my car. Don't go ninety."

"I promise."

Mitch tore down the stairs and called Sandy as she started Rebecca's car.

"How are things?"

"Really busy. It must be, 'Take your lesbian girlfriend out for a drink' day. We're packed." "Still no sign of Marge?"

"Nope."

"Call me when you need a drink recipe."

Mitch drove carefully, staying in the slow lane even though the fast lane looked oh so tempting. She had to keep reminding herself that it was a bar, not a baby. It wasn't an emergency, just a damn nuisance. Images of being lovingly held captive by Rebecca not more than ten minutes ago made this all the more damnable. She would track down Marge just as soon as she settled down the two brand new bartenders. The phone buzzed.

"What's a 'Between the Sheets'?" Lisa asked without preamble.

"It's the place I want to be with Rebecca."

"Get serious. Some guy wants a 'Between the Sheets.' I thought he was making a pass and almost slapped him. Then, I saw his boyfriend."

"Okay, let me think. Take about four ice cubes, put them in a shaker with ¾ ounces each lemon juice, triple sec, brandy and rum. Shake it together and sift it into a glass. See if that passes the test."

"What's your ETA?"

"Still about ten or fifteen minutes."

"Geez, Mitch. Shut up and drive, for God's sake."

Lisa hung up without further pleasantries. Mitch wondered if they were breaking any rules, having two unsupervised novices running the bar. They were only a phone call away, Mitch rationalized. It rang again.

"What's a Flying Kangaroo, and I don't need another smart-ass answer from you." "Put Sandy on the line."

"Okay."

Sandy picked up as Mitch swerved to avoid a stalled car in her lane. If she wasn't careful, she'd be a flying kangaroo.

"What the hell is it? Rum Night?"

"Who knows? They just keep asking for weird drinks."

"Okay, mix together ice, sweet cream, coconut cream, pineapple juice, orange juice Galliano, vodka and rum. Don't argue with the customer if they say it tastes funny. Offer to remix anything and give them an extra bowl of pretzels."

53

"Thanks."

Things must have quieted down. Mitch pulled into the parking lot before the phone could go off again. She breezed in the back door and found a trio. Marge had finally arrived. "We need to talk," Marge informed Mitch.

"We certainly do," Mitch agreed adamantly as they went into Marge's tiny office. "I guess the adults are going to have a fight," Lisa said to Sandy.

Sandy ignored the comment. She was too busy for gossip, innuendo or small talk.

"You promoted Sandy?" Marge began the conversation quietly.

"I needed to do something. Where have you been?"

"I ran late."

"So did we."

"Now we have two budding bartenders."

"You shouldn't have promoted Lisa over Sandy."

"Sandy doesn't have the charisma."

"But she has the experience. They sound like a good pair."

"So who's gonna take Sandy's place?"

"I will. Or you will. Somehow, this will all work out."

"One more thing," Marge said in her best businesslike way. Uh oh, thought Mitch. Here it comes. The lecture.

"Sign these papers."

Mitch was now truly puzzled.

"Sign what papers? Why?"

"I'm handing the Lucky U over to you."

"What do you mean, handing over?"

"Handing over, you know, transferring, selling."

"Selling?" "Selling."

"How much?" Mitch asked, boldly.

"Don't know yet."

"Marge, you don't hand over or sell a bar just like that." "I know. That's why I need you to sign these papers. This is preliminary paperwork."

"Preliminary?"

"It's what my lawyer said I had to start with."

"I'm not going to sign anything until we get a chance to talk."

"You promoted Sandy. You got what it takes."

A knock on the door interrupted their conversation.

"Anybody in here know how to make a Swimming Pool?" Lisa asked.

"Well, first, you dig a really deep hole?" Mitch joked.

"And don't add too much chlorine," added Marge.

"Would you two get serious! We have a business to run!" Marge led the parade back behind the bar and started school in earnest. Things hummed along about normal and by nine, when the place suddenly emptied out for the night, Marge dismissed class. Lisa took Mitch's car to the spare house, where she promised to do laundry and ironing before going to bed. Marge pushed Mitch out the door and locked it behind her. Sandy would stay to help prep the place for tomorrow. Mitch arrived back at the mansion just about the time that Rebecca awoke from a nap. She looked absolutely fetching.

"You home already?"

"Got time off for good behavior," Mitch explained as she crossed over to the bed and sprawled on her side, still fully clothed and everything.

"Maybe I can interest you in some bad behavior?" Rebecca quizzed coyly.

"I'm always interested," Mitch said as she reached out to touch her true love.

"Why do I get the feeling that you're still wound up from your day?"

"Oh, maybe because I still have my shoes on, I guess."

"That, and those scowly furrows across your forehead."

"Would you believe me if I told you that things just got weirder as the day went on," Mitch said as she felt her forehead for furrows. They felt more like craters.

"I'd believe anything, now that Lisa's back."

"It's even more than that."

"You still haven't told me the first part, about the chicken salad baptism."

"I want you to know something," Mitch kicked off her shoes and pulled Rebecca close. "Okay. What?"

"Every time I closed my eyes this evening, I saw you. I saw you smiling at me and hovering over me. Kissing me. Holding me down. God, I hated to leave!"

"Well, you're back now."

Mitch's thoughts wandered back to the mysterious paperwork that Marge had produced. They hadn't had time to discuss it further, but it weighed on Mitch's mind. "What's wrong?"

"I still have my clothes on."

"And?" Rebecca asked with a teasing tone of voice.

"How are you ever going to make love to me when I still have my clothes on?"

"Why don't you get undressed while I think about it."

"Why don't you help me?"

"Thought you'd never ask."

Mitch's pulse raced as Rebecca's hands traveled over her skin. "Is it my imagination or do I still smell salad dressing?" Rebecca asked as she teased one of Mitch's nipples erect with her index finger. It was a habit she had acquired as of late. She had mastered the fine art of teasing the nipple erect, and then, through the same kind of touch, relax it, and then, as if by magic, make it erect again. After about the fourth time, Mitch couldn't even remember her name, let alone the day and time or anything about salad dressing right off the bat. She struggled to think.

"I had honey mustard vinaigrette drizzling between my breasts."

"Oh really? And was it sensual?"

"Don't you even think about it! If I so much as see a bottle of salad dressing in this bedroom, I'm calling a cab."

"How about a warm oil massage instead?"

"You're kidding. Right?"

"I wouldn't kid about something like that. You want a warm oil massage or don't you?"

"What did you do, hire a masseuse for the night?"

"No, I can do this all by myself," Rebecca reassured her. "Really?" Mitch sounded very interested. Very, very interested.

"Oh sure, I've been giving warm oil massages for years. Everyone has their little secrets. This is mine."

"Gee, I hope I can live with the revelation," Mitch laughed.

"Come on. Turn over and stretch out on the bed crosswise."

Never one to argue with the boss, Mitch followed orders. After a slight delay, she felt Rebecca straddle her. Warm, liquid hands

56

rubbed her neck and shoulders. Rebecca's hands were a lot like her opinions: strong, to the point, but eventually assuaging in nature. It was the first time Mitch had ever groaned without even getting close to a climax. "You are as tight as my grandmother's corset," Rebecca breathed in her ear.

"This is great. Why didn't you tell me you had this kind of talent?"

"You didn't ask."

Mitch chuckled, feeling more relaxed by the minute.

"Yeah, like I'm going to come up to you and say, "Uh, excuse me, Governor, but do you give great massage or what!?""

"You didn't mind talking about oral sex."

"That's different."

"How?"

"Anybody can do oral sex. Massage is a whole different ballgame." Rebecca laughed quietly as she worked her way down Mitch's back. By then, Mitch was ready for a lot more than a back rub. Sensing this, Rebecca held her down even more firmly, not giving her a chance to turn over. Mitch didn't struggle. Rebecca had her plans set in her mind and Mitch could be patient. Yeah, right.

"You're still really tense."

"It's for entirely different reasons than when I first got home."

"I see."

Rebecca carefully maneuvered her hand under Mitch, touching her other tension sensitive place. It was a wonderfully unique treat to work through an orgasm via this different angle. As Mitch sought her release, Rebecca held her as close as she could. Only after she realized that she had a death grip on the sheets did Mitch know how hard she had come. Even her breathing was ragged and uneven. As Rebecca resumed the regular massage, Mitch fell into a deeply relaxed state of mind and body. This was usually the point where lovers blurt out something stupid like, "Was it good for you, too?" Mitch silently congratulated herself for avoiding this trap and remarked instead, "That was lovely."

"You were very ready."

"That's the word, all right. Ready, ready, ready," Mitch smiled at her private joke.

Mitch turned over, still in Rebecca's loving embrace and said, "I thought I was supposed to be making up to you for running out earlier in the day?" "You look worn out."

"You have me so relaxed that I can't keep my eyes open."

"Then, don't fight it. Here, let me tuck you in."

Rebecca fluffed pillows and rearranged sheets and blankets until Mitch was downright cozy.

"You're spoiling me," Mitch said.

"You deserve it."

"What time do you have to go into the office tomorrow?"

"About eight. When are you due at the U?"

"About then. If you wake me up early, I'll send you to work with a smile on your face."

"You always do."

"Okay, I'll shoot for a grin, then."

"You got yourself a date."

Chapter 4

As promised, Mitch woke up early and stroked Rebecca's arm until she stirred awake. Sometimes, Rebecca came out of a deep sleep ready for a fight. Not that she was cranky, but rather easily startled. Given her nature, when choosing between fight or flight, Rebecca could land a right hook with the best of them. Thank goodness she aimed in her sleep. It usually gave Mitch a chance to duck. This morning, however, she was calm and collected, at least until Mitch raised her sexual awareness to a fevered pitch. It didn't take long. She must have been dreaming about it all night. Morning lovemaking was full of energy and freshness and as Rebecca stretched back in bed to soak up the tingly feelings, Mitch disappeared downstairs to scrounge for something portable to eat. The staff ignored her. Remembering her recent episode with the dog food, she gathered only what she recognized as truly edible. Bagels, bananas and coffee. By the time she zoomed back upstairs, Rebecca was already in the shower. Mitch sipped coffee in her robe as she waited for the privilege of watching Rebecca dress for work. Normally, most people enjoyed watching other people undress. Mitch had this reverse preoccupation. Rebecca could put on clothes in the most sexy way imaginable, and if she knew this had an effect on Mitch, she would probably find any excuse to draw the process out even more, if for no better reason than to send Mitch clear off the edge.

"You going to shower, too?"

"No, I don't think so," Mitch said casually. She didn't want to miss the show.

"You probably still have some oil on your skin from last night."

"I think it all soaked in."

"Well, don't blame me then if you slide out of your booth at work."

"Whatever," Mitch answered absentmindedly. She was watching Rebecca slide on her pantyhose.

Rebecca stopped in mid-slide. The best base stealer in baseball would have been envious.

"You know, one of these days, I'm going to spend about two or three hours getting dressed just to see if you'll drool."

"You found me out."

"You love watching me dress and undress. Is there anything you don't enjoy watching me do?"

"Can I think about it, until, oh say, the year 2034?"

"Sure. In the meantime, get ready for work yourself. I feel like I'm on stage."

"Okay."

They dressed, munched on their continental breakfast and kissed goodbye at 7:45. It was a morning for the mental book of memories. Once again, Mitch took a cab to her other home. Once again, she scrounged through her pockets for cab fare. Thank goodness it was a different driver. When she finally located a mangled, slightly torn twenty-dollar bill and offered it as a tip, the driver took hold of it by one corner like it was infected with smallpox or something. Lisa was waiting by the door. Gee, she was probably "ready." "Good morning! Don't *you* look refreshed!" Lisa kicked off the conversation, chipper as ever.

"Don't even start. We really need to get this transportation thing figured out."

"I *could* take the bus," Lisa offered.

"You? Take the bus?"

"It goes right by the house. One transfer and forty-five minutes later I'd be right at the front door of the U."

"Problem is, the bus doesn't run at three in the morning. Besides, I don't want you taking the bus. And *don't* call me mother hen! I just need you to be fresh and safe and ready to work when you get to the U."

"The bus is safe."

"Buses break down."

"Cars break down."

Lisa was in a mood to argue. Maybe not argue so much as pick at Mitch. Maybe Mitch deserved this. She had been picking at Lisa for about three days straight. Their prior relationship had never gotten to this point, the picking stage. They had still been in the throes of bliss when Lisa walked out. Perhaps Mitch had stored up enough acrimony to finally fully engage in the picky stage. All she seemed to need was a catalyst. Any issue would do. Today, it was transportation.

"Let me think about it while we drive to work."

"I'll drive if you need the sleep."

"I don't need any sleep!"

"You look sleepy."

"I'm chronically fatigued. Mostly from arguing with you!" Lisa shrugged her shoulders and walked to the car. She unlocked both doors and handed the keys to Mitch when she got behind the wheel. Silence engulfed their drive. Although the vehicle was equipped with a CD player, Mitch craved the quietude to ponder the oncoming traffic and day. Her thoughts got stuck in some sort of feedback loop concerning the paperwork that Marge had produced the day before. The transportation issue that she was pretending to think about was easily solved. She would buy another car. Having millions at her disposal made some things easy.

"What kind of car do you want?" Mitch tossed the question out with honest concern.

"A safe one, I guess," Lisa sounded like she was thirteen-years old.

"Fine."

By two o'clock that afternoon, several events had come and gone. A new car had been delivered to the U. Insurance, title and license were being tended to. Lisa was on an errand to the department of motor vehicles to tidy up the legalities. Mitch had discreetly asked Sandy for her clothes size and then placed an identical clothing order to match Lisa's new wardrobe. Marge and Mitch had a brief if important meeting about Marge's pending paperwork. Mitch signed the documents after listening to reassurances from Marge that her Texas millionaire relatives didn't give a hoot about the Lucky U. Marge likened it to Mitch owning a gum-ball machine in New York. It just wasn't worth their time and effort to care one way or the other. One more event took center stage after the lunch rush. Judy and Trish arrived with flowers and a heartfelt apology from Judy. Mitch accepted all this and a hug as well.

"Trish explained things to me. I'm sorry I overreacted."

"It's okay. Believe me, I understand your shock and anger. I'm still working through it myself."

"Is Lisa here?" Judy asked, trying hard to make the question sound like an off-the-cuff remark. Even Trish heard otherwise.

"I sent her on an errand."

"I see."

"She'll be back soon."

"I just wanted to take the opportunity to apologize to her as well."

"Come on and sit with me. We can have some wine or something while we wait."

"Who's serving drinks?" Trish asked.

"Me, actually. Marge is training two new bartenders, Lisa and Sandy."

"So, is that a promotion?" Judy inquired.

"It's a whole lot of dirty, messy, exhausting work. Whoever is still standing at the end of the day gets to start all over again tomorrow. What do you want to drink?" "Beer's fine for me," Trish reassured.

"Scotch and water, thanks," Judy ordered.

"Single or double?"

"Double."

It might take a triple or quadruple to get up the courage to face Lisa again. Especially with an apology. Mitch went to the side of the bar and caught Sandy's eye. She hurried over to get the order.

"How you doing?"

"A little nervous, still. But so far, I've only spilled three drinks and broken one glass."

"You're a ballerina compared to me."

"You need an order?"

"A good bottle of beer and a strong scotch and water."

"The good stuff?"

"Yeah, and I'm buying. That's Lisa's most recent ex-girlfriend over in the booth."

"She's due back any minute."

"I know. This could really get interesting."

"I thought you were Lisa's ex-?"

"I am. Just not the most recent."

"Here you go. Beer, scotch and water. What about you?"

"A pillow and blanket. I'm worn out!"

Sandy laughed, nodded and then hurried back to her other customers. Mitch delivered the drinks to the booth of honor and then went to check on things in the kitchen. Other than the fact that they were all out of arugula, things were humming along. Marge was nowhere to be found and when Mitch took it upon herself to check her office, she was sound asleep on the emergency cot. Anybody who could sleep on that thing deserved all the shut eye they could catch. Mitch emerged from the office in time to witness Lisa breeze in through the back door and stop dead in her tracks at the sight of Judy. Mitch went over and caught her by the arm to prevent an equally hasty exit. Judy had also caught a glimpse of Lisa, as if she had built in radar where the exgirlfriend was concerned. Judy tried to turn her attention back to Trish. Even Mitch knew this hadn't happened. Judy may have turned her eyes back to Trish, but her mind was still fully and completely inundated with Lisa.

"Judy has something she wants to say to you."

"What's she armed with this time? A tuna sandwich?"

"A scotch and water."

"Does it sponge out of silk?"

"How the hell would I know. I'm just an expert on honey and mustard."

Lisa laughed. Weakly. They took their final steps like someone was testing wattage on an invisible electric chair. They arrived, with Lisa pushed ahead just a little by Mitch. Judy took her time looking up at Lisa and when she did, for Mitch it was like looking in a mirror. Did Lisa even have the slightest clue how she twisted up people's hearts? Mitch's grip on Lisa's arm tightened inadvertently, and only a nudge and pointed look brought Mitch back to the moment. Here they were, three people in a room who had been the beneficiaries of Lisa's magnificent kisses, and nobody could think of a thing to say. Mitch more or less pushed Lisa into the booth next to Trish. The recoil was barely noticeable. Nobody talked, still. Judy just watched Lisa, with perhaps not nearly enough disgust to suit Trish.

"I wanted to say something," Mitch announced awkwardly.

It was the necessary catalyst that stirred both Judy's brain and mouth. "No, let me go first," she jumped in. "I just wanted to apologize to you, Lisa, for causing that scene yesterday."

More silence. If anyone had noticed the long pause between the words "wanted" and "apologize," nobody was venturing a comment. After about three seconds, Trish had had enough. And when Trish had had enough, everyone found out real quick that Trish had had enough.

"Lisa, don't you have something to say to Judy?"

"Apology accepted," Lisa replied, matter-of-factly.

"Is that all," Trish demanded to know.

"Well, I could tell her that, you, Trish, are a great kisser," Lisa replied with a benign smile.

Mitch envisioned a bar-clearing brawl was the next step in this conversation and jumped in with both feet.

"I still have something to say-" It

didn't matter. Trish was on a roll.

"Just a second," she interrupted, "You've got one helluva nerve, Lisa."

"Oh, you're right," Lisa seemed agreeable. "After all, Judy here found out days, maybe even weeks before I did what a great kisser you were. Isn't that right, Judy, Trish?"

As planned, the remark stopped further rebuke from Trish. Judy just averted her eyes, having no true defense.

"I may have taken the money," Lisa confessed happily, "But at least I didn't fool around."

"We weren't fooling around," Trish responded.

"I'm sure you were dead serious," Lisa retorted coldly.

"You made your point, Lisa," Judy said quietly. Even after all that had happened, this one sentence from Judy seemed to quell Lisa. Sensing that things were going to finally quiet down, Mitch, again, began her speech. It was directed toward Lisa, but everyone felt they had permission to eavesdrop.

"In front of witnesses, I want you to know something, Lisa." The silence became so deathly that it may have already been reincarnated and come back as a fly on the wall.

"I just want you to know that because I still care for you, in spite of all the heartache you've caused, I'm going to absolve you here and now of all your debt to me. You have new clothes, a car, and a drawer full of capital to start over somewhere else. You can leave now and know that you're free and clear."

"You think that's it!" Lisa replied hotly.

She was angry all over again, and at the oddest times.

"I just thought…." Mitch tried to explain.

"I don't give a damn what you just thought. You don't determine when my debt is paid back. I decide! You got that! I decide when my debt is paid in full. And as of right now, it isn't! You understand?"

"Well...."

"Good!" Lisa jumped on ahead, "so while the three of you are relaxing, I believe I'm on duty. Judy, what are you drinking?" There was no reply. Still waters ran deeper in some more than others. Lisa took a not-so-wild guess. After all, they had lived together. "Scotch and water. And another fancy import for Trish, and what about you, Boss?" "My on-duty usual, I guess."

"Oh yeah, water. Coming right up."

As Lisa stood up and marched away, Mitch asked no one in particular, "When exactly did I lose control over that conversation?"

"Before you even opened your mouth is my guess," Trish surmised, correctly.

"I think you're right. Seems like it happened to all of us. Lisa has an answer for everything."

Trish didn't seem to have an erudite reply and Judy was still inspecting her fingernails for invisible chips and dents. Mitch stifled a yawn and would have dropped off to sleep had Trish not jolted her back to wakefulness.

"You look tired!"

"I'm exhausted."

"Working hard?"

"It's a tough life. Up all day, up all night."

"I forgot you were a newlywed, so to speak."

"And how is the governor?" Judy asked, suddenly interested in more than a manicure.

"She's fabulous," Mitch admitted, inadvertently putting way too much emphasis on fabulous.

"Hmmm," Judy voiced, and then shook her head.

"Hmmm, what?" Mitch asked.

"It's just something you wouldn't expect, a right-wing conservative lesbian."

"She's not so right-wing anymore. I'm not convinced she ever was."

"And the conservative part?"

"She's convertible."

"Isn't that a car?"

"Oh, please, don't give her any more ideas! We've done it everywhere *but* in a car!"

Only one event could've stopped the laughter in mid giggle. Mary had incredible timing. "What's so funny?"

Mitch sobered up first and waved Mary to the spot vacated by Lisa. As if the giggle gods hadn't already caused enough trouble, the bartender-in-training gods were about to descend. Lisa approached with a perfectly balanced tray of drinks. Not even the arrival of Mary seemed to bother her. She quickly and efficiently set down the drinks and asked Mary, "What's your pleasure?"

"You in a maid's uniform."

"And they promised me they burned all those porno tapes," Lisa bantered back, not missing the proverbial beat.

"I'll have a root beer."

"Ooooh, living the wild life, are we?"

"Just driving, that's all."

"Whatever."

Lisa scooted over to the bar to decant a bottle of locally produced root beer. Mitch stocked it just for Mary. She hadn't seemed shocked at the reappearance of Lisa. Mother and daughter must have talked about it by now. "So, you all seemed to be having a great time. What's going on?" Mary asked again.

"Uh, oh we were just discussing the finer points of tossing a salad," Mitch made it up as she went along. It wouldn't do for the governor's daughter to hear about having sex with her mother. Some things you just didn't talk about over root beer. "And what's so funny about tossed salad?"

"I guess you'd just have to be there," Trish tried her hand at explaining. Badly.

"And in the way," Mitch muttered under her breath.

"What?" Mary asked. It ran in her family. Curious nature. "I need to check the kitchen, see if they're on the way to getting dinner ready," was Mitch's way to escape the question. She made her way to the kitchen and performed a series of round-robin type chores to ensure that everyone got a decent break before the dinner rush. Marge woke up about four o'clock and after imparting more bar-tending lore to Lisa for about an hour, left for the day. It was either a case of the late flu or early spring fever. Judy and Trish were long gone by the time Mitch got a break herself, but Mary stuck around. She seemed to be at loose ends. Either that or she just couldn't tear herself away from the sheer ecstasy of watching Lisa work like a dog. Well, maybe more like a cute, frisky puppy.

Mitch carried two plates of the dinner special, Cornish game hen stuffed with wild rice, over to the booth and cajoled Mary into eating dinner with her. It didn't take too much cajoling. Somewhere between, "How about dinner?" and "You want salt and pepper?" Mary was overwhelmingly agreeable and ate in silence.

"How's Hilary?" Mitch had asked in between bites, only to hear a simple, "Okay."

"And how's Mary?" Mitch followed up, sensing something unspoken.

"I'm okay, too."

"I guess your mom already warned you about Lisa showing up."

"She mentioned it."

"All things considered, I think she took it well."

"You make her really happy."

Mitch thought back to the night before.

"It's mutual, believe me."

"And that's what was so funny earlier, wasn't it? Your sex life?"

"Your mom and I can't get enough of each other. Considering the fact that she couldn't stand having me around a few months ago, yeah, I think it's pretty damn hilarious."

"I guess you're right," Mary lapsed back into silence.

"What's going on, Mary?"

"Do you always do everything my mother tells you to do?" The question dumbfounded Mitch.

"I'm sorry," Mary followed up quickly. "It's none of my business."

"How do you know? I haven't even answered the question yet."

"Your silence spoke volumes."

"I'd jump off a cliff backwards if your mom asked me to. Why did you want to know?"

"Just curious."

"But, then again, I'm probably not the best example."

67

"What do you mean?"

"I guess I'm just a little too codependent for my own good." "I doubt that. I know that if my mom asked you to do something that you didn't want to do, you wouldn't do it."

"I'm sure it would generate a discussion, depending on the issue. What's the issue between you and Hilary?"

"It's tough to get everyone where they want to be in their lives." Mitch nodded like a wise sage. She hoped to hell that they weren't talking about sex.

"This isn't kinky or anything, is it?"

"Depends on how you'd categorize working with cadavers."

"That's a little on the kinky side, if you ask me."

"Hilary wants to go to medical school."

"That was my next guess. There's a couple of schools here in Colorado."

"She's looking at California schools, but mentions schools out east from time to time."

"And you don't want to move?"

"I do have *my* work. It's important."

"Absolutely critical."

"Don't patronize me. I'm not in the mood."

Mitch nodded again, feeling a lot less sage. Even though she hadn't meant the remark to be condescending, it must have touched a nerve. This Mary was, truly, a different Mary than the one who had solicited Mitch for funds the first day they met. Even though she had dressed like a babe in the leather hood, she was a blushing virgin in disguise. It wasn't too long after Mitch introduced Mary to Hilary that the virgin condition vanished. However, the blushing still resurfaced from time to time. As Mary found her own two feet, she became more like her mother, not afraid to scrap if need be to make a point.

"I'm sorry I snapped," Mary said when Mitch remained meditative.

"If snapping helps, please feel free to snap away."

"If my mom wanted to move to California, would you go, too?"

"Mary, if your mom wanted to move to Orion, I'd pull up stakes and follow."

"You'd move east?"

"You bet," Mitch smiled. Astronomy must not be a required course in social work?

"You really must love her."

"I don't have anything or anyone in my life that's more important."

"The Center is important to me."

"There are abused children in California. Anywhere you go, you will do good things for kids." "That isn't it."

"What is it, exactly?"

"It's just that she *expects* me to go. It's *expected*."

"Like how a wife is expected to follow a husband?"

"Yeah."

"Have you talked this over with her?"

"No."

"Hey, you two," Lisa appeared from Mitch's blind spot. "How about another root beer for the road?"

Mary looked into Lisa's eyes. She tried to appear annoyed, but her efforts fell far short. It was as if Lisa absorbed and neutralized the bad feelings between them. Marge was right, Lisa had what it took to be a bartender. All she had to learn now was how to mix drinks.

"No thanks."

"Oh yeah, I forgot, you're driving."

Lisa picked up their dishes and offered to bring dessert.

"No thanks," Mary tried to sound dismissive. "I need to get home."

"Sure." Lisa nodded, "Say 'hi' to Doc for me."

"Sure, yeah," Mary stood to leave. Mitch waved and then looked around for something to do. Something that would keep her occupied so that she wouldn't have to go home and avoid talking. That would really make Rebecca suspicious. What was she going to say? Mary and Hilary might be moving far away? Sad but understandable. Or perhaps Mary and Hilary are maybe splitting up? Too drastic. Rebecca would hit the parental roof over that. What could be worse? How about, Mary is hot for Lisa and doesn't even know it? If Mitch sensed it and Lisa, oh yeah, Lisa knew it, how long would it take for Mary to figure it out? Maybe California was a pretty good idea after all. Orion? Even better.

"Why don't you go home, Lisa. I'll take over from here," Mitch suggested.

"Now that I have a car, I'll take you up on that generous offer."
Lisa put her arm around Mitch's shoulder. It made Mitch wince.
"Don't touch me!"
Slowly, Lisa drew her hand away. She knew when Mitch meant business.
"Don't ever touch me again."
"Sure, no problem. I just appreciate all your help."
"Fine. Go home."
Sandy and Mitch buttoned the place up by eleven and Mitch drove the long way home. Rebecca had to be zonked out by midnight. Mitch crept into the bathroom, stripped, showered, and slid naked between the sheets by half past midnight.
"Hey, you," Rebecca uttered her standard sleepy midnight greeting.
"Hey, you back," Mitch replied. This was usually enough to lull her back to sleep.
"I love you."
"I love you back."
This was enough reassurance to send Rebecca back to sleep. Mitch breathed a silent prayer of thanks and then dropped off herself. It felt great.
When she awoke, it was quiet, cool and light. She checked her watch and cursed. It was almost lunchtime. Her first thought was to call the U.
"Lucky U, this is Lisa."
"It's Mitch."
"Hiya sleepyhead."
"Is Marge there?"
"Everybody's here but you."
"I overslept."
"So, you want to talk to Marge?"
"No, just tell her I'll be there soon."
"Sure."
Lisa hung up, too busy to say goodbye. This would work out great. Mitch could work the night shift again and avoid talking to Rebecca until she had a better bead on the Mary-Hilary story. She was just drawing the sheets back to get up when the door opened. Thank

goodness it was Rebecca and not the snooty staff. Maybe? It depended on how many questions she had this morning.

"Well, good morning," greeted the most gorgeous honorable governor in the whole universe.

"What are you doing here?"

"I live here!"

"And that's not all, I've heard!"

"What about you? What's going on down at the U that you're able to sleep in all hours?"

"Not much," Mitch tried to sound nonchalant.

"What's going on?"

Rebecca sensed when Mitch was troubled. She searched for a believable response.

"Marge wants to sell the U to me."

"Sell the U to you?"

"It even sounds comical, you know, U to you."

"Why does she want to sell?"

"She won't say."

"So, that's what's been bothering you."

"I confess, it's been on my mind," Mitch could honestly admit.

"Will you be home for dinner?"

"I don't know. I doubt it."

"Mary and Hilary are coming over. I'd hoped you could come." "You always hope I come," Mitch couldn't resist the tease.

"Okay, you! I have a whole twenty minutes left on my lunch break. You got any good ideas?" Rebecca said as she closed the door behind her.

"Give me about five minutes and then I'm yours for the next fifteen." Ten minutes turned hope into reality. Thank goodness for lunch breaks.

"I'm beginning to figure you out," Rebecca boasted after Mitch had gathered her wits back together. "A little at a time."

"If you figure me out any more, I may never leave this bed again."

"That might be an interesting situation for the next governor?"

"I'll amend my statement. I'll never leave your bed." "Lucky me," Rebecca replied.

"Lucky me," Mitch echoed, not yet able to get enthused about going to work.

"What about dinner?"

"I'll see what I can do."

"Thanks."

Rebecca left the bedroom after one last long goodbye kiss. Mitch dressed quickly and vanished as quietly as she had appeared the night before. The U was cooking, literally and figuratively. The lunch special was fettuccini Alfredo. The sauce bordered on sinful and everyone smelled like they were going on a field trip to Transylvania right after dessert.

"You're just in time to do the paychecks," Marge greeted. What may have been a nasty chore for some stingy bosses was actually a treat for Mitch. She admitted it. She enjoyed paying people. They made enough money at the U to comfortable support everyone. Even Lisa. When Lisa received a check, she had the audacity to argue with the hand that was feeding her.

"I'm really working for free, remember?"

"I just can't get that little nagging detail past the IRS," Mitch used the government for an excuse.

"Yes I know...you have to pay me."

"It would be illegal otherwise," Mitch played along.

"Well," Lisa huffed, really overplaying her part, "I'll just pay you back in cash!" "Do me a favor instead."

"What?"

"Run an errand for me during your break. I need two servings of some kind of decadent dessert, something that we don't serve here."

"Uh oh, problems at home," Lisa intoned wisely.

"Why would you say that?" Mitch queried, frankly sick to death of Lisa being more psychic than Kreskin.

"Just sounds like trouble to me. Dessert is a peace offering in many cultures." "Name one."

"Shut up."

"It's not a peace offering. But you'd better make it four servings just in case."

"If I'd known you were in that much trouble at home, I'd a never fussed over the paycheck." "I am not in trouble at home!"

The "yet" was added on. Silently.

Mitch scooted home about eleven. She wouldn't have admitted to dragging her feet, but if under oath in court, wouldn't have lied about it either. The downstairs lights were still on. She peered around the corner and found Rebecca sitting on the couch in the parlor. This is the place where they had exchanged their first 'real' kiss.

"Hi there. You're up late."

"Come sit here."

Most days, that kind of invitation had an irresistible lilt to it. Tonight, it was more like a summons to the principal's office.

"I brought dessert," Mitch held up the bag and forks that she had just now filched from the kitchen. Mitch's other favorite hobby was making sure the staff had to count the silverware at least once a day.

"A peace offering?" Rebecca said, rather coolly.

Mitch shook her head, frankly unbelieving the way Lisa and Rebecca were so tuned in to each other. Maybe they were lovers in a past life?

"Why would you say that?"

"I think you know why."

Mitch walked over and sat down. She placed the bag and forks, aka peace offering, on the table. "You're angry?" Mitch asked, taking the lead.

"I don't know."

"Close to angry?"

"Hurt. Maybe hurt?"

"Okay, as in hurt feelings?"

"You had dinner with Mary yesterday?"

"I wouldn't categorize it as having dinner. She showed up at the U and hung out for so long that when I put a plate of food in front of her, she ate."

"What's going on between Mary and Hilary?"

"I'd say they're having a couple of bumps in their relationship."

"And you didn't bother to tell me."

"When was I supposed to do that? Between the two minutes at midnight or the twenty minutes at lunch?"

"You could've called."

"Yeah, right."

"What's that supposed to mean?"

"Have you talked to yourself lately on the phone?"

Rebecca pondered the question, wondering if there was *any*, let alone a good answer to the question. "Tell me what you mean."

"I mean, you're pretty monosyllabic on the phone."

"I'm usually in a meeting." "Right, you're in a meeting or going to a meeting or on another line. And you want me to call you up and tell you that I have this vague feeling that your daughter and her lover are maybe splitting up?" "Are they?"

"I really don't know. Mary didn't say, I didn't ask. It was like the Mitch Tanner, Mary Fairbanks' version of 'don't ask don't tell'."

"But you listened."

"So, crucify me for that. I listened and then I made the decision to let Mary talk to you. Wouldn't you rather hear stuff like this from Mary anyway?"

"You're right."

"I don't want to be right nearly as much as I want you to not hurt."

"She tells you because…?"

"Because I'm there. And I'm here now with mocha cheesecake. You want a fork?"

"Sure."

Mitch pulled the Styrofoam containers out of the bag and handed one to Rebecca.

"You know," Rebecca confessed, "if I had the choice between talking to you or talking to me, I'd rather talk to you."

"And if I had the choice between making love to you and making love to me, I'd rather make love to you."

"Here?"

"Here?"

"I asked first!" Rebecca smiled.

"I'll do anything you ask."

"That might get you in trouble one day."

"Soon, Lord, soon."

Five days passed without incident. Unless, of course, you included the search for the missing two forks. When would the staff think to look under the cushions on the couch in the parlor? Otherwise, Mitch was convinced she had died and gone to Boringville. Lisa was soaking up the skills of mixology like a bar rag. Marge was reliable if somewhat preoccupied with the real estate and liquor license issues. Rebecca was giving much better phone, but whatever was going on between Mary and Hilary had reached an impasse. That was French for nobody wanted to talk about it. That wasn't entirely correct. Rebecca and Mary had talked a little, but there seemed to be nothing earth shattering about their conversations. Mitch would have sensed otherwise. Just when things had become routine, Mitch rolled in one night on time for dinner to find the mansion quiet. No one cooking dog food, no surly guard counting the silver, no recalcitrant staff member to drag Rebecca away. Mitch, in fact, wondered for a moment if Rebecca hadn't already been dragged off to some meeting. Then, she smelled something wonderful and followed her nose to the bedroom.

"Honey, I'm home!" Mitch called out.

"I'm in here."

Mitch peeked in to find Rebecca pouring wine. A beautifully set table had a feast for two carefully laid out.

"What are you up to?" Mitch said, knowing full well this wasn't an anniversary day, she hoped? "Gee, that's a romantic statement if I ever heard one!" Rebecca answered, not at all unkindly.

"Sorry. I'll try again. You look lovely. This is wonderful."

"That's better. Have some wine?"

"Thanks."

"You still look suspicious."

Mitch tried to relax her face. It was sometimes hard after spending an entire day smiling at people. It was like her face was permanently cramped.

"How's dis," Mitch said through a slack jaw.

"You look ridiculous. "What's for dinner?" Mitch changed the subject. Food would be safe to talk about. Right?

"Home cookin."

"You cooked?" Mitch mustered up as much enthusiasm as she could in her question.

"I cook," Rebecca answered assuredly.

"Of course you do."

"Sit down."

"Thank you."

Mitch sat dutifully as Rebecca uncovered a chafing dish filled wall to wall with lasagna. This was enough for the both of them and the entire Osmond family. Mitch had to admit, it looked great. It tasted even better. Remembering that it was always a challenge to compliment someone's cooking without sounding surprised that they could even light a stove, Mitch searched for just the right thing to say.

"This is wonderful. Better than the stuff we serve at the U."

"Thank you."

Mitch exhaled, and then said, "I'm glad I wasn't running late tonight. That would have been a major problem."

"Oh, not really," Rebecca answered nonchalantly. So nonchalantly in fact that Mitch wondered if the Osmonds were waiting in the wings for the leftovers.

"I think it very important to understand and be flexible when work situations are concerned, don't you?"

If this seemingly innocuous question would have been any more loaded, it would have fallen face first off a barstool.

"Uh huh," Mitch nodded, curious as to what "work situation" she was soon going to be asked to be flexible about. Let's see, Rebecca already worked about eighteen hours a day. Were we going for twenty? Mitch worked her way through lasagna, salad, and bread before holding her hands up in mock surrender.

"How about dessert?" Rebecca asked.

"Maybe later. Do we have coffee?"

"Of course."

Like two sophisticated aristocrats, they took coffee sitting in the armchairs that furnished the master bedroom. Putting her feet up in the ottoman, Mitch felt ready to talk.

"So, what's going on at work that I am going to need to be flexible about?"

She prayed it wasn't some issue that they would disagree about. They tried to keep politics out of their bedroom. Sometimes it worked, and sometimes it didn't. What was that French word again? Impasse?

"I'm going on a business trip."

Mitch smiled brightly, happy to hear this good news. "Where? To Grand Junction? Aspen? Points beyond?"

"Points beyond. Points way beyond. I'm going to Japan."

"To Japan!" Mitch exclaimed. "How wonderful!"

"It is."

"Oh, the food, the scenery, the culture. It will be so great!"

"You can't go," Rebecca delivered the news abruptly.

Mitch looked over to see honest concern on Rebecca's face. "I know that," Mitch said with eyebrows up, "but I'm really excited for you."

"I've been worried how you would take the news."

"I understand that significant others, particularly of the lesbian persuasion, aren't allowed on these types of junkets."

"I floated the idea."

"And now it's at the bottom of the ocean, I bet."

"Right down there somewhere between the Titanic and Davy Jones' locker."

"And you went to all the trouble to cook this nice dinner in order to cushion the news? I appreciate it, really, but you don't need to go to these lengths. Anything I can do to help your career, short of moving out of the mansion, I'll do. Gladly! Without hesitation."

"Mary asked me if you do everything I tell you to do."

"And what did you tell her?"

"I lied. I said, of course not."

Mitch chuckled and then asked, "Why did you lie?"

"Because I don't think it's okay for her to do everything Hilary tells her to do."

"But it's okay for me to do everything you ask?"

"It's not okay. It's just true."

"I'd do anything for you as long as my self-esteem is allowed to remain intact."

"Mary said you told her that you'd jump off a cliff for me." "I would. My self-esteem would still be intact. Can't guarantee the rest of me!"

"Backwards?"

"Think of the view. Sky, clouds, sun. Or stars at night."

"I miss you already."

"When are you going?"

"In about a week."

"That soon! Are you going to need a traveling wardrobe?"

"I hadn't thought about it."

"Shop early, avoid the rush. That's my motto."

"That's Trish's motto!"

"Okay, then, Ms. Smarty Pants Governor, what's my motto?" "Oh, I don't know, how about, 'You haven't lived until you've been drenched in salad dressing'?"

"Shut up!"

"So, how are you going to stay out of trouble while I'm gone?" "Well, I think I'll organize a fork-finding scavenger hunt for the staff, and then maybe at night I'll attend a course in 'salad ducking 101' at the community college."

"Did I tell you that I miss you already?"

"You must have pretty bad aim. That's twice already and I've been sitting still." Mitch winked.

A couple of quiet moments crept by.

"This is nice," Rebecca noted.

"Is this what marriage is like?" Mitch asked.

"I'm not an expert on the topic," Rebecca answered bluntly.

"You've been married."

"So?"

"I just thought you'd know."

"Maybe if you asked me what a bad marriage is like, I'd have an answer," Rebecca said with an edge in her voice.

"Was it always bad?"

"I know why you're asking this."

Mitch knew why she was asking this, as well. She brought the subject up from time to time to check on the depth of the emotional scar tissue. It still seemed about as deep as the Marianas Trench and almost as wide.

"Why am I asking?" she played along.

"Because I asked about Lisa."

"I guarantee I don't want to know about sex with Jeff."

"Good! My long term memory isn't what it used to be." "I guess what I was really wondering about was how to tell a comfortable silence from an uncomfortable silence?"

"Ours is comfortable."

"Like a good marriage."

"I'll bow to your expertise on that."

"Where's that dessert you mentioned a few minutes ago?"

"You ready?"

"Oh, yeah."

They made short work of the warm peach cobbler and tucked into bed at a relatively early hour for them. The silence became comfortable again. Apparently, however, the thought of Jeff had put a damper on Rebecca's sex drive. This was not such a horrible situation for Mitch. She enjoyed every bit as much just snuggling side by side. With one week until Rebecca's business trip, they would have time to store up on affection. "What are you thinking?" Rebecca asked.

"I was thinking that when you leave politics, I should hire you to cook at the U."

"How's that paperwork going?"

"Okay, I guess? I keep signing documents. Marge keeps paying lawyers. How usual does that sound?"

"Very usual. Especially the part about paying lawyers."

"Is it going to be a problem for your political career if you're sleeping with the proprietor of a bar?"

"It might be the only thing that saves me."

"Oh, I don't think so. You're a brilliant woman and an outstanding politician."

"You are *so* good for me!"

"It's my job. That, and hiding silverware."

"This is what marriage should be." "Mmmmm," Mitch replied, suddenly sleepy.

"Goodnight," Rebecca said.

"Night," Mitch answered.

The following week was a blur. A flurry of activity enveloped both Mitch and Rebecca. Getting the state prepared for Rebecca's impending absence was more challenging than originally expected. For years, Colorado had struggled to find a balance between tax breaks for citizens versus tax breaks for businesses. When the bombastic campaigning about family values was a distant memory, the real issues came into sharper focus. It was easy to attract business to an area if you promise the moon in tax credits. Some saw this as shortchanging the entities that rely almost entirely on taxes, like public schools, for instance. Rebecca's job was to convince businesses that Colorado had enough to offer without tax breaks. Looking out the window at the Rocky Mountains every morning was all the benefit she needed. So along with briefcases full of information, she packed a photo of the view from her bedroom window. It was a breathtaking sight, visible for miles.

Meanwhile, activity was heating up at the Lucky U for Mitch. Marge must have set a fire under her lawyer. The U was ready for sale and the authority to own and run the bar was bestowed to Mitch. There had to be a bribe somewhere. Nothing in licensing moved this fast. The price asked and paid was ridiculously low.
"Are you sure this is okay with your family?" Mitch had asked one more time before she signed the check. "I'm sure," Marge answered. One more time.
The sale and transference happened quietly. No champagne, no confetti. no nothing. There were customers waiting to be served. It was no time for self-indulgent partying.

Mitch found herself suddenly in charge of researching, mixing and teaching exotic drink combinations to Lisa and Sandy. She selected a dozen every day, printed them on a computer, gave printouts to Lisa and Sandy and then tested them each morning. They had to recite the ingredients from memory and mix the drink. Lisa referred to the process as doing "orals." Mitch tried not to show any reaction to this rather accurate terminology. In fact, she tried to block it clear out of her short term memory, particularly when Rebecca would ask, if somewhat distractedly, what was new at work. She could just imagine the problems when she answered with "Lisa is doing great on her orals!"

Kaboom!

Today's "oral" included the famous Tequila Sunrise. It sounded easy: ice, two ounces tequila, one-fourth ounce grenadine, and three ounces of orange juice. The trick was to add the orange juice and grenadine slowly so the colors could stay separate and then mix them so that the customer could see the "sunrise." Sandy had the touch. Lisa screwed it up three times and was about ready to begin drinking the mistakes. Mitch stopped her.

"I'm not getting this!" she sounded truly upset.

Mitch had to agree, but did so in a sympathetic way. After all, Lisa had been trying hard. "You will. Let me show you."

Mitch gave Sandy a well-deserved fifteen minute break as Mitch walked behind the bar. Lisa lined up a new set of ingredients and then Mitch, without even thinking twice, gently but surely guided Lisa's hand as she poured the ingredients. Although it was a minimum of contact, it still affected them both. Lisa admonished, "You fussed about me touching you, so this doesn't seem quite fair." "You're right," Mitch pulled her hand away. Even so, the close proximity stunted her response time. "It isn't fair," she continued, "It won't happen again."

"It's okay, I just like to know the rules before I play the game."

"Why don't we take a break."

"I don't need one." "Maybe not, but I do."

Lisa wandered back to the kitchen, leaving Mitch to stare at the sunrise. She took one sip, then another. It was good. The third swallow went down the wrong way and she was blowing orange juice out of her nose when the phone rang. Sandy had come out of the kitchen when she heard Mitch coughing and sputtering and picked up the call.

"Lucky U, this is Sandy."

"Hi Sandy, this is Rebecca."

"Yes, your honorable, Ma'amness," Sandy struggled with the title. Mitch glanced up, still dribbling grenadine syrup. It looked like an anemic bloody nose. "Is Mitch there?"

"Yes, your honorable governess. She's choking on a drink right now. She'll be with you in a moment."

"Are things okay?"

"Oh, yes ma'am. Orals are going great!"

"Orals, right," Rebecca replied, as if she knew what Sandy was talking about and carried on the conversation so that Sandy would keep informing her of the latest news.

"Right, Lisa calls it orals."

"She would."

Sandy noticed that Mitch was looking even more distressed than before. Mitch tossed the rest of the drink down the drain, blew her nose which stung like hell and then reluctantly took the call.

"Hi," Mitch still sounded snotty, only literally, of course.

"So, you're choking to death?"

"Have you ever had tequila come out your nose?"

"Not for at least a week."

"You're lucky."

"So, I hear that *orals* are great."

"With you, they're terrific," Mitch bantered, trying to figure out how much trouble she was in.

"*Orals*?"

"We have a test every morning on how to mix certain drinks."

"Sounds like it should be called 'mixology.' Anything but orals."

"I'll put your idea in the suggestion box."

"You're sure you're okay?"

Mitch realized that she was being defensive, for no reason that would be halfway close to explainable let alone understandable. The old girlfriend was in the kitchen, the new one was on the phone and her sinuses were soaked with something distilled from agave sap. The combination made her feel prickly all over. She inhaled, exhaled and sat down.

"I'll be okay in a minute."

"I called to see if you can have lunch with me today?"

"Love to…."

"But?"

"But nothing. I will need to change my shirt, but I think I have a spare. Is a shirt okay?"

"They usually don't let you into most nice restaurants without one."

"I'm not dressed for nice, like dress or skirt nice."

"So, I should take you somewhere informal?"

"You should probably take me to the hot dog stand on the corner."

"I could bring a change of clothes for you from home."

"How's that going to work if we meet somewhere?"

"I'll pick you up there."

"You'll pick me up here?"

"Is that a problem?"

"No, but you sure have a lot of time on your hands for leaving for Japan later today."

"I have nothing better to do than hang out with you this afternoon."

"Things are that bad, huh?"

"I didn't mean it that way."

"I know. Come and get me when you can."

"Okay."

Mitch rinsed out her shirt in the bathroom, Lisa only barged in once through the changing process, catching Mitch in a state of semiundress. It was as if destiny was playing one long practical joke on them. Meanwhile, Sandy had put the bar in good order and the early lunch crowd began to drift in. Marge showed up, looking better than she had a week ago. Maybe selling the bar was the best decision she could have made. Mitch warned her that she had a lunch date with Rebecca. Expecting a lecture on the serious responsibilities of being a bar owner, Mitch was pleasantly surprised to find her agreeable. "It's important to spend time with loved ones," she declared.

"That's why I spend every day with you," Mitch answered back. "I hope the governor isn't the jealous type." "Me, too," Mitch replied, a little too fervently.

"When you get back, we need to do inventory."

"Sure."

"You are coming back?"

"Rebecca leaves today. I'll be back. Sometime."

Mitch worked the tables and bar, talking to customers, filling orders, and paying attention to everyone's stories. It seemed more intense now that she owned the place. She hoped her attitude appeared to be as genuine as it truly was and not just a show. Rebecca arrived about two in a private limo. She brought a garment bag in and chatted amiably with Marge while Mitch changed.

"You ready for Japan?"

"I've done everything I can think of except learn Japanese." "How long are you going to be gone?" Lisa interjected her way into the conversation. Butted in might have been a more accurate description.

"About five days," Rebecca replied cordially.

"Won't that be fun!"

"It's a business trip."

"Sure. By the time you get back, I'll know how to mix something exotic for you, like a September Morn, or a Black Widow, or maybe even a Sweet and Hot!"

"I'm a wine person."

"Okay, suit yourself. You want a glass while you wait?"

"No, thanks. I won't be long." "Guess not. Here comes your date now."

Mitch, dressed to go upscale, approached the gabby trio. "She sure cleans up nice, don't she," Marge remarked from the sideline.

"She sure does," Rebecca agreed, watching Mitch for a clue as to public displays of affection. They had to be so careful at the mansion due to the staff. What was the protocol around a former girlfriend? Mitch kissed Rebecca chastely. A step up from a peck on the cheek and miles away from anything they had shared in the last two evenings. They maintained eye contact for a moment, which allowed gawkers to put their eyes back in their heads.

"I'm ready," Mitch said quietly.

"Me, too."

They walked out without looking back.

"They make a cute couple, don't they," Marge noted for the record.

"Umm," was Lisa's full and complete reply.

Rebecca held the limo door open for Mitch and indicated where to sit. Of course, there were seats for ten or more, but Rebecca pointed to a love-seat style arrangement. Room for two. How romantic. When they were settled in, Rebecca pushed a button and the vehicle moved forward slowly.

"You want something to drink?" Rebecca inquired.

"Anything but a Tequila Sunrise."

"We have wine or wine!"

"What kind?"

"White or red."

"White is okay."

"Just okay?"

"Sorry, I'm feeling a little surrounded by liquor lately."

"Want a soft drink, instead?"

"Sounds great."

Rebecca poured a cola and a Chablis. They toasted an entire mid afternoon together. Mitch sipped down some of the drink, and then put it in a cup holder. Rebecca noticed her pensive mood and asked outright, "You're a million miles away. What's wrong?" "I don't want to do the airport thing. I hate public goodbyes."

"Okay."

"Is it okay? Really?"

"It's really okay. I'll have an entire entourage with me."

"I just don't want to cry in front of your staff."

"You're going to cry?"

"Probably."

"I told the staff that they had to be on their very best behavior while I was gone."

"No dog-food casseroles?"

"No."

"No fussbudget attitudes when I'm late for dinner?"

"No."

"No interrogations about missing silverware?"

"No!"

"Gee, maybe you ought to leave town more often!"

"Shut up!" Rebecca giggled.

Mitch laughed, a welcome sound to Rebecca.

"Hey," Rebecca said suddenly, "You ever make out in a limo?"

"No!"

"I told the driver to keep on driving until he heard differently."

"Would you just hold me for a while?"

"Of course."

They cuddled close together for fifteen or twenty minutes. Mitch lost track and nearly dozed off. What little she had of the tequila had that effect on her. The limo glided to a stop, and they disembarked at the Briarpath. Apparently, Rebecca had buzzed the secret code to the driver during Mitch's nap, signaling perhaps that making out was off and eating lunch was on. Mitch was glad that she had changed her clothes. The Briarpath was upscale. Extremely upscale. Feeling a twinge of guilt for falling asleep, Mitch not only stayed awake all through lunch, but even managed to be good company. She patiently listened as Rebecca summarized the last minute preparations for her trip and offered all her traveling expertise in one simple sentence, "Go to the bathroom every chance you get."

Dessert was cherries jubilee, one of Mitch's favorites. In fact, every course had been perfect.

"You called ahead on this menu, didn't you?"

"I wanted to celebrate your ownership of the U. Since you didn't throw a party for yourself, I decided to do it for you."

"A private party?"

"As private as a Governor can arrange."

They had gotten used to over the weeks of the ever-present aura of paparazzi in their lives. The crush of media had subsided several days after they realized that there just wasn't one more story in the day to day doldrums of the most out couple in the state. But the fringe photographers still shadowed them, waiting for an incriminating or embarrassing photo op. The simple act of opening up your mouth to take a bite of food could make most people look absolutely inane.

Don't even think of picking your nose! Imagine how boring your life would have to be to lay in wait for people to eat their dinner and pick their noses? Mitch didn't give it another thought, and felt ridiculous that she had given it any at all. She licked her spoon in such a sensual way that even Rebecca, distracted by her upcoming trip, took note.

"I'm supposed to check in at the airport in an hour," she explained the time constraints they were under.

"No time to stop by home for something you forgot?"

"I didn't forget anything."

"Well, you know that and I know that, but nobody else knows it."

"It would be cutting it too close."

"I'll make love to you in the limo."

"I think I'd be too nervous."

"Okay. I understand. When you get back, I'll rent a limo and we'll see what we can do about those nerves."

"You got yourself a deal. Now, stop licking your spoon!"

Rebecca arrived at the airport with a few minutes to spare. Her snippy staff was waiting, and after one quick kiss, Rebecca was swallowed up in official business. The limo driver returned Mitch to work. She managed to put on a happy face for at least two hours. By then, most of the dinner crowd was gone and she took a break to go back to the mansion just to shower and rest for a few minutes. There was no dinner in sight, not even dog food. So much for the staff paying any attention to Rebecca's directives. She showered and then stretched out on the bed for a moment. It felt so incredibly lonely and quiet that she went directly back to work, not even bothering to steal a teaspoon. Sandy had gone home for the night, needing to attend to child issues. Apparently, her two-year-old had developed a fever. Being a single mom navigating the mine field of work and day care had been manageable so far, but one glitch, like a simple common cold, could upset the apple cart. They had to find a better schedule for Sandy. Mitch scrawled a few notes on a cocktail napkin. If Sandy came in early and worked eight hours to correspond with normal day care hours, then Lisa could come in later, and stay up half the night. Mitch and Marge could fill in during emergencies with no problem. After she ran this plan by Lisa, she knocked on the office door to see what Marge was doing. She was turning blue and Mitch started shouting orders.

"LISA! CALL 911!"

"What did you say?" Lisa hollered back, unable to hear clearly from behind the bar.

"CALL 911. Get an ambulance here. Then get in here and help me do CPR!"

"Okay."

Lisa, bless her little heart, remained calm during emergencies. A plus for such a sweet young thing. Together, they wrestled Marge into a position where they could administer mouth-to mouth resuscitation. As Mitch cleared Marge's windpipe, Lisa prepared to apply the correct rhythm of pressure on her chest. Mitch puffed air into Marge, Lisa pushed with sure, steady hands. They heard the distant sound of sirens cutting through the otherwise still night air. Lisa went to hold the door open as Mitch hovered over Marge. She had responded to the CPR, but her pulse was thready and her color was still spectrums removed from healthy pink. In one minute, more men were in the office than Mitch believed could fit. They squeezed her out of the way and one team member pulled her aside to ask about prescriptions.

"What medications does she take?"

"I think estrogen, but she is really a private person where her health is concerned."

"The ER personnel will want to know any information you can find."

"I can send someone to her home to find her medication."

"You may want to check around here as well."

"I'll take a look when you clear out."

Paramedics worked a fine line between saving lives and stabilizing patients. They hadn't wasted one movement in hooking Marge up to a variety of monitors and tubes. Mitch didn't take stock, she was too busy giving instructions to Lisa. These included going to Marge's house, getting recent pills from the medicine cabinet, and then driving carefully to the hospital.

"None of that going ninety crap."

"Okay, I'll meet you there safe and sound."

"Thanks."

Mitch followed far behind the ambulance. It would do Marge no good for Mitch to arrive feet first herself. She thought that she should have told Lisa to search for anything that might have contact information on Marge's relatives. Her Texas kin were rich, and Mitch searched her memory to come up with a last name. They would need to be notified to make decisions about medical care. Traffic was light and by the time Mitch parked the car, locked it, and walked into the emergency room waiting area, papers were already being thrust at her.

"You want my signature?"

"We need somebody's signature!"

"Okay, but her family lives in Texas."

"The doctor will be out to talk to you after she's completed a preliminary examination."

"Thanks."

Twenty minutes crawled by on the clock. Lisa arrived, out of breath, but with a sack full of prescription vials and an address book.

"I thought it would come in handy."

"Let's hope for positive news to convey."

Mitch handed the prescriptions over to the desk personnel and then took her phone to place a call to Texas. A somewhat sleepy person answered the phone on the fifth ring. Between the sleep and the Texas drawl, it took Mitch a second or two to establish that this was indeed Marge's sister. They had never met, but Mitch knew Marge and her sister were on good terms. Mitch explained the situation as best as she could to this point in time. Then, by lucky coincidence, the doctor appeared with an update. Lisa pointed in the direction of the phone, and Mitch explained that she had the next of kin on the line. The doctor took the call and as Mitch stood nearby, she caught a phrase here and there. It didn't sound good. Marge most likely had heart damage and not the kind you get from being jilted. This was life and death stuff. Mitch wandered away, glad to be removed from the decision-making role. When the doctor hung up, she informed Mitch that the sister was flying up and Marge was going straight into emergency surgery. Neither bit of news surprised Mitch, but she still had to sit down to alleviate the shakiness in her legs. Lisa sat next to her and without touching her, still imparted a calming effect.

"You want me to scrounge up a couple of cups of coffee?"

"I don't think I can stomach the stuff they have here."

"Maybe we could go somewhere close?"

"I can't leave."

"Give them your phone number. It's not like you can actually do the surgery and the decisions are out of your hands."

Lisa was using her head and making an effort to be helpful. The least Mitch could do was to be cordial and cooperative.

"Okay."

They would stay in touch via cell phone. It could be hours. Lisa drove Mitch to an all-night diner that thrived on hospital situations just like this. The mocha was to die for. Mitch prayed it wouldn't come to that. She didn't want to eat, the knot in her stomach wouldn't allow it anyway. Lisa had no such condition and she chowed down on bacon, eggs, hash browns, biscuits, jam, coffee and a milkshake. She was eyeing the pie menu when the phone went off. Mitch answered. Marge was out of surgery. This was too fast, something wasn't right, but no more information would be given over the phone. Mitch settled the check and Lisa drove them back to the hospital. They located the area where people waited for news from surgery. Marge was in recovery but due very soon at the critical care unit. Mitch wouldn't be allowed in. Ditto Lisa. That privilege was strictly reserved for family members. It didn't matter much, Marge was still unconscious, and hanging on to life by a thread. If the stories were true, Marge was probably having an out-of-body experience anyway. Mitch gazed at the ceiling for a fleeting glimpse. Nothing so far.

"So, what do we do now?" Lisa asked.

"You go home."

"I'm staying."

"What time is it?"

"Eleven."

"Go home. Be ready to open the U tomorrow."

"We're open tomorrow?"

"I think we should have the doors open. Talk to people. Tell them what's happened. Sandy will probably still be tied up with child care issues."

"I didn't know she had a kid."

"Cute as a button, too."

"Give me the keys."

Mitch handed over the keys to the U and walked Lisa to her car. They stood awkwardly for a moment. Lisa commented the obvious,

"You've had one helluva day."

"I'll call you if anything happens."

"Okay."

Now that they had figured out the rules on physical contact, or lack thereof as the case may be, they parted ways without even standing close. Mitch wandered back to the waiting area. The lighting was florescent and annoying. Despite this, Mitch dropped off into a restless sleep. She had no other choice, exhaustion had replaced adrenaline. When she awoke at three, someone had mercifully dimmed the lights and covered her with a standard issue hospital blanket. She stretched her legs with a trip to the restroom and then wandered around to see who was on duty. New nurse, same old rules, but she managed to get an update which was also nothing new. She rested more and only knew she had fallen asleep when she was awakened by Marge. It was a miracle. Except that between last night and now, Marge had found time to recover from critical condition and dye her hair red.

"Are you Mitch Tanner?"

The Texas accent was unmistakable. It was Marge's sister, Scarlet. It was like Gone with the Wind had moved from Georgia to Texas.

"Yes, I am."

"It's nice to meet you, Honey, I just wish the circumstances were different."

"Me, too. Have you been in to see Marge?"

"Yes, dear, and she's still sound asleep."

Sound asleep must have been her euphemism for coma. The husband/brother-in-law was behind her, fidgeting from foot to foot.

"Sit down or take a walk, Ace." He
grunted and sat down.

"Nice to meet you, Ace," Mitch extended her hand. He grasped her hand in a paw the size of a catcher's mitt.

"I could stand some breakfast. You two mind if I take a break?" Mitch asked.

"You go right on ahead, Sweetie. We'll spell you."

"Can I get you anything while I'm out?"

Ace looked like he was about to recite a long list of needs. "Don't you fret none," Scarlet declared, putting a sudden stop to Ace before he even got started. She only had to make eye contact with him to convey her thoughts.

"You just relax and take care of business."

"Where are the two of you staying?"

"We hadn't planned that far ahead."

"I have a dinky house out west a little ways. You're more than welcome to stay there."

"Oh, Honey, we wouldn't dream of putting you out."

"It's no problem, but then again, it's nothing fancy either," Mitch explained, trying hard to keep the Texas affectation from invading her speech patterns as well.

"Got land?" Ace found his voice.

"One acre." "Sounds
little."

"It's my little bit of heaven. Why don't you mull it over and we can talk after breakfast."

"Sure thing."

It was a few minutes after six a.m. They must have chartered a jet, Mitch thought as she walked to the diner that Lisa had practically cleaned out the night before. The place was more crowded than it had been at eleven, and Mitch called Lisa after she placed her order.

"Morning," Lisa answered between yawns.

"You up?"

"Almost."

"What's that mean?"

"It means I'm groggy. What's new?"

"Marge's sister and brother-in-law are here."

"That was fast."

"I told them they could stay out there at the house."

"Sure, no problem."

Mitch figured that Lisa was still very groggy.

"Well, there will be a few things to sort out," Mitch began to explain.

"Why don't I just call a furniture store and get another bed bought and delivered?" Lisa volunteered.

Mitch's suspicious nature where Lisa was concerned thought this was too good to be true, but kept that opinion to herself. She guessed that any excuse to spend Mitch's money was a good enough excuse for Lisa to shop.

"And where will you stay?" Mitch had to ask.

"There *are* two bedrooms," Lisa huffed, obviously annoyed at having to explain the floor plan to the owner.

"I know that, but maybe they would like a little more privacy. They are used to living in a mansion."

"I remember. So, you have any good ideas?"

"You want to sleep at the Governor's mansion?" Mitch suggested in a moment of delirium.

"No, thanks!"

"Yeah, me neither."

"Maybe they could stay at the mansion?"

"Oh, please! The staff treats me like crap. Imagine what they'd do to Texans. Besides, somehow, word would get back to Rebecca and I don't want her to know about this yet."

"Why not?"

"She's got enough on her mind."

"Oh yeah, she's got the whole state to worry about. Why do I keep forgetting that?"

If there was a twinge of sarcasm, Mitch let it pass.

"I have an idea," Mitch gave fair warning.

"Uh oh."

"What do you mean 'Uh oh'?"

"I mean 'Uh oh'. Anytime you have an idea in that tone of voice, it's usually a wild one."

"Well, I hooked up with you once, didn't I!"

"Proves my point!"

"Listen, let's go out and buy one of those recreational vehicles."

"Like the kind Judy and I rented to go to Texas?"

"Right."

"I know just where to go, but what about the U?"

"Go open the place and wait for my call."

"Sure. I can order bedroom furniture from the U. Anything else?"

"Not that I can think of."

"How's Marge?"

Mitch winced with guilt. "I guess I should have talked about her first."

"It's no problem. It's just how your mind works."

"Marge is still in the critical care unit. I can't get in to see her."

"And that's not good, is it."

Mitch didn't want to think about it. The long pause gave her away.

"You still there?" Lisa asked into the silence.

"It's not good."

"Call me when you need help."

"Thanks."

Mitch disconnected the call. Breakfast had arrived piping hot and had cooled enough by now to eat without pain, which worked out great because Mitch was so distracted by events that she ate without thinking. And too fast to boot. She got back to the hospital and swallowed two antacid tablets with an orange pop. So much for dessert. Scarlet and Ace were not in the designated waiting area, so Mitch checked at the desk. They were in with Marge. Mitch sat down in a different chair than she had slept in. Might as well get her entire rear end sore as long as she had to wait. If the report was good, she'd go into work. If it was bad, well, she hadn't figured it out yet. Scarlet came out in tears. It was time to start figuring. Five tissues later, Scarlet had cleared up enough to talk.

"She's goin downhill."

"I'm so sorry."

"You go in and see her."

"I don't think I'm allowed."

"We managed to get you allowed this morning. They don't stick so close to the rules when people are dyin."

Scarlet made it sound like she did this once or twice a month. Break the rules, that is. Mitch drained her poor excuse for an orange juice and girded her loins. The last time she did this, it was her mother dying by inches. She walked back to the hallowed halls of the CCU. Marge was there, and yet she wasn't. She had been gone to Mitch since she found her blue and gasping in the office. The gasping was alleviated somewhat, replaced by a ventilator. Sickly gray had replaced blue. Death was replacing life and the only factor that was up for grabs was timing. This could go on for days. Doctors tug one way, death the other, and ultimately the hearts of all involved were pulled apart in the process. Mitch watched Marge breathe for a moment and then went back out to the waiting area. Scarlet was knitting, Ace was restless. Guess he forgot his yarn at home? By the time Mitch had sat for a couple of rows of knit one and purl two, she had decided on a plan. She'd go in to the U. Anything but this.

"I need to check in at the Lucky U."

"You go right on ahead, Honey," Scarlet patted Mitch's knee. "We'll stay here."

Mitch looked over at Ace, who was looking thirstier by the minute.

"I'll try and come back down at lunchtime, so you can get something to eat. You could go out to the U, as we call it, for short."

"She sold the place to you?" Scarlet asked.

"Yes," Mitch answered somewhat guardedly.

"Thank goodness for that! I'm glad she got that tended to before, well, you understand!"

Mitch nodded. Otherwise, the bar would be stuck in "estate limbo" for months. Ace didn't look nearly so thrilled. It seemed to Mitch that he would have welcomed a bar in the family. Then again, he probably had his favorite hangouts back home.

"You two have a car?"

"We rented a hunk-o-junk." Ace grumbled his way into the conversation.

"It's nice enough!" Scarlet retorted.

"Junk," mumbled Ace, not wanting to concede the point.

"What would you like to drive?" Mitch asked Ace.

"A truck," he answered in a tone that suggested, "What else?" was added on in his mind.

"You want me to find one for you?" Mitch asked directly. "If you have time," he answered politely, but had a look in his eyes like he was just named "Rancher of the Year."

"Sure thing. I'll be back."

Mitch drove to the U and gathered the staff together for a heart-to-heart talk and update. Since they had already heard the worst of the news from Lisa, they mostly had specific questions. As a group, they agreed to split up the impending duties. Regular customers would be notified and asked to convey the news. Staying open would give people a place other than the hospital to congregate. Food would be kept to buffet style for now to give the wait staff a bit of a break.

When Mitch offered to compensate them for lost gratuities, they waved off the offer.

"You need anything else, boss?" Sandy asked.

"How's your boy?"

"He's better. Well enough to go back to daycare."

That was saying a lot since daycare was picky, and rightfully so, about these things.

"I need an RV and a truck."

"As long as Sandy's here, I could help with that," Lisa volunteered.

"Then I could come back in time to do the night shift."

"Okay. One more thing, we may need to think about holding a wake. I hate to say it, but you all deserve the warning." "I'll order the turkeys," said Just Joe.

Just Joe was Mitch's cook. He got the nickname from his unpretentious nature. Anywhere else they would have called him the Chef. Here, he was Just Joe. The moniker stuck.

"That would be what Marge would've wanted."

Everyone set about their business, fending off the pall that was threatening to descend. Mitch and Lisa went to the RV dealership and after touring several models, picked out what could only be described as a mini mansion on wheels. If Mitch ever decided to get out of the bar business, she could always take up country music singing. An entire band could travel in this behemoth. Yee Haw!

Through a combination of coy smiles and witty remarks, Lisa managed to get a deal. The salesman never knew what hit him as Mitch made out the check. It was still a hefty amount, but worth it. "At this rate, you're liable to get us a truck for free," Mitch remarked as they left the lot. They had arranged for the vehicle to be delivered later, hopefully by bedtime. Maybe that's why the salesman was so happy to take a little off the top. Hoping, perhaps that Lisa would follow suit later. He would have had better luck if he was the only gay guy at a eunuch's convention.

Two or three salesmen circled them like sharks at the truck dealership. Honestly, when was the last time two women went truck shopping together and decided to fool around with men?

"Let's just buy something and get out of here," Mitch instructed Lisa. "I told Scarlet I'd be there at lunchtime."

"We could always take the truck there for a test drive? That way, Ace could get a good look at it."

"Why do you always have the best ideas?" Mitch tried her hand at a compliment.

"Been hanging out with you too long, I guess."

After Lisa crossed and uncrossed her legs a couple of times, the salesman would have agreed to a test drive to the moon and back. With Lisa behind the wheel and Mitch riding shotgun, he was more than happy to instruct Lisa in the finer points of four wheel trucking. At least she didn't go ninety. She usually saved that for the third test drive.

Mitch remembered her pattern well. When they first met, Lisa either didn't have such finely tuned seductive skills or she simply didn't need to use them on Mitch. It had been an interesting period in Mitch's life. Once Mitch had figured out that she was gay, it had become her best kept secret. She kept it from her parents, friends, enemies and every other person on the planet for good measure. By the time she had started college, she was an official member of the "Orphans Club", having outlived both parents. She had inherited enough money to squeak her way through college, and met Lisa in her freshman year. Their first meeting was by accident, sharing a table in the student union. Mitch remembered thinking along the same lines as Humphrey Bogart, of all the tables in all the world, she picked mine. Their second date was more formal, dinner at a quaint little Italian place. Checkerboard tablecloths, candles, wine, and enough garlic to course through their veins for a week. They closed the place at two a.m. and walked back to Lisa's apartment, where Mitch had left her car. Back then, Lisa loved walking. And walking. And walking. And then, they were at the front door and Lisa imparted a kiss that tasted like a drop of water in the Sahara. So precious, and not nearly enough.

Their third date was of the strained variety, but only for about the first fifteen minutes. Mitch was a mess of nerves, virgins were like that sometimes. Lisa was soothing and sensual and Mitch paid the tab.

They had driven this time and ended up parked on a hill overlooking a bucolic municipal golf course. Mitch would have been content to talk, which was how she had remained a virgin up until this point, but Lisa had other ideas. She was ready, there's that word again, ready to explore their total relationship.

The desert of loneliness that Mitch had wandered through for years was now a flourishing oasis. And as they say, "jump in, the water's fine." Mitch jumped. The truck bounced over a speed bump at the hospital entrance.

"Rides real nice, doesn't it," the salesman was on sell mode every minute.
"Sure does," Lisa winked.
Mitch slid out the passenger door and stretched her legs.
"You were quiet," Lisa said as she walked in beside Mitch.
"I was thinking."
"About Marge?"
"No," was all Mitch would say.
They left the salesman behind to cool his heels and any other part that needed cooling. Like the radiator? Ace had had quite enough of watching Scarlet knit and nearly two-stepped out to the parking lot with Lisa to look over the goods. Mitch helped Scarlet pack up her bag of knitting. At least the woman came prepared.
"Are you okay, Honey?" Scarlet asked.
"I'm getting through it," Mitch answered glumly.
"Nothing's changed since mornin,"
"Okay."
Everyone converged in the parking lot and surrounded the truck. Ace was beaming from ear to ear. Mitch instructed the salesman to take Ace and Scarlet to the Lucky U and then begin the paperwork. He seemed heartbroken for a moment that Lisa was staying behind at the hospital, but brightened considerably at the thought of a sale.
Squeezed in between Scarlet and Ace, the salesman grimaced as Ace revved the engine and sped out of the parking lot. He was certainly earning his commission.

"Come on. Let's go check on Marge," Mitch said as she led the way back into the hospital and down the previously forbidden corridor. Scarlet was right, nothing much had changed except that Marge seemed to be shrinking. She looked so small and vulnerable next to the machinery that was keeping her alive. Only when Mitch looked over at Lisa did she realize that Lisa was crying. Mitch entered into the great debate with herself on how to handle this. Her good angel told her to take Lisa into her arms and comfort her. Her bad angel told her to take Lisa into her arms and comfort her. Mitch felt slightly outnumbered at this point. She patted Lisa on the shoulder and then more or less caught her when she fell into her embrace.

"You gonna be okay?" Mitch asked quietly. Why do people ask questions at a time like this when they already know the answers?

"No," Lisa snuffled.

"Come on, let's go back to the waiting room."

Together they ambled slowly back down the hall. Thankfully, the area was deserted. Lisa could grieve in relative privacy. They sat together on the couch and Lisa more or less soaked the upper left quadrant of Mitch's shirt. Once or twice she sniffed out a sincere apology, but Mitch just shushed her and handed over more tissues. She owed her this much. After that thirst-quenching third date, Mitch had invited Lisa to live with her. One open door led to another and the night that Mitch talked about the death of her parents, Lisa couldn't have been more comforting. She let Mitch cry until the phase passed and then made tender, sweet love to her. Emotionally and physically drained, Mitch stayed in bed for two days, waited on hand and foot by Lisa.

Mitch sighed audibly. So much so that Lisa noticed.

"God, here I am blubbering away and you're the one who needs to cry."

"I'm okay right now."

"Marge was like a mother to me."

"She's not dead, yet," Mitch reminded gently.

"I'm scared."

"Of what?"

"Of death. Of losing people."

Mitch couldn't figure this one out. The woman famous, or infamous in this case, for walking out on people, and taking their liquid assets with her, was crying about losing people. It was either a good act or a great beginning.

"You wanna grab a bite?" Mitch asked.

"Who's gonna watch over Marge?"

"God."

"I guess we can trust her for a while."

Not ready to go back to the diner, they walked to a mid-priced Chinese restaurant two blocks away. As Lisa studied the menu, Mitch made a mental wager with herself. Didn't matter how much time she took, Lisa's order would still be the same. Sesame chicken. It had been every other time they had gone out for Chinese. After they moved in together, their schedules were full. School and work absorbed time and energy. Making love sapped the rest. Since Mitch was an elder among her classmates, she struggled to keep up academically. At least a hundred times she wondered why Lisa was so enamored with her when she had so many other younger, prettier, smarter students to choose from.

In spite of tight schedules and tighter budgets, Mitch treated Lisa to dinner out at least once a week. Lisa had eaten enough sesame chicken to set a world's record, but it did something marvelous to her sex drive. It was her own private aphrodisiac. Most nights, Mitch barely had time to check out her fortune in the fortune cookie before Lisa was tugging her out the door. Why bother reading; it was always the same. "You are about to get lucky!" In bed.

Usually, Mitch drove while Lisa would distract. If it were up to Lisa, they would have still been in the parking lot. Mitch was sort of a stick-in-the-mud where that was concerned. She made a point to keep her private life private. So, Lisa would behave herself until they arrived home, and then Mitch was all out of excuses. Not that she wanted any more reasons to hold Lisa at bay. When Lisa went on these wild rides, she took Mitch right along with her. She would tease until Mitch couldn't hold back any longer. It was Lisa's own brand of control, she always brought Mitch first, and then and only then did she allow Mitch to satisfy her. If Mitch didn't come, Lisa didn't come. Ever. Thank the gods and Chinese for sesame chicken.

"I'll have the sweet and sour shrimp," Lisa informed the waitress as Mitch snapped out of her reverie.
"Sweet and sour shrimp?" Mitch restated in disbelief.
"Two sweet and sour shrimp," the waitress repeated dutifully.
"And egg drop soup," added Lisa. The
waitress looked at Mitch.
"No soup for me, thanks."
She left with the order and menus.
"Since when do you like sweet and sour shrimp?" Lisa quizzed.
"I don't, much."
"Then why did you order it?"
"So you could eat off my plate, just like the good old days, I guess."
"Your plate always was a lot of fun to eat off of," Lisa nodded.
"I planned it that way."
Mitch was taking a vow of avoidance where sesame chicken was concerned.
Lisa's soup arrived and kept her busy for about three minutes. Mitch added way too much sugar to her tea and drank it down in one gulp.
"Still using way too much sugar in your tea, I see."
"I can't drink it otherwise. It sets my teeth on edge."
"Even more than I do?" Lisa asked with one eyebrow cocked. This was a skill that Mitch had never mastered, the 'cocking-of-oneeyebrow' thing. She gave up, blaming in on genetics.
"You're a not so distant second."
"It's too bad that we didn't stay together longer. I'm beginning to enjoy your wry sense of humor."
"I've always had it."
"I never saw it."
"You didn't stick around long enough!"
"A decision I regret."
"But only in hindsight."
"Is there any other?"
"There's foresight."

101

"I had better uses for the prefix *fore* when I was with you. Sorry I didn't think of *sight*.

Their meals arrived, providing Mitch with a good excuse to stop talking. She ate slowly, even though the food was delectable. Lisa polished off her portion and eyed Mitch's progress with more than passing interest.

"Help yourself." Mitch pushed the plate her way as she refilled her teacup and added a little less sugar. Maybe a microgram less. "Thanks."
"Why did you take the money? The first forty-thousand." Mitch clarified.
"$42,851.32," Lisa corrected.
"Yeah."
"Because I knew you'd have more to spare, someday."
"You what?" Mitch wasn't buying this lame excuse.
Lisa fell silent. This was odd, the queen of the snappy comebacks without a syllable in her mouth. Mitch asked another question.
"What did you know?"
"Nothing."
"Were you psychic? You had a premonition that I'd win the lottery?"
"Yeah," Lisa brightened at Mitch's suggested answer.
"Try telling me the truth."
"I knew that Marge was going to give you the Lucky U."
"But you didn't know that until a few days ago."
"Actually, *you're* the one who learned about it a few days ago."
"How long have you known about it?"
"About two years."
Mitch didn't even realize that she had knocked over her teacup after hearing this pronouncement. The stain grew on the brilliant white of the tablecloth like a giant drop of brown blood. "No, you didn't," was all she could think of to say.
"Marge told me she was leaving you the place in her will. Apparently, she changed her mind and sold it to you outright. On the cheap." Mitch thought for a moment. Something didn't add up.
"Even if I believe that you were privy to Marge's last will and

testament, that still didn't mean I'd have the asset anytime soon. For all we knew, Marge would have lived for years."

Lisa didn't answer except with a small shrug of her shoulders. She wouldn't look up much less meet Mitch's eyes. It was a very quiet thirty seconds, and Mitch just watched and waited. It was far more effective than bright lights and brass knuckles.

"Marge knew she was dying two years ago," Lisa finally explained.

"No, she didn't."

"Yes, she did."

Their bill arrived with two fortune cookies. Lisa cracked hers open and read it out loud. It said, "A stranger will soon hold your heart in their hands."

"Pretty asexual, if you ask me," she said and then asked, "What does your fortune say?"

Mitch hadn't even glanced at it before Lisa snatched it away from her. She read it out loud as well, "You will have more fun atoning for your mistakes than you have making them."

Mitch didn't listen closely, something still nagged at her about Lisa's sudden insights. She had to be lying to rationalize her actions.

"What's wrong?" Lisa asked.

"You're lying to excuse your behavior."

The accusation hit a nerve with Lisa. She stood up, said, "Fuck you," and walked out of the restaurant. Sensing another sudden departure, the waitress came over and collected the money. Mitch tipped extra for the spilled tea she had finally noticed. Giving Lisa at least five minutes head start, they didn't meet up again until they were back at the hospital. Lisa was sitting with her arms crossed. Mitch checked in at the desk. Marge's condition had been downgraded to grave. The news stabbed Mitch's stomach like an icicle. She went back over and sat next to Lisa. It was icy here as well.

"I'm sorry. I was wrong to call you a liar."

"Yes, you were."

"Marge is in bad shape. We should track down Scarlet and Ace."

"Yes, you should."

Mitch called the Lucky U, and Sandy answered. She put Scarlet on the line.

"I think you should come on back down," Mitch said. It was a hard call. Grave condition could go on for some time, but if Mitch stalled, it could be over. Soon. "She's goin downhill worse?"

"A little. Could you put Sandy back on the line?"

"Sure, and we'll jump in the truck and be there in a jif."

Mitch apologized to Sandy for running late.

"I'll be there soon."

Lisa interrupted, "I'll go in. You stay here."

"You sure?"

"I just want to be as helpful as I can be."

"Okay."

Lisa was in a cab and gone in five minutes. Mitch tried to sit and wait for the family but was too nervous to stay still. She walked a couple of laps around the interior corridors of the hospital, absentmindedly sifting through the remains of the bombshell that Lisa had dropped at dinner. If Marge confided in Lisa, why did Marge ever think that Lisa wouldn't recognize her in Texas? It didn't make sense.

Mitch lost track of her aerobic exercise. Before she knew it, Scarlet and Trish were in the waiting room. Ace was probably parking the truck.

"Hi, Honey," Scarlet yoo-hooed from her spot.

Mitch gave Scarlet a hug and Trish a longer one. It was precious to have friends like her.

"Did you go in yet?"

"Thought I'd wait for my hubby," Scarlet said. "You can go in now, if you want," she directed the comment to Trish, who obviously, wasn't waiting for her own hubby.

"I'll wait," Trish said quietly.

"If you want to go in, Scarlet, I'll send Ace in right away."

"I'd rather wait."

"I understand. This must be quite the shock," Mitch nodded.

"Well, it isn't easy, but it ain't a shock."

"What do you mean?" Mitch asked with heightened awareness.

"Marge been dyin for a coupla years now," Scarlet said matter-offactly.

Mitch just nodded like she knew it for a fact. Just because she knew it for a fact only thirty minutes ago didn't need to be blabbed. Trish looked puzzled, but Mitch shook her head, sending an important signal. So, Lisa had had the inside track on this story. Mitch swallowed her sense of betrayal. How dare Marge not tell her she was dying? Damn her! Even if she lived through this crisis, she was still dying anyway. Mitch resisted the urge to throw two or three chairs across the room. Ace showed up, trying hard to smother the giddy feelings associated with truck driving. Clams weren't *this* happy.

Scarlet and Ace went in to see Marge. Trish sat with Mitch long enough for her to tell the story about how everyone on earth except those present knew that Marge was dying.

"Did you know?" Mitch demanded of Trish.

"No, absolutely not."

"Lisa knew."

"She did not."

"She told me an hour ago, before Scarlet broke the news."

"She probably heard it from them."

Mitch tried to think back if there was a time when Lisa had Scarlet and Ace all to herself. Her mind wouldn't clear. Trish didn't press.

"What happened to your shirt?" she asked instead.

"My shirt? Oh yeah, Lisa had a few tears."

"Looks like she drenched you. High tide on the Mississippi doesn't leave that much residue!" "Does it show?"

"Only with the light on."

Mitch laughed. Trish was always able to tug at Mitch's funny bone, even in the worst of times. Some might think it irreverent. Mitch and Trish knew better. She stayed for about an hour, and then Mitch walked her to her car. "You going to stay all night?"

"I don't know what good that will accomplish. I planned to take Scarlet and Ace back to the house. Lisa and I bought an RV for extra sleeping space. And a bed as well.

"Sounds like you're going to have the zoning commission on your ass before too long."

"I'll work it out. As long as my woodpecker neighbors don't complain, I think I'll be okay for a while."

"You take care and call me if I can help."

"Thanks,"

Mitch trudged back to the waiting room. Things were beginning to be surreal. It was like a nightmare. Knit one, check on Marge, purl two, watch Ace fidget. After three hours of torture, which included dinner in the hospital cafeteria, Mitch talked Ace into driving everyone out to her house in the woods. "Sounded like Robert Frost's residence," Scarlet declared as they pulled up in front.

Lisa wasn't there, but an RV was parked out back. An electric cord stretched from it to the main house. Mitch directed traffic in the house, pointing Scarlet and Ace to the master bedroom, complete with new bed and sheets. Mitch went in and laid down on the bed vacated by Lisa. It still had the same sheets, and Mitch could smell the faint aroma of the "perfume" she used, eau de shampoo. It kept her awake for a few minutes, deep in thought. Lisa had always smelled nice. It wasn't something Mitch had noticed with the thinking part of her brain. But it was always there, subconsciously pricking at her. It was all by design, Mitch now realized. While Mitch had never been one to do a lot of the feminine things that most women do, Lisa was an expert at this form of chemistry. She looked natural despite the makeup she always wore, she smelled wonderful although it never seemed to overwhelm and in bed, the sheets and pillows would absorb the soothing fragrances. When Mitch had a cold, or flu, or just a case of the lazies, she would hold Lisa's pillow close. Of all the things Mitch missed, even more than the money, when Lisa left, was the care she took to make things nice. For some reason, Mitch felt that Lisa had always done it just for her. Everything had been perfect. Mitch had died and gone to Lesbian Heaven. She slept like the dead, even though it was tacky to say so.

When she woke up, everyone was gone, but Mitch still had Lisa's pillow. Otherwise, there was no note, no trace, no mess in the kitchen. Mitch set forth on her morning routine, feeling no sense of dread or panic. Things were truly out of her hands. She dressed and drove to the U. Sandy and Lisa were prepping for the lunch buffet crowd.

They practically pushed her back out the door to check on the "knit one, purl two" crowd. Scarlet and Ace were on their best guard duty behavior and had no news to report. If it wasn't so tragic, it would be a colossal bore. Dying was dramatic on TV. Not so in real life. At least, not in this real life. If Marge couldn't get well enough to get up and tend to things, she would want to be dead. With what felt like great selfishness, Mitch prayed for a speedy end.

Who says God never listens? Marge died the next day, during Lisa's watch. Things moved quickly after that. Since the body was going to be shipped to Texas for cremation, there was little left to do but plan a gathering at the U. Word had spread about Marge's wake, now scheduled for Friday. The doors would open at noon and close at three p.m., not a.m. Three hours of grief was enough, and the staff needed a break. Mitch and Lisa had dragged in Friday morning at five to begin work. Just Joe was already there, along with a mountain of turkeys. The turkeys were stuffed and roasted, a grueling job when the mood was good, like at Thanksgiving time. Today it was arduous. Mitch buried herself in the task, hoping that the distraction would alleviate the pain. It did, a little. She kept telling herself that this was great practice for when Rebecca would need her to feed the homeless closer to the holidays. So she practiced for about two or three hours. Rebecca. Mitch had thought about her at least a hundred-thousand times in the past few days. It kept her going. She hadn't called to tell her the sad news. What was the point? It would distract her, and she couldn't help anyway. When she got back, Mitch would fall into her arms and she would catch her and make everything okay again.

It was noon before Mitch realized that she hadn't sat down in hours. Trish, Judy and Lisa were setting up the final details. The tables were set, the bar was ready, the door was open and Lisa was hostess. People who hadn't stopped in for years showed up to pay their last respects, and insisted on passing a hat for donations. Scarlet took the money and with Mitch's okay, divided it equally among the staff. It was a decent bonus for such a caring group. Three hours passed quickly and after they locked up for the day, the place was scrubbed down by people working through their residual grief. By five, everyone had been given a week's vacation with pay. It was down to Mitch and Lisa, sitting in Mitch's booth, soaking up the calm.

"A lot of people showed up," Lisa remarked.

"It was nice."

"Nice is a strange way to look at it."

"Why?"

"You just don't usually associate death with nice." "I wasn't," Mitch snapped, suddenly feeling the emotion of the week. "I was just pointing out that so many people respected Marge enough to be here."

"And eat and drink for free," Lisa said dryly.

"That isn't why they came."

"So, why did they come?" Lisa demanded to know in a way that irritated Mitch further. Maybe that was her plan. She had already fixed her a Flying Kangaroo that was way too steep, and now she was being a royal nag.

"They were here because they needed closure," Mitch said through the rum that was soaking into her brain in record speed. She hadn't really eaten and the booze was making up for lost meals. "Closure?" Lisa quizzed. If the prize for knowing the definition of closure was a trip to Hawaii, Lisa would have been stuck on the mainland.

"Yeah," Mitch stood up to get another glass of wine for Lisa. No use having just one roaring drunk on the premises. "Closure is important to people. Not everyone can waltz away from relationships as easily as you seem to be able to do."

Mitch could hear the bitterness in her own voice and didn't care.

"What sort of closure did you want with me?" Lisa asked, softly, to absorb the anger.

"Nothing," Mitch waved it off.

"No, tell me! You've gone this far. What did you want from me?"

"I'll tell you what I missed most!" Mitch said, gathering up the rest of her courage.

"And what's that?" Lisa answered back, defiantly.

"I missed not being able to give you a …"

"A what?"

"A goodbye kiss. How's that for needing closure?"

"Well, here's your chance."

"What are you talking about?"

"Kiss me now. At least you'll get off this inner child obsession so you can get on with your life!"

"It's a little late."

"Better late than never. If you don't care about me anymore, then it won't matter."

Mitch thought she had heard this kind of logic somewhere before. Too bad she didn't think a little deeper. Instead, she followed the rather inane advice of her bad angel and took Lisa in her arms. Instead of recoiling, which would have signaled the intent only of a groundless dare, Lisa stood her ground and waited. The kiss was everything Mitch had remembered. And more. Between the two of them, they had both learned a thing or two in two years and were now more than happy to try to impress the other. However, that was about the extent of the meaning for Mitch. It gave no thrill to kiss Lisa one last time. In fact, it kind of made her feel queasy.

"Just what exactly is going on here?"

Mitch recognized the voice. Oh, damn!

She slowly pulled away from Lisa to see Rebecca standing just a little inside the front door.

"Back from Japan so soon?"

"Apparently not soon enough!"

Lisa quietly slipped out of the room and hid out in the kitchen, where there was canned food, of course. This might be a long siege.

"I'm glad you're home," Mitch took a step.

"Don't even come near me!"

"Okay."

"Why were you kissing Lisa?"

Mitch's mind wandered around in that two or three ounces of rum that seemed to be gelling her thought process.

"It's been a long week, I can explain."

"The truth will do!"

"I was working through my residual feelings for Lisa," Mitch stated matter-of-factly. Rebecca had always wanted the truth. Maybe she was big enough to handle it.

"Leave me alone!"

"What?"

"You heard me, leave me the hell alone!"

With that pronouncement, Rebecca turned on her heel and walked out the door.

Lisa reappeared, munching on a celery stick. Where she found that after three hours of nonstop wake was anyone's guess.

"I guess that'll teach her to come back early."

"Don't start."

"I could go out and scrounge up another couple of pieces of mocha cheesecake for you to take home."

"You heard her, she wants to be left alone."

"Whatever."

"And so that's what I'm going to do."

"What are you talking about?"

"I'm going to go away for a while. Bring me the checkbook out of the office."

"Sure."

Mitch took the time to make out another month's worth of paychecks for everyone and signed a few blank checks as well before she handed the ledger back to Lisa.

"If there's an emergency, you'll still have the petty cash drawer, except for what I'm about to borrow."

"Borrow. That's a good one. Where are you going?"

"I don't know."

"You'll call when you get there?" Lisa trailed after Mitch, who had gone into Marge's office.

"I don't know."

"How long will you be gone?"

"I don't know," Mitch said as she unlocked the two-million-dollar drawer.

"So much for closure."

Mitch counted out a hundred thousand, give or take a thousand.

Lisa tried one more time, "You'll be back?"

"I'll be back, sometime."

Sensing that it was now safe emotionally, she pulled Lisa into a brief hug. Then she left. Pointing her car due generally south, she drove until she was tired. If the truth were known, she shouldn't have been out on the road at all, having been tired since two days ago and a little bit too much rum on the brain. She checked into a flea bag motel for six hours sleep. They had given her about two minutes of grief about not giving them a credit card imprint. Mitch, trying to avoid a paper trail, handed over double what the room rate was. They still informed her snottily that they would have to disconnect her phone. She didn't say it out loud, but thought to herself that it would save her the trouble of ripping it out of the wall anyway.

The next morning, Mitch had a choice. Well, not at first. At first, she had two over-the-counter pain killers to quell her headache. Then, she had a choice. Go north and rejoin life as if nothing had happened. Go south and take a well-deserved break. Mitch realized that she really hadn't had a break since she'd won the lottery and now seemed to be as good a time as any. Her good and bad angel agreed. Her inner child, dormant until now, put the final stamp of approval on her decision. Ensuring that it wasn't a total temper tantrum, she called the Governor's staff secretary from a pay phone. Since they were never overjoyed at her calls, Mitch just left a message before hitting the road again. She knew it was just her imagination that she had heard paper crumpling and being tossed into the waste basket on the other end of the phone. They never wrote down her messages anyway, let alone toss them out! Whatever!

By noon, she was well past the Colorado state border, driving along I-25 through northern New Mexico, the Land of Enchantment. It didn't look quite so enchanting with a hangover, but that wasn't the fault of the landscape. As the highway curved west and then north-west, Mitch's stomach grumbled again. She had heard about the culinary delights of Santa Fe from patrons at the U, so she pulled into the city limits in time for a late lunch. The peacefulness of the desert settled on Mitch's soul like a comfortable dust, and after she scorched her tongue on fiery green chili burritos, she asked the waitress about rental information.

There were several real estate businesses to check with, but "if she was serious," the waitress stated firmly, there was a place within walking distance. Mitch copied the address and spent the next hour finding her way through the confusing streets that entwined the town like a web. If she had walked, it might have taken five, maybe ten minutes. But no…she had to drive. If anyone wanted to lose themselves, it sounded so sixties when Mitch thought about it, Santa Fe was just the ticket. After an exhausting but adventurous search, Mitch finally found the rental. It looked modest on the outside, so what was the big deal about being serious?

Mitch knocked on the door. A small woman opened the door just a crack.
"Hello," Mitch said.
"Wha jou want?"
"I heard this home was for rent."
"Come back with anajint," was her reply as she closed the door. It thudded back into place, sounding more final than the end of most novels.
Undaunted, Mitch knocked again. The door opened. Again.
"I'm sorry," Mitch said, "But I didn't understand."
"Jou got anajint?"
"Anajint?"
"Ajint!"
"Oh, agent, like a real estate agent. I get it."
"Jeah, anajint."
Mitch pulled one of the bundles of hundred-dollar bills out of her pocket.
"I have cash." "Three
thousan down."
Mitch peeled off thirty bills and handed them over.
"Jou come in."
"Thank you," Mitch said, happy to be out of the sun.
"Wipe jou feet!" she instructed.
"Of course."
Mitch could see why. The tile in the entranceway was imported from Italy and polished to a high shine. From where she stood, the

house exuded a cool airiness. Dust was afraid to land in this place. She didn't need to see any more. She was hooked. "Three thousan a month," the woman was getting out the paperwork. She certainly was businesslike.

"Okay."

Apparently, the lack of argument deflated the woman, just a little. Perhaps she had expected a fight. Mitch wasn't in the mood for any more conflict.

"Jou sign here," she pointed to the six-month lease agreement.

"And you'll give me a receipt for the cash."

"Of course."

Ten minutes later, the paperwork was complete.

"I clean once a week. Only once." She held up her index finger like she meant business.

"Do you cook?"

"Thas extra."

"How much?"

"Five hundred a month. Jou buy the groceries."

"Okay, let's try it for two weeks."

"Five hundred minimum."

With each transaction, her mood was improving.

"You drive a hard bargain, Ms…," Mitch tried to decipher the signature on the cash receipt. It began with an L, and after that it was anyone's guess. "La, Le…."

"Bella."

"Bella, I'm Mitch."

"Meech?"

"Close enough. Well, Bella, what do people do for fun in Santa Fe?"

"Don jou know! Everybody an artist." She pronounced the word artist like she was French.

"Artists? Hmmmm. Sounds relaxing."

"I got no time for art. I gotta go to the store and cook."

Mitch had noticed the plethora of art in the town as she wandered around lost like Moses. Artist, huh? It sounded like just the tonic Mitch needed to unwind after a long couple of weeks. Mitch managed to backtrack to her parked car and then drove it to her new rental. Once the Subaru was safely tucked away in the enclosed garage, Mitch unpacked what little she had brought with her, which comprised of putting her cash in a drawer in the bedroom. She admired the paintings on the walls. They were soothing. Ideal for lulling her to sleep. Then, for lack of anything else to do, she tested the bed for firmness. It must have been perfect, she slept for twelve hours in between fresh, crisp sheets while still in her clothes. When she could no longer ignore her stomach, she dragged herself to the kitchen. Food, which tasted a damn site better than dog food casserole, was waiting for her. She ate, showered, and then slept again, this time without clothes. Another ten hours slipped by. It was heavenly.

When she awoke, her money was intact, her clothes were clean and lunch was served. Mitch took time to eat before shopping for clothes. At least two changes of wardrobe were necessary since she hadn't bothered to pack. But first, another call to Rebecca's chief of staff to allay any worry she might have. The message would be passed on. Uh huh. Mitch wasn't buying it. What she was buying would be at the mall. She drove to a shopping area and walked around, picking out beautiful articles of clothing here and there, even finding a couple of things to take back home to Rebecca. Whenever that was safe. She was outfitted for a life of desert living by four and scurried back home in time for dinner. Bella was just putting the finishing touches on one of her specialties, shrimp paella. Mitch would have crawled across glass for this back at the mansion.
"It smells wonderful," she told Bella.
"Of course it does. I cook it!"
"Tell me something, Bella," Mitch asked, "You will join me for dinner, won't you?" "I don eat with my employers."
"Do you eat with friends?"
"Sometime."
"If I say we're friends first, will you have a bite with me? Please?"
"One bite, then I gotta go."
They sat down and she served and then ate a couple of bites.
"I wanted to ask you a couple of questions, Bella."
"Then I go."

"First question, you mentioned that I buy the groceries. So you would prefer that I shop, correct?"

"Of course not! What kinda question is that? How jou know what to buy if I cook!"

"So, you could make me a list."

"I do the shopping! Next question."

"Where would I sign up for art classes?"

"In town."

"Where in town?"

"Lotsa places. The Painter's Group is a good place to begin."

"That's a good idea. Thanks."

Bella shook her head side to side.

"What?" Mitch asked.

"Any woman got a pocket fulla cash don know where to sign up for art classes must be from a long way away." "You're right, Bella. I'm from a long way away."

During the night, it felt just like that. She felt universes away from Rebecca. She had called the mansion twice, and hadn't heard back. Maybe being in single orbits for a while would help. Art class would be a kick. Mitch hadn't dabbled in paint since kindergarten finger painting day. She'd go sign up tomorrow.

By the next afternoon, Mitch was sitting in front of a blank canvas surrounded by a dozen talented artists. Or as Bella would say, "Artistes?" Is *this* what seemed like such a relaxing idea just yesterday? Now, she felt her stomach clench as she observed everyone else creating beautiful bowls of fruit with mere brush strokes. Mitch couldn't draw an inference most days, let alone a banana.

"Start slowly," her instructor sounded soothing behind the doubting eyes. Come to think of it, she looked a lot like Mitch's kindergarten teacher, complete with the doubt. Mitch obeyed authority well, it had said so on all of her reports cards. Well, not word for word. It had said something like, "Respects authority" and "Doesn't run with scissors." Okay, so she made the second one up. She could make things up now that she had that artistic license that she paid for. They called it a fee. Fine. Anyway, Mitch obeyed, and created a god-awful mess. Well, at least it was *her* god-awful mess. It was fun once she got started, and slowly, the knot in her stomach dissolved.

Speaking of fees, by paying extra, Mitch had smooth-talked the Painter's Group into allowing her to attend class every day. By the third day, not only had Mitch created three more god-awful messes, but she also managed to get on a first-name basis with a few of the other students and accompanied them to a coffee party at the local espresso shop, aptly named, "Espresso Yourself." Oh those clever artists! They were an eclectic bunch and Mitch did her best to blend in. She paid the tab. That helped with the blending. Artists were starving everywhere, but nowhere was there a more excited bunch of artists than at this gathering. They could hardly contain their glee. Next week was "Nude Week!"

Oh gee. Mitch looked mostly thunderstruck. She hadn't checked the curriculum. Before the weekend, Mitch left another message for Rebecca, including the phone number of her rental. Since she had forgotten her cell phone at the U, there was only one way to find her. If Rebecca wanted to talk, she could call Santa Fe. And say what? "Gee, I'm sorry I barged in on you and your girlfriend kissing up a storm?" Guilt washed over Mitch. Maybe nude painting was just the thing to keep her mind off her mistakes.

Over the weekend, between sleeping and eating, Mitch frittered away her time meeting the art group at the local paint supply store. Up until this time in her life, Mitch had only bought paint in the gallon size, enough to do the exterior of a house and a matching garage if you were rich enough to afford one. Paint by the gallon and a couple of rollers and 2 or 3 four-inch brushes usually filled the bill. This artistic stuff was a whole different ballgame, and just how ignorant she was, she tried desperately to hide from her new artistic coffee friends. It was okay, they could spot a novice a kilometer away. The store was fascinating. The minute Mitch walked in, it was as if she was transformed into another dimension. Colors and hues and brushes and canvases were packed along aisles. It would take a lot of guidance to buy the correct material.

Brushes. That sounded like a good place to start, unless Mitch wanted to revert back to finger paints. There were brushes for oils and acrylics and watercolors. They, her new friends, and Annie in particular, gave her help. "The softer brushes are for watercolors. The harder, stiffer brushes are for oil and acrylic, in a general use way."

Annie had to be seventy if she was a day, so she should know this stuff. Right?

"So, do you paint nudes in oil or acrylic?"

"Depends."

Mitch decided to stay on the safe side and buy a variety of ten or twelve of each type of brush. They ranged in price from three to seventy dollars. Apiece.

Annie rolled her eyes. Mitch noticed.

"What?"

"Are you taking an art class or opening a store of your own?"

"I thought I'd give them away as Christmas presents."

"I'll go home and hang my stocking up tonight."

Mitch smiled. Annie was too cute. Any seventy-year-old lady interested in painting nudes was okay in Mitch's book.

"Now what?"

"Paint," Annie said.

Mitch knew they were talking noun, not verb. The next display had acrylics. About every color in the world, in fact. It was more confusing than buying a couple of gallons to redo the living room. There was Cerulean Blue and Medium Magenta and Unbleached Titanium. This sounded more like a chemistry class than art. "Here's a good nudie color," Annie pronounced. She held up a tube of Titan Buff. It even sounded sexual. Mitch was beginning to feel like she should go home now. Not to the villa, but instead to Colorado. Right back to the mansion, where naked people stayed behind closed doors. "Here's another good flesh tone, Light Portrait Pink. Mix it to ten to one tint and it might be just the ticket," Annie mused.

Mitch nodded, recognizing that math was now involved and cringed.

"Too light, too pinky," said Bill, who himself was more of a earth-tone kinda guy. "I'd buy more along the lines of Flesh Ochre or Yellow

Oxide."

Annie nodded. He left.

"That's great if you're trying to match a flower pot!"

"A flower pot?"

"Too earthy for me."

"Oh, Annie, I didn't think anything was too earthy for you?" Mitch teased.

"Start picking out your colors, young lady. My stocking will be up tonight!"

Mitch poked around, knowing full well that all the taste she ever had was truly in her mouth. Still, the colors pulled her close and tempted her to buy. She picked up a set of one-hundred forty-four oil colors, each tube containing enough paint to get her started. The set alone was hundreds of dollars. Good thing she had brought cash. Between the brushes, paint, canvas and easel, the total bill was close to one thousand dollars. So much for school supplies. She barely had enough change to treat Annie to dinner. They parted at nine, which gave Mitch plenty of time to set up her new paint studio. When she had rented the villa, she knew it was right the moment she walked in the door, but if she had seen the "studio" as Bella referred to it, she would have signed a year lease. It was a beautiful room with a hard wood floor that begged to be painted in. The double windows let in the light of the day but not the heat. At night, the moon poked in to see what was new. Tonight, there was something new. Mitch, her easel, her brushes and paints, and her soul. This was the vacation she needed. Mitch relocated the mattress and slept in the room. If Bella objected, she kept it to herself.

Actually, the only thing that Mitch and Bella fussed about was food. Mitch ate out more than suited Bella, who obviously liked to cook. If Mitch wasn't careful, she would need to shop for clothes again. Another part of Mitch felt that she was getting too good a bargain with Bella, paying only five-hundred a month. So she tried to cut back on the woman's work, since she had already flatly refused a pay raise. Things seemed to be backfiring, as more and more food piled up in the refrigerator. It was all delectable. To offset the extra calories, she took long walks every evening. Her new jeans were breaking in beautifully, and the material was soft and soothing, just like the town.

Nude Monday rolled around, with just a quiver of anticipation. Mitch did her best to not blush and was relieved to discover that it was *male* nude week. Now, *that* was something Mitch could be dispassionate about. Besides, it was far more interesting than a banana. Mitch looked over at Annie, who winked back. Ah yes, Titan Buff. After class, Mitch made a beeline for the changing room and waited for the model to dress. He came out, and seemed genuinely surprised that he had a groupie waiting.

"Hello, my name is Mitch Tanner."

"Hi, I'm Tim."

"Hi, Tim. Say, I need to ask you a favor. Would you go out and have a cup of coffee with me?"

"Well, I have a girlfriend," he said with the perfect touch of timidity.

"Oh, so do I," Mitch said, "So we have one thing in common."

"Uh, I guess it would be okay then."

They went to the coffee bar, where Mitch endured the notoriety of "hitting on" the model the first night. Ohhhhh.

"You said you needed a favor?" he said after a long sip of something latte.

"I stink at painting."

"I see."

"And I was wondering if you would help me with my homework." "I dunno."

"This isn't a come-on. I'm really a lesbian who's really on vacation who really stinks at painting. If I could pay you double your fee to do some overtime work at my house, it would help me out a lot." "I have a girlfriend." It was like an echo. What a sweet young man. "She's more than welcome to come over. We can have dinner. She can read. She can watch. She can give me pointers? She does know you do this, doesn't she?"

"I charge one-hundred for the art class, and yeah, she knows."

"I'll pay you three hundred."

"Per sitting?"

"Per hour if that helps you to make a decision."

"I'll ask her."

"That's always a good idea to get these things talked over with the better half," Mitch intoned her recent discovery.

"The better what?"

"It's an old saying."

"Uh, okay. Give me your phone number."

"Sure thing."

Mitch had Bella set the table for company the very next day. Not only had the girlfriend agreed, but was willing to let him come over all by himself as long as Bella was the designated chaperone, something Bella had begrudgingly agreed to during the preliminary phone call to Mitch's rental. She, the girlfriend, would be out window shopping with the extra fee money. Who knows how many windows you can get for that kind of money? As she waited for her guest, Mitch called Trish, just on a lark, to see if Colorado was still there. Her voice mail picked up. Oh well. Mitch didn't even leave a message. She'd wait and talk later.

Tim arrived promptly at six and ate about fifty-dollars worth of food before they got started. Where did he put all that? Oh, yeah. Mitch remembered now. All those muscles needed lots of protein. He posed and Mitch painted for an hour and then they made an appointment for the following afternoon, early, around tea time. It seemed like a good and civilized idea at the time.

Mitch woke up early the next day with the intention of spending time on Canyon Road. This is where the real artists resided in Santa Fe, at least according to the travel brochure. As a child, Mitch had limited exposure to the arts. Her parents hadn't been wealthy patrons of the arts and now they were dead and gone. It wasn't a cause and effect thing, it was just how things had turned out.

Annie confirmed what the travel brochure had stated. If Mitch wanted to see the most amazing collection of art anywhere in the world, it would be found on Canyon. Perhaps Annie and the local chamber of commerce were prejudiced, but honestly, wasn't everyone prejudiced where art was concerned? Maybe discerning was a softer word to use, but it was still a fact of life that people appreciated different mediums of art. Mitch had truly never evolved beyond her childish fascination with finger paints. Blue blues, red reds, mixed together yielding the purplest purples.

Canyon Road was less of a road in the common usage of the name and more of a small paved trail leading up into the hills from the Santa Fe Plaza. Canyon Road started from a more major road called Paseo de Peralta, which itself completed a three quarters circle around the downtown scenic area, which included the Loretto Chapel and the Palace of the Governors. If the governors here really had a palace, Mitch wondered if that would ever be enough of a selling point to convince Rebecca to relocate and run for office here.

Mitch's Canyon Road experience was an eye opener indeed. There were paintings that looked like someone else had also been caught up in the primordial goo of finger paints. But there were also very sophisticated works of painted art as well. One only had to walk from shop to shop, gallery to gallery in order to visually feast on these paintings. However, where the real depth of art revealed itself was in the various mediums through which artists channeled their creative talents. There was sculpture, ironwork, brass, fabric and a few things that frankly defied categories. It was, after a while, overwhelming to the senses and the feet.

A coffee/teahouse was situated strategically near the top of the hill and Mitch stepped inside for some much-needed liquid refreshment. Expecting beatniks and smoke, there instead was an eclectic group of people enjoying a break from their day. Honestly, Mitch needed to get out of her bubble more often. Or maybe just the sixties viewpoints she grew up hearing about. Rebecca would know more about that time in history, but probably had experienced none of it firsthand growing up in rural Kansas.

At moments like this, Mitch was tough on herself. Prejudice in any form was an ugly thing, and her own prejudice seemed even more hideous, considering the source. Artists and tea drinkers didn't need to also be beatniks and smokers. So she waited in line for a minute or two, which gave her time to study the offerings on the chalk board suspended over the counter by thin nylon filament. Okay, there was tea. Some that she had heard about and some that she had no idea what it was. When had it happened that someone had invented a bunch of new kinds of tea and Mitch had been left out of the loop. She knew there were different kinds of coffee. Like, for instance, Folgers and Yuban. But now, there were coffees she didn't know about either. Something like Ethiopian? And what on earth was Yerba Mate. Was it Australian?

Mitch had hoped to have enough time to study all these possibilities by the time she got to the front of the line, but that hadn't happened. She was still translating without a guide when she arrived at the counter to order. The consternation of the people behind her was evident. So she did what people usually do in similar circumstances. She ordered something familiar.

"Just a small coffee, please."

"Roomfermilk?" came the reply.

It sounded like German to Mitch. "Pardon?"

"Roomfurcream?" came a different word from the person behind the counter.

Mitch wasn't understanding either inquiry. The line behind her was growing impatient. A lady behind Mitch decided to be helpful. "She wants to know if you are going to put cream in your coffee?" she explained as if to a two-year-old.

"Why would she want to know that?" Mitch had never before been asked about this and wondered if it was a reflection on her perceived coffee-drinking skills. Like, if you needed water in your scotch. You know, a lightweight.

"Because if you're going to use creamer, she won't fill your cup up all the way so you will have room left for the cream."

The woman had enunciated every single word like it was Mitch who had been the German tourist.

"Oh! I get it now! Room...for...cream!"

The woman who had been helping Mitch understand this concept now enthusiastically nodded her head like Mitch had been potty trained or something.

"Yes," Mitch turned back to the patient clerk. "I do! I will need room for cream!"

The entire line breathed a sigh of relief. These folks were serious about their caffeine and needed a fix. Mitch took the cup over to a counter that had different types of cream and sugar products. There was half-and-half, whole, skim, and soy in the milk department. Sugar wasn't any simpler either. Mitch took what she recognized as plain white sugar and passed on the cinnamon and nutmeg and vanilla. There were times when she enjoyed plain coffee and other times when she wanted something more exotic. Like chocolate syrup. But if she wanted spices like this, she's stick to eating pumpkin pie. She took her cup to a table by the window and enjoyed looking out over the rugged scenery. She thought about Rebecca. Mitch had called what? Two or three times by now? The staff had taken the messages. The object lesson had been made pretty clear, never kiss your old girlfriend when your new girlfriend was in the same room. Maybe time away was good. Mitch could spend time mourning Marge.

Rebecca could debrief from her trip to Japan.

Meanwhile, Mitch could learn to paint. There wasn't enough time left in the Universe for that to happen, but it was pleasant enough to be among those who could: Young adults, moms with kids, senior citizens. Talent was a funny thing. It came out of nowhere, evidently. Landed, took root where it could flourish, and making life worth living in its wake. Mitch drank her coffee in a peacefulness surrounded by noise and hubbub. For the first time in a long time, Mitch felt relaxed. Like she had made peace with a lot of the recent events, and at the same time, it was as if she found a place where she felt comfortable, if not completely at home.

Chapter 6

The next day, feeling rejuvenated after another good night's sleep, Mitch prepared to once again attempt the impossible. Paint a nude man and make it look like something besides ridiculous.

Bella had once again fixed a snack that would have lasted to the moon and back. Tim helped himself to the food and then shed his shirt and jeans. There was a knock at the door. Bella went to take care of whoever it was.

Rebecca knocked on the door, again. Louder. A small Hispanic woman answered. "Hello," the woman said, suspiciously.

"Is Mitch Tanner here?"

"Meech Tanner?"

"Yes, is she here?"

"Who are jou?" the woman held her ground, not opening the door any more than she had to.

"I'm the governor."

"No jou not!"

"Yes, I am!" Rebecca answered back, holding on to the last of her patience with tired nerves.

"Jou not the gubernor of New Mexico!"

"You're right," Rebecca nodded, a small smile crossed her lips. "I'm the governor of Colorado."

"Whas jour name?"

"Rebecca."

"Rebecca what?"

"Rebecca Louise Fairbanks."

"Kay. Jou wait here," the woman opened the door and pointed emphatically to a spot just inside the door. Not looking back, the woman walked to a doorway and disappeared. Rebecca, never one to be hesitant, followed behind at what she considered to be a safe distance. As she turned the corner, she abruptly found herself in a rather large sun dappled studio, with three people staring back at her. The first was the Hispanic woman, with a look of disapproval on her face. The second was Mitch, beaming ear to ear at the sight of Rebecca. The third person was a buck-naked male model. He must have been six foot two, if he was an inch. His muscled shoulders and torso slimmed down to a trim waist, where his hands were placed as he stood akimbo. He turned to face Rebecca, and as he viewed this beautiful woman, he became more male. A lot more male. Rebecca tried to focus on his deep brown eyes. Oh those eyes.

"Hello, Dear," Mitch said, mostly to break the spell.
Rebecca remembered now that she was angry. It had only taken five, maybe six seconds.
"Don't 'hello, dear' me! I have been looking everywhere for you!"
"I'd like you to meet Bella, my household engineer." The Hispanic woman nodded to Rebecca, although she was still mightily upset that Rebecca hadn't stayed put in the foyer. "And this nice man is Tim. He has been kind enough to be a model for my painting class homework."
Tim held out his hand, and they shook like they were at a cocktail party. There were those eyes, again. So penetrating.
"I have a feeling that we're done for the day, Tim. Thanks for your help."
"Will you need me tomorrow?"
"Tell you what," Mitch said, glancing at Rebecca. Why don't we take tomorrow off. I'll still pay your fee, of course."
"Thanks."
He turned and walked over to his clothes, which were hung perfectly at the far end of the studio. Oh yes. Perfectly. Mitch waited for Rebecca's full attention. It happened. Gradually. "You found me. Took you long enough."
"What in the hell do you mean by that remark!?"
Mitch studied Rebecca, surprised at the degree of her anger after the passage of time. "You're still upset?"
"You're damn right I'm upset! I've had the police looking for you for days!"
"Why?"
"Why? You disappeared, for Christ sake! I thought something had happened to you! I checked the hospitals, the morgue…"

"You told me to leave you alone."

"I what?"

"You told me to leave you alone. I'm just doing what you asked me to do," Mitch answered quietly.

Mitch's quiet manner sent a message to Rebecca. It wasn't often that she was this reticent. Her mind searched back through the conversations she had had with Mitch just prior to her disappearance. The argument came back to mind.

"Are you talking about the argument we were having?"

"I didn't think it was an argument, as such." "You were kissing Lisa," Rebecca said.

"I explained that."

"I remember. You told me you still love her."

"I said I still had feelings for her and I was working those out."

"And then I told you to leave me alone. I remember now."

"So I did."

"I didn't mean for you to leave me *this* alone. I meant for you to leave me alone for a few minutes. An hour, maybe."

"I left you alone. You shouldn't ask for things you don't want."

"You had me worried."

"I called and checked in."

"No, you didn't!"

"Yes, I did."

"No, you didn't!"

"Yes, I did!" Mitch wasn't yelling yet. It was getting harder not to.

"You did?"

"I gave your staff the messages. Didn't they give them to you?"

"No, they didn't."

"Well, when you go back to Colorado, I suggest that you check with your staff. Hell, check the phone records."

"That's how I found you, but it was through Trish's phone records."

"You didn't think to check your own?"

"No, I didn't."

"I'm sorry. If I had known you were worried, I would have done something. When I called in, and you didn't call back, I just assumed you still wanted to be left alone."

"How did you ever end up clear down here in Santa Fe?"

"It's a pretty part of the world, isn't it!"

"The men are certainly good looking."

Mitch laughed. "Tim is a nice guy. He's working his way through school."

"Nice work, if you can get it."

"You made quite an impression on him."

"What do you mean?"

"He's been posing for me for two days with no reactions. You walk in the door and he practically salutes. I thought for a minute that I was going to have to run down to the art supply store and stock up on more penis pink."

"Penis pink?"

"It's a shade they sell. They use it a lot in art class."

"I expect so, if Tim's the paid model."

"So, I suppose you expect me to take you out to a nice dinner," Mitch said as she put away her painting supplies. Bella had left the room earlier, to see Tim to the door, and was now back and fretting. She had let her guard down and now Mitch had been bothered. Such too nice a woman to be bothered!

"Bella, why don't you take the rest of the day off?" Mitch suggested.

"Oh, no ma'am! I cook you dinner. Both of you."

"That's alright, Bella, you don't need to do that."

"I cook better than you get going out."

"I know that Bella, but if I don't go out once in a while, I forget that. Tell you what, you take tonight off, and tomorrow, we'll treat the governor to one of your fabulous meals."

"I go shop now." "Thank you, Bella."

She hurried through the front door, happy to be on a mission. Mitch and Rebecca still stood apart. It wasn't like them to surrender so easily after so much anger.

"You still love Lisa."

"I still have feelings."

"I don't see why you still love her?"

"Love isn't something I turn on and off. It doesn't come in faucet form." "She hurt you."

"That's right. What do you want me to do? Would it be easier if I lied and said that I hated her? Is that what you want? You want me to hate people?"

"I just don't want you to…I don't know what I want."

"Okay. Maybe you just didn't frame your questions right. I still love Lisa, I always will. I still love you. I always will. I want to be with you. You just haven't been very easy to be with lately. You weren't there when we had the grand reopening of the Lucky U. You weren't there when Marge died. You weren't there when it was important for me to have you there. Lisa was there. She was comforting. She listened. And yes, we kissed."

"You kissed her back?"

"You were there. But you didn't want to hear about it. When you and Jeff get together to talk about Mary, I don't throw a fit."

"I don't kiss him."

"But I wouldn't mind if you did, because I know that you have a lot of history with him." "The kiss meant nothing?"

"The kiss meant, 'I'm sorry one of your best friends died.' It was more than I got from you."

Mitch didn't mention that it was a good-bye kiss of sorts. Maybe she would try and explain it later. "I was out of town."

"You still are," Mitch remarked quietly, doing her level best to scrub all anger from her voice as she tossed the last of her paint supplies in a box.

Rebecca walked over to Mitch and held her face in her hands. Mitch gazed up into her eyes, searching for an indication of things to come. A kiss came. A deep, soft kiss. The kind that Rebecca had become famous for, if only to Mitch. Mitch stepped closer, to hold this women, this lover that she had missed so achingly in the past few days. Rebecca managed to elude most of the embrace and slowly but gently turned Mitch around so she could hold her from behind. Mitch didn't question. Rebecca had her mind made up. She unzipped Mitch's dusty jeans and maneuvered her hand inside, touching Mitch where it would bring back so many feelings so quickly. After a moment or two, she stopped.

"You forgot how?" Mitch asked, hanging somewhere between great and magnificent in the foreplay.

"No, I just wanted to give you an appetizer. You're still going to take me out to dinner?" "You are such a tease!"

"I just want your full attention the rest of the night. We still have serious things to discuss." "Let me change for dinner."

"You can't go in jeans?"

"I can do almost anything in jeans, as you're finding out! But I want to look nice for my wonderful companion. Besides, if we're going to continue arguing, I want to do it in style."

Mitch pulled Rebecca's other hand to her lips and kissed it. One finger at a time. This was almost as teasing as what she had done to Mitch a few moments ago and Rebecca was apparently enjoying a taste of her own medicine.

"We'd better go eat. I can tell we're going to need our strength."

It was as close as you could get to a standing reservation in Santa Fe. Mitch and Rebecca were at what had become "Mitch's table" in the most expensive restaurant in all of New Mexico. Not that it was ever planned that way. Mitch had only arrived a few days ago, but word traveled fast. She had money. Lots of it. And she was nice to people, too. Two or three wait staff had trundled all over themselves to ensure Mitch's good favor, bringing wine, water and appetizers. When Mitch remarked that she liked Rebecca's appetizers better, Rebecca only smiled. As Mitch ate, Rebecca talked.

"I can't stop being governor."

Mitch looked up. As far as arguments were concerned, this was the best place to continue.

"I don't want you to stop being governor."

"And I don't want to break up."

"We're not breaking up!"

"You leave town for days on end and don't tell me where you're going? It felt like we were breaking up."

"Well, we're not. If, and you notice I said 'if' we ever break up, there's not going to be any question about it. It's going to be loud and on the ten o'clock news! I gave you some time to yourself. I figured that's what you needed."

"I need you."

"You need to fire whatever staff person lost my messages on purpose."

"I'll do that, when I get home, which must be soon." "You can't stay down here for a while? I rented the house for a month, with an option on five more. I'm thinking about buying it outright. I know it's expensive, but isn't it beautiful?"

"I haven't seen all of it, yet."

"But what you did see, you were very impressed with, weren't you?" Mitch arched an eyebrow and Rebecca laughed.

"I want you to take me to the art store before I leave town. I want to see what other shades of pink they sell."

"They sell the shade that you're turning right now, as well as a beautiful color called nipple rose."

"Dare I ask?"

The second course of crisp salad graced their table, and they began to talk of other things that had been ignored. Mitch had never truly gotten the entire story about the trip to Japan. Lisa's kiss had squelched that conversation. Rebecca tried at first not to brag, but it didn't go over with Mitch. Mitch had always encouraged Rebecca to boast about her talents, and before the main course of shrimp fajitas was devoured, Rebecca had gone into excruciating detail about her accomplishments. Mitch smiled, nodded and listened through cheese enchiladas and quesadillas as she heard about the business deals that would be forthcoming from the trip. Rebecca was indeed a masterful negotiator and tough but fair businesswoman. Colorado was lucky to have her, even if it always seemed that they needed constant reassurances.

After a dessert of fruit and ice cream, they walked leisurely back to the rental, now couched in darkness. No more sunshine to poke through and protrude into private activities. The bedroom was smaller than the studio. The builder must have been more interested in art than sleep. When Rebecca noted this, Mitch took her by the hand and led her out to the studio, where she slowly undressed her.

"Here? In the studio?"

"I'll bring a mattress. It's comfy. I sleep out here when it gets hot."

"What if someone comes by?"

"They could just as easily look in the bedroom windows."

"I guess so."

Rebecca relaxed in a little while as she and Mitch lay next to each other in the room. Outside, a soft breeze stirred the trees, and they heard the distinctive sound of crickets. "This is beautiful," Rebecca stated. "You're what's beautiful," Mitch clarified.

"I didn't know you could paint." "I can't!"

"You seem to be doing okay."

"I'm terrible. I would need about ten year's lessons just to get to the rank of nearly hopeless." "You could do that back home?"

"What? Be hopeless," Mitch sighed.

"Why don't you tell me what's wrong?" Rebecca wanted to get to the root of Mitch's mood.

Mitch looked at her and shrugged. "I feel like I'm always underfoot when I'm at the mansion."

"You're not underfoot. You're hardly ever there when business is brisk at the U."

"But when I'm there, I'm a nuisance. You don't notice it, but everybody else does. That's probably why the staff so conveniently lost my messages. They probably hoped that if I stayed away long enough, I would stay away for good. I'm as useless as a back pocket in a shirt at the mansion, and everybody but you knows it." "That's not true. When you're not at the U, you're more than welcome at the mansion."

"I'd spend more time at the U, but there, I'm getting into trouble with Lisa. She's underfoot there as much as I am at the mansion, and we can't seem to get out of each other's way."

"You brought that on yourself."

"It took me a few days down here to figure that out."

"How much longer is it going to take you to figure out a solution?"

"About another two days."

"The art store is going to run clear out of penis pink by then."

"Well, then, I'll just have to improvise, won't I? I'll just have to mix nipple rose with something lighter!" Mitch teased with more than her

131

voice. Her touch sent shivers of delight through Rebecca. Mitch touched with more than her fingers, and Rebecca stirred and moved in sync with Mitch. After a few minutes, when Rebecca was building to an orgasm, Mitch slowly stopped and straddled Rebecca, holding her hands gently but firmly just above her head as she kissed her lips.

"You're not stopping, are you?" Rebecca asked with a husky voice.

"No, I just wanted you to know what my idea of an appetizer is." Mitch spent the next few minutes kissing Rebecca intimately around the face and neck as her excitement waned a little. Mitch was careful to not wait too long, and when the time was right, she nuzzled Rebecca back to a long and satisfying orgasm.

The bedroom was now cool and quiet. They had moved there after Rebecca had cooled down from her climax. She relaxed so quickly that she slept the rest of the night away close to Mitch, seeking her body even in sleep to be next to. By the time Bella arrived to fix breakfast, Mitch was up and dressed. Rebecca was still sleeping, exhausted from lovemaking, emotion and travel.

"She still here?" Bella asked in a whisper.

"Yes, thank goodness," Mitch replied.

"You two good friends?"

"We're lovers, Bella."

"You and the gubernor?"

"Me and the governor."

"Well, she's a lucky girl," Bella stated as she set forth to cook.

"She's watching her diet, as usual. We better cook healthy until she leaves."

"When she leaves, you go too?"

"Yes, I'm afraid so. But I want to pay you for extra time."

"You buy the place, I keep it nice for you. All the time."

"I'd like that, but I can't pay you full time wages."

"Thas kay. I get another job to help along."

Rebecca came in on the tail end of the conversation, and Bella busied herself even further. "So, you're staying?" Rebecca asked, without emotion.

"After last night, do you think I could?"

"Well, you're talking about buying the place?"

"As a vacation home. Wouldn't it be nice to come down here once in a while and make love again in the studio, in the daylight?" Bella busied herself with cooking chores, but kept one ear on the conversation.

"It would be heaven on earth. Can you afford it?"

"I'll look into it. In the meantime, how would you like a tour of the city, such as it is?"

"I'd love it. Come and help me pick out something to wear." Rebecca had been selecting her wardrobe since she was two years old, so Mitch could only wonder. Rebecca caught her in a full embrace when they got to the bedroom.

"You let me fall asleep again last night. You shouldn't let me get away with that!"

"Why not? You were exhausted."

"I want to make love."

"To me?"

"No, to Madonna's bodyguard!"

"Right here? Right now?"

"Why not?"

Mitch couldn't honestly think of a good reason why not. Rebecca took the silence as agreement and guided Mitch back to the bed. The tour of the city would have to wait.

Rebecca had, over the course of their short relationship, learned the benefits of taking her time. Mitch had been an excruciatingly patient lover, teaching her about the wonderful benefits of soft and tender touching as well as the harder, more needful kisses that would show up from time to time. Never boring, never routine, and always honest, Rebecca had become bolder as time went on. Bella had prepared breakfast and then left to take care of other errands. Noting that neither one of them had eaten since dinner the night before, Rebecca took a few moments to forage through the kitchen for food. She found the fruit and bread that Bella had left behind for them. Rebecca settled back into bed and hand fed oranges to Mitch as if she were a goddess, and then experimented, to Mitch's wonderment, with the leftovers. First, Rebecca squeezed a little of the orange juice on Mitch's neck and then chased it down with her tongue. The neck was just a convenient starting point and before Mitch could say "orchard", she had dribbles of orange juice on the most sensitive parts of her body. It was as if Rebecca had had a vitamin deficiency, so great was her appetite for this nourishment. Mitch could only lie back and enjoy the fulfillment. Rebecca snuggled up close after bringing Mitch to a climax and they rested for such a long time in comfortable silence that Mitch had dropped off to sleep.

"Remind me to put oranges on the shopping list," Mitch said after she woke up from a nap. "At least a dozen."

"Maybe I could plant a tree?"

"Maybe a grove?" "I love you."

"I love you, too."

"And you don't ever need to worry again about anyone else or anything else taking that love away."

"I know."

"She isn't even in your league."

"She's so . . ."

"Blond?"

"So beautiful." "So are you."

"Not in that way. That twenty-two year old drop-dead gorgeous way." "This is another one of those trick questions, isn't it?" Mitch asked.

"Like what?"

"Like, 'Gee, I don't like drop-dead gorgeous women. I like you' kind of trick question."

"I see your point. Does it seem like I'm begging for compliments?"

"No, but it does seem like I should make things clear. The problem is, I don't know how."

"Give it your best shot."

"Lisa is gorgeous, no doubt about it. And you're gorgeous. But in a different way. In a genuine way. The beauty that makes you gorgeous radiates from your eyes. You're gorgeous in a deep down way. A way that doesn't come off at night with cold cream. A way that doesn't depend on your hairstyle. A way that haunts me even when my eyes are closed. That kind of way."

"That's beautiful. Not only are you a painter, but a poet as well."

"I'm neither, you flatterer."

134

"What did you want to tell me about the kiss with Lisa that you couldn't bring yourself to say yesterday?"

Mitch looked at Rebecca in the best puzzled way she could muster. "I'm beginning to hear what you're not saying about as clearly as what you do say."

"It would have sounded strange yesterday, that's why I waited." "It was a little more than a sympathy kiss. I could tell that from the doorway."

"I'd had one too many Flying Kangaroos."

"What a beginning to a story," Rebecca smiled. "Sounds like a great first line if you ever write a novel!"

"I'll keep that in mind. It sounds better than 'I was drunk' doesn't it?"

"So, about that kiss." "Lisa and I were talking about closure. It had been a terrible week. Before you even got a good start on your business trip, I found Marge almost dead in her office. There was the hospital and Marge's Texas relatives, and the wake. It was a walking nightmare. When everyone finally went home, Lisa mixed me one drink and that's about all I needed. We got to arguing, maybe bickering is a better word? Anyway, Lisa knew that I needed some release, so we got to picking at each other about our past relationship. I opened my big mouth and said something about never getting a chance to kiss her goodbye and she dared me to do it and that's about the time you came through the front door."

"You were kissing her goodbye?"

"From years ago. I know it sounds strange."

"Did it work?"

"I don't know yet. I haven't been back."

"I'm trying to be very modern about all of this, but it's difficult."

"I know. And you're doing better than I know I would be doing, under the circumstances."

"Would you have told me about it if I hadn't walked in?"

"Eventually."

"I need you to make a promise."

"Okay, what?"

"Being a powerful politician has one drawback. People stand in line to tell you what they think you want to hear. Everyone's a spin doctor. If no one else in my life tells me the truth, I want to know that I can count on you to be honest with me. All the time. Even if it hurts." "I'm not a perfect person. This could end up hurting a lot." "I doubt that. I just want to know where you are emotionally. You didn't call me in Japan. I had no idea what was going on."

"I didn't want to distract you."

"My joy in life is being distracted by you. Don't ever take that away from me."

"You got yourself a deal. Let's get dressed and take a hike. I want to show you something."

"I want to show you something first," Rebecca said as she pulled Mitch closer. So much for distractions.

Thirty minutes later, they dressed in comfortable clothes for the heat of the day, but respectful as well so that they could visit Mitch's favorite place, Our Lady of Light Chapel. Mitch had heard about the place as a child, and only now as an adult had made the pilgrimage. The interior was small, cool and quiet. The spiral staircase was remarkable, in a subdued sort of way.

"You know the story?" Mitch asked Rebecca in hushed tones.

"Vaguely. Tell me more."

"This is what religion is all about."

"What is?"

"This," Mitch gestured to the staircase. "This is. Or at least it should be. The story is that the Sisters of Loretto built the chapel but neglected to leave room for the stairs that they needed to go up to the choir loft."

Rebecca gazed up. The loft was small and yet so lovely.

"So, one day a mysterious carpenter showed up and built the only staircase that would fit, which was spiral in design, and he did so without any nails. Legend, or belief, depending on your point of view, was that the mysterious carpenter was Jesus. Of course, he wouldn't use nails, having been nailed to the cross. So, it's a miracle of sorts." "It's awe inspiring."

"And this is what religion should be about."

"Why do you say that?"

"Because religion should be about helping people, not about chiding them or scaring them or judging them. If we all used the scarce resources we have to the best of our ability to help each other out of a tight pinch, we'd be much better off as a society than spending days and weeks in churches fretting about the salvation of our little soul."

"I'm beginning to appreciate your view of the world."

"I'll admit, it is a little 'out of the box' but it's what gets me through."

"Can we talk more over lunch? I'm starved."

Of course she was, she had only had a little orange juice for breakfast.

"Sure. You want something with green chili?"

"Absolutely!"

They wandered through the downtown mall area until Mitch zoned in on another favorite hangout. At least Rebecca could be sure of the fact that Mitch had eaten well during her retreat. The green chili was stunning. It hurt so bad and yet tasted so good that it was hard to know when to stop. Mitch hadn't found that perfect balance yet and was sweating out of the top of her head by the time she got through the main course. Rebecca had been a little more conservative, no surprise there, in her order and was only in mild discomfort. What a showoff! They drank heavy duty margaritas and were ready for a nap by the time they arrived back at the house. It was cool and still. Cool and still enough to make Mitch want to talk about one other thing.

"I want to tell you something else," Mitch started down the path of Honest Truth. A map would have helped.

"Something else?"

"But I don't know where to start."

"It's about Lisa."

"And sex," Mitch tacked on.

"Lisa *and* sex."

"Right."

Rebecca raised up on one elbow to hear this loud and clear.

"I wasn't completely honest about something we talked about earlier."

"How earlier?"

"A couple of weeks ago. Maybe longer."

"Okay, so it's an old lie."

"Just well-aged. Like a good wine."

"Whatever. What's the lie?"

"You remember when you asked about frequency of orgasms?"

"Like how you were missing them?"

137

"Yeah, and then you asked if I'd ever missed one with Lisa."

"Uh huh."

"That's the lie."

"You always had one. I knew it."

"But that's only part of the story."

Mitch stopped talking long enough to organize her thoughts.

"You didn't want to share Lisa's sex hints with me."

"There isn't much to share, really, but she always made me come first. Always."

Rebecca nodded, waiting for more explanation.

"Do you realize how much pressure that puts on someone? It was like being a guy and having to, well, perform, I guess?"

Rebecca just kept nodding, obviously afraid that any remark would stop this stream of monologue.

"After a while, it dawned on me that it was more of a control issue and what started out as great fun soon deteriorated into looming anxiety."

Mitch stopped talking after this revelation. Rebecca knew that she had something else to say, and only after another quiet moment prodded with a non-committal, "Okay."

"And so, here's the honest truth," Mitch picked up again after making eye contact with Rebecca, "Not having an orgasm every time with you is so much more fun than it ever was having one every time with Lisa, that, well, I guess I hope I miss a lot more. With you." "When you say it that way, it makes perfect sense. But I don't want you to miss too many?"

"When I get concerned, I'll talk it over with you. Deal?"

"Deal. Now, I want to talk to you about something," Rebecca intoned.

"Okay."

"I feel partly responsible for driving you back into Lisa's arms."

"You're not."

"Let me finish! I think that me having all the say so in our sex life causes problems. It's every bit as bad as Lisa's control, and maybe worse." "Okay."

"And so I want you to take over for a while."

"If I have control, I may not do anything for a while and probably not at the frequency that you need?"

"Really?"

"If I didn't have sex again for twenty years and then died, you could still have my headstone inscribed, 'She was totally satisfied.'" "I'm that good?" Rebecca couldn't resist a grin.

"And more. Why don't we just sort of split up the sex initiation. You tell me what you need and when, and I'll tell you what I need and when."

"I'd like that."

"And then, if our schedules or libidos aren't in sync, we can start a 'dollar jar'."

"A what?"

"A 'dollar jar'. If you want sex and I'm too tired, I put a dollar in the jar. Same for you. Then at the end of a week or month or year, we'll take the money and do something fun. Splurge on dinner or a movie or a new car."

"What an original idea! I love it! I'm not sure we would end up with a car...."

"Twenty years is a long time."

"Maybe a skateboard?"

"Maybe a couple of bus tokens?"

Bella arrived later in the day in time to cook dinner. Of course, it was far superior to anything they had eaten out. When Rebecca engaged in pre-dinner chit chat with Bella, she finally managed to decipher her last name, which happened to be Lugosi. Mitch strained a muscle trying not to laugh.

"You mean I've been in the same house with Bella Lugosi for a week!"

"Let me check your neck for bite marks."

"Better yet, let me check your neck and leave a bite mark!"

"Put your fangs away and let's eat."

They supped on seafood paella. It had to be Bella's prize-winning recipe. After dinner, they took one last walk together before Rebecca's impending departure. She was leaving tomorrow. Mitch would stay behind to close things up.

"You'd like to live here, wouldn't you?" Rebecca half asked, half stated as they walked arm in arm down the dusky street. "I don't know if I'd want to live here, but I wouldn't mind dying here."

Rebecca looked over, puzzled.

"Haven't you ever thought about it?" Mitch asked.

"About where I'd like to die? Not really in a geographical sense." "I guess you're too busy living to be concerned. But me, I've thought about it a lot. And if I could really have control, I'd want to die here when the time came."

"But that's just it. We don't have that kind of control." "I guess it all boils down to the fact that if you really want to be absolutely sure about dying in Santa Fe, you have to live here."

"You're wrong about one thing."

"Just one?"

"I don't care where in the world I die, as long as I'm in your arms."

"Does eating seafood paella always make you this romantic?" "Oh, always!" Rebecca laughed.

"Then I'm just going to have to steal Bella's recipe."

"I wrote it on my hand."

"Cheater!"

They managed to keep the giggling down to a roar as they turned the last corner to home. No reason to wake up the neighbors, at least, not yet.

Chapter 7

By the time Mitch returned from Santa Fe, which was about three days after Rebecca had to report back, she knew what she had to do. She called Mary and set up an appointment. Of course, that's not what she called it. She called it lunch.

After hugs, they settled in with menus and chit chat. Mary was working tirelessly at the Center, a place where she helped abused children. She raised money and did intervention. That was a fancy term meaning she gave food, clothing and shelter to abused women and children while they tried to get their lives in order. It was more than work, it was a divine calling of some sort and Mary had the talent and compassion to make it all come together.

"How's work?" Mitch asked with a little more interest than normal. Fishing wasn't her strong suit.
"Busy, why?"
"Just wondering."
Mary looked concerned and this facial expression, more than any other, made her resemblance to her mother uncanny.
"I heard you ran away from home."
"I did."
"Aren't you getting a little old for that sort of thing?"
"I'm getting too old to run, period!"
"You had my mother worried."
"I fixed that problem."
"You didn't call."
"The staff didn't pass along my messages."
"You're kidding!"
"Nope."
"I see. Sorry I jumped on you."
"It's okay. I need a favor."
"You do?"
"A big favor."
"How big?"

"I need you to give Lisa a job."

"No way in hell!"

"At least hear me out."

Mary looked earnestly at Mitch. If she hadn't felt so strongly that Mitch was family, she would have walked out without further comment.

"You have two minutes."

"Okay. Lisa is good at working with people. She could get good donations. If she worked for you, your mother wouldn't need to be concerned about Lisa being constantly underfoot at the U. If Lisa raised a certain amount of money for you, I would convince her that she's truly absolved of all of her debt to me and then she can leave town to start over. Is that two minutes worth?" Mitch paused to take a breath.

"She treated me like shit on purpose in Texas."

"Now is your chance to repay her. If you want, make her clean toilets for a week. Or a month."

"If she alienates any of my long term donors, I'll personally drive her to the state border and leave her to fend for herself." "Is there a 'Yes' hidden somewhere in that statement?"

"Only because it would make things easier for my mother." Mitch couldn't help but smile. Mary and her mom were on such good terms lately, it made her heart sing.

"So it's a 'yes'?"

"It's a 'yes'!"

"Thanks! You won't regret it."

They ordered diet food and ate like rabbits, each munching greens and yellows with a couple of reds thrown in for good measure. It was as close to a salad-a-thon as Mitch could endure.

"When can she start?"

"Might as well start tomorrow."

"I owe you one."

"You owe me about ten!"

"I'll find a way to pay you back, I swear."

Lisa's first day at the Center was every bit as grueling as Mary had planned. She had to do every duty expected in boot camp except

142

march twenty miles in full pack. Well, maybe it wasn't quite that bad. Mary did give her a toilet brush instead of a toothbrush to clean the bathrooms. When Mitch had informed Lisa of her new occupation, she had just shrugged her slender shoulders and took it in stride. Work was work. She scrubbed the floor, changed sheets, did laundry and washed walls. And all before noon.

Mitch had reminded Mary about Lisa's voracious appetite, so when lunch break came around, Mary arranged to see this for herself. They ate in relative silence and Mary, for lack of anything better to do, studied Lisa's table manners. If she were to eventually graduate to the banquet circuit, this would be important. So far, so good.

"What are you doing?" Lisa asked, catching Mary off guard.

"Nothing."

"You were staring at my hands."

Mary didn't reply.

"You have some sort of hand fetish?"

"No!"

"I wouldn't blame you. I do have nice hands."

"Ummm."

"Soft and smooth."

"Time to go back to work," Mary announced, practically snatching Lisa's plate out from under her.

"I'll do the dishes," Lisa volunteered.

"I'll take care of them."

"I can help."

Mary remembered the last time someone offered to help her with the dishes.

"I'll do it! You just go...do something else."

"Okay," Lisa surrendered.

She left the kitchen and started to vacuum the floor from one end of the Center to the other. It took a long time to move all of the furniture, and by the time the task was complete, the dust was thick enough to write a message on the table with your finger. She chased the dust away and polished the furniture to a high shine. Mary nagged her three times to take a break and finally brought her a cool drink at three fifteen in the small den. It had two comfy chairs.

143

"Sit, drink, take a break," Mary tried to sound stern.

"Just don't ask me to shake, roll over or play dead and we'll get along just fine."

Mary swallowed any hint of a smile.

"Don't worry, I won't."

"Why isn't anybody here?" Lisa asked, ever curious.

"We usually vacate the Center one or two days a month to do a proper cleaning."

"Wouldn't you know, my first day is a spring-cleaning fest. So where do the women and children go during this time?"

"I find other shelters with room."

"That doesn't sound easy."

"It isn't."

"Well, I'm glad to be helping you on spring-cleaning day."

"It's two days, actually. You know how to clean a hardwood floor?"

"I've done it once or twice."

"Good. It's a dying art."

"I'll do it now."

"You'll take a break now."

"Fine. I'll take a break. It's more than I ever gave you in Texas."

"I'd like to think that I'm above exacting revenge for that." "Right."

"You sound unconvinced."

"A hotdog stand doesn't have this much relish. You're enjoying every moment and that's okay. Just let me know when I've earned forgiveness."

Lisa cleaned the hardwood floors to within an inch of their lives, whatever that meant. Mary resisted oohing and aahing and instead blandly announced that it was quitting time.

"I'll buy you a drink at the U," Lisa offered.

Mary was so taken aback by the invitation that she agreed without argument. They walked in together after meeting up in the parking lot. Mitch's booth was empty, so they sat there.

"Hey, you two," Mitch came over to check on them.

"We're celebrating," Lisa chirped.

"Oh really?" Mitch inquired, looking more at Mary than Lisa.

"Yeah, we managed to work together for eight whole hours and haven't scratched each other's eyes out," Lisa teased in such a way that she even coaxed a small smile out of Mary.

"We got through the day," Mary nodded agreement.

"Good for you. By the way, Hilary called here looking for you. She wants you to give her a call."

"Sure," Mary said. She looked a little like she was just handed a summons.

"Meanwhile, what are you drinking?" Mitch asked.

"Something exotic. Maybe a couple of Tequila Sunrises!" Lisa suggested.

"I'd better call Hilary before I decide. I might need to get home." Mary went over to use the phone in the office while Lisa hovered over the mixing of the drinks. "Couldn't have done it better myself!" she declared to Mitch, who guffawed at the remark.

"Just don't blow it out your nose!" Mitch laughed. "Gee, ruin all my fun!" she shot back, not bothering to stifle a giggle. They had time to goof off, business was still slow after the two week closure. Mary came out of the office and headed straight for Lisa.

"I can't stay," she explained, eyeing the two drinks with unmistakable envy.

"Not even for a quickie?" Lisa held up the drink.

"If I drink that, I won't be able to crawl home, let alone drive." "Sorry you have to run off," Mitch said.

"See you tomorrow, then," Lisa added.

"Right."

Mary took off practically at a run.

"Oh the ball and chain…" Lisa said between sips.

"The what and what?"

"Ball and chain, you know, a committed relationship."

"A real drag?" Mitch quizzed.

"Depends on who you're committed to."

Mitch tried to keep her mind on the bookkeeping, but found her attention drawn back to Lisa's comment.

"Was I your ball and chain?"

"Didn't seem like it at the time."

"What did you use to drug me?"

"Benadryl," Lisa answered as easily as if she was commenting on the weather.

"And you feel no guilt about that?"

"I do, now. At the time, you got some great sleep."

"You understand that that's the hardest thing for me to forgive. How far would you have gone?" "Benadryl did the trick."

"But what if it hadn't?"

"It did," Lisa finished off one drink and started on the one they had fixed for Mary, just in case.

"You better eat something to soak up all that booze."

"I wouldn't have hurt you permanently."

"I was struggling to study for exams."

"You didn't need to study, you were so smart."

"Oh yeah, real smart."

"Just not as smart as me."

"Grab yourself some dinner."

"Why don't you let me take over the bar for a while so you can spend dinner with Rebecca."

Mitch thought this over as she wrote down a few more figures in the ledger. Then, she called the Governor's office. The brand new secretary patched her right through with no hint of snootiness. Must have hired a Democrat.

"Hey you," Mitch greeted, testing the phone waters.

"Hiya, gorgeous," Rebecca came back friendly.

"What are you doing for dinner?"

"Eating."

"Care to do that with me?"

"But where will we go afterwards?"

Mitch chuckled. "You must *not* be in a meeting!" she surmised.

"That's for me to know and you to find out."

"Shall we eat in or dine out?"

"I'll come down there," Rebecca was being so flexible.

"Let's do that new seafood place out north," Mitch hedged.

"You need a break from the U?"

"Lisa said she'd watch the place for a while."

"I see. And you don't want the distraction."

"Only one woman distracts me, and that woman is you."

"Beautiful woman."

"Huh?"

"That beautiful woman is me."

"Absolutely!"

"Meet you at The Net in thirty minutes?"

"Yeah, would you make the reservation? They never give you any grief."

"Okay. I love you."

"And I love the most beautiful gorgeous wonderful governor in the universe."

"And that would be me."

That was Rebecca's form of goodbye. When Mitch hung up, she could sense Lisa's invisible antennae retract. Eavesdropping was an art. Lisa was no Picasso. "Listening in, were we?"

"I thought I'd take notes just in case I ever needed a pick-up line for a governor."

Mitch cast a pensive look at Lisa. When Mary had left so quickly a few minutes ago, Mitch had sensed no sparks of any kind in either direction. Maybe she had been wrong weeks ago about sensing an attraction between them. As long as Lisa wasn't taking notes on how to pick up a governor's daughter, things might get back to normal.

"You're supposed to laugh. That was a joke." "I'm hysterical, on the inside." "You have a nice dinner," Lisa said.

"You want a doggie bag?"

"Only if having dinner with the governor makes you lose your appetite. For whatever reason."

"You'll be okay here?"

"Go!"

Mitch left after locking up the financial records. Better safe than sorry. Traffic snarled the highway between the U and The Net. The circumstances of Mitch running a good twenty minutes late allowed Rebecca to get settled at a quiet table and sip down two glasses of Chablis. One right after the other. "I'm late," Mitch greeted with a grimace.

"No problem, I'm ahead by … one." she held up her nearly empty glass. A waiter reappeared to refill and take Mitch's drink order.

"I'll have coffee, thanks."

"Regular or decaf?" "Regular."

"Everything okay?"

"Just the traffic. You're the governor. Can't you clear the highways when I'm trying to get from where I am to you?"

"I can't even clear them for my commute!"

Mitch settled into the chair which was a lot more comfortable than it first appeared. "You look tired."

"I've been doing the books. That's always a brain drain for me."

"And Lisa's helping?" The tone was there. Mitch could hear it loud and clear.

"Watching things for an hour or two."

"After a busy first day at the Center?"

"I guess."

"She's a real super woman, isn't she? Maybe we should buy her a cape." "A cape?"

"Yeah, so she can be Super Lisa and fly around rescuing everyone."

"If you can find a cape that does that, get one for me. I'd like to fly over traffic on a day like this!"

"How about I buy you a set of tights to start?"

"Blue to match my eyes?"

"Deep blue."

Mitch smiled and tried to relax with the menu. It didn't last long, this quietude.

"I thought that your plan to have Lisa work at the Center was going to keep her pretty busy," Rebecca tried to sound casual. Mitch's ears began to tingle, and not in a good way.

"You mean, keep her away from the U and away from me as well, right?" Mitch clarified pointedly. "I meant busy. I said busy. I meant busy."

Mitch looked at the nearly empty third glass of wine. She didn't need to, she knew what a couple of glasses did to Rebecca. One was fine, two was interesting, three was the bell for round one.

"You meant not underfoot at the U. Why can't you just admit that that's what has you bugged."

148

"Whatever."

"Don't 'whatever' me," Mitch kept her voice even-tempered, although it was a huge struggle.

"Forget I said anything."

"Ever?"

"Don't be a smartass!"

"I'll be a smartass if I want to be a smartass!"

"Well, do it quietly. People are beginning to stare."

"We should be used to that by now."

"But not for this reason!"

"Translated means I'm picking a fight?"

"Exactly."

"Which in reality *you* started," Mitch's ears were turning rosy.

"Me! Asking about your day constitutes starting a fight?" "You didn't ask about my day, you asked about Lisa's day and what the hell was she doing at the U." "Fine. How was your day?"

"Great until about two minutes ago."

"Do you plan on ruining this entire dinner?" That did it. Mitch's ears were bright red.

"No, I don't."

With that, she calmly stood up and walked out. Anyone within close proximity may have guessed she was just taking a trip to the ladies' room. She was in her car, headed back to work in three minutes. Three blocks before she got back, she drove through one of those fast food places and bought a fish sandwich and fries meal. Lisa would be suspicious if there were no leftovers. Everything was cool and quiet, including Lisa who was holding court with four lovely ladies. One wrapped around each finger on one hand with a thumb to spare. They traded jobs. Lisa munched the food while Mitch refilled drinks. "This stuff is pretty bad. What was the name of the place you met Rebecca?"

"The Net."

"Remind me not to go there anytime soon!"

Lisa went home and soon afterwards, the four lovelies followed suit. Mitch had hours of work left to do. With Lisa under new management, so to speak, Marge dead, and Sandy working day shift, there was no one left to close up shop. Business was still slow, so the kitchen crew was gone for the night. Mitch left the door unlocked while she restocked and cleaned the bar. After the third trip out of the stockroom she noticed Rebecca waiting patiently at the bar.

"Hi," Mitch said.

"Hello," Rebecca answered. "How was your day?"

"Exhausting," Mitch answered honestly as she wrestled the cases of liquor with one and a half good arms. It made her look clumsy. She hated it.

"And yours?"

"I'm hungry."

"You didn't have dinner?"

"No, I didn't."

"I'll rustle up something in the kitchen for us."

"No, don't do that. Let's try the 'eating out' thing again."

"Maybe we should try the 'talking thing' first."

"That's a good idea. But first, what *is* that smell?"

Mitch noticed the remains of Lisa's dinner and smiled sheepishly.

"It's Lisa's doggie bag. I promised her the leftovers and when I didn't have any, I stopped and got something. Just so she wouldn't have a hundred questions."

"And she didn't notice you were back so soon?"

"She was entertaining four customers. If she noticed, she kept it to herself. What she didn't keep to herself was how bad the food was. She's not going to The Net anytime soon, and I hope they don't find out that I did a switcheroo and sue me for defamation or whatever." Mitch mercifully cut short her run on answer.

"I see."

"One more place safe from Lisa, which is probably what this argument is all about. Right?"

"You tell me," Rebecca pulled Mitch over to their booth.

"Lisa and Mary came in for a drink after work. Mary had to go, Lisa offered to watch the place. We didn't kiss. How much else do you the hell need to know?"

"I didn't even ask about a kiss."

"You haven't forgiven me, have you?"

Rebecca didn't answer for a full minute. Chess matches were won and lost in less time. The polar ice cap was melting. Y3K was creeping up on them.

"I've forgiven you."

"But?" "I

hate her."

"You hate her?"

"Pretty strong talk from a politician, I know."

"Pretty strong talk from anybody."

"I don't want her around you."

"You don't mind her being around Mary."

"Mary's going to work Lisa's fingers to the bone, isn't she?"

"Of course," Mitch nodded sagely, like she understood, which she didn't.

"I'm not trying to be logical," Rebecca explained. "I'm just telling you how I feel."

"Keep going."

"I hate her because she had you first. And everybody knows you never forget your first. You're never going to forget her. Never."

"And when you saw us kissing?"

"I hated her even more."

"Maybe you could try to just pity her for a while."

"Pity her?"

"Well, she did walk out on me," Mitch said, realizing how terribly conceited it sounded only after she said it.

"A little full of ourselves, aren't we?" Rebecca teased when she saw the look in Mitch's eyes. "Look," Rebecca followed up, "I know we don't have this settled all the way, yet, but can we do dinner now?"

"Sure. I think we've gotten past the worst of it."

Mitch locked up and trailed Rebecca in her car to a quiet suburban restaurant. Traffic had thinned as had the crowds. They were seated immediately and shared a shrimp cocktail while waiting for steak and lobster.

"Can we please fight every day?" Mitch asked.

"What?"

"Please! If we get steak and lobster as a reward?"

"You haven't seen what's for dessert, yet."

"In that case," Mitch said, catching Rebecca's drift, "can we fight every hour?"

"Maybe we need a secret code word."

"A secret code word?"

"I didn't mean to start a fight earlier, but I know now how things got going. By the way, your ears went bright red." "I could feel them heating up," Mitch admitted.

"And you did handle things very well." "Particularly when you called me a smart ass."

"I was way out of line with that remark."

"It's okay. I baited you."

"So, we both struggle with this."

"What do you suppose would have happened if we had had this discussion earlier tonight, at our first dinner?"

"Tell me more."

"Well, suppose when we were at The Net earlier, what would have happened if you had just said that you were still upset about Lisa and the kiss?"

"I didn't know I was."

"Okay, but you weren't happy about Lisa hanging out at the U after work."

"Okay, I can admit to that."

"So tell me straight out when you feel that way. I won't crumble or snap or cower or bite your head off. I'm pretty reasonable, aren't I?"

"Yes, I guess you are, except when you disappear for days."

"That really bothered you?" Mitch asked calmly. "You can always run away. I have to stick around and be responsible."

"And you don't think that burying yourself in your work constitutes a form of escape?"

"It's socially acceptable."

"And damn convenient. And effective. Very effective."

"Being governor is a demanding career choice."

"And I love you."

"That came out of the blue."

"I'm testing code words."

"And 'I love you' popped into your mind."

"Only because I do, love you."

"That won't stop every fight."

"I agree. But at least we can help each other to make our fights productive. We wouldn't be fighting if we weren't so helplessly in love."

"I'll try my best to get my feeling to the front."

"Me, too. Our love is too precious to undermine it with unspoken anger or concerns or disappointments. I know you felt all that and more when you witnessed the kiss."

"You're right."

"And you know what's so ironic?"

"What?"

"You had more feelings associated with that kiss than I did. The fire's gone between Lisa and me. The only sparks that ignite all my passions come from you and only you."

Dinner arrived after this profound announcement. They ate slowly, savoring the food and the company of each other. Deep down, they were compatible. They just needed to get deep down more often. They skipped dessert, a sure sign that passions were running high. Only one thing ranked ahead of chocolate on their list of favorite things. When they arrived home, Mitch wouldn't be rushed. She kissed Rebecca tenderly until she was fully convinced that Lisa no longer mattered. Nothing else mattered but having Mitch touch her. Here, there, there. Oh, yes, there. Mitch loved doing this; taking her time, touching so gently, kissing so softly, making things go so slowly. Rebecca surrendered to the merciful climax and then soon after, to sleep. Mitch smiled to herself. It had been a roller-coaster ride. A very fun ride. A very necessary ride.

Chapter 8

The morning dawned bright and clear. Rebecca kissed Mitch awake early, knowing that she had left stacks of cases of liquor behind the bar. Work was awaiting both of them.

"I love waking up like this," Mitch whispered in Rebecca's ear.

"Me, too," Rebecca stretched long and slowly.

"It's going to be another long day," Mitch thought out loud.

"Are you going to try and hire someone to take Lisa's place?" "I'll have an ad in the local paper today, and I'll put up a Help Wanted sign in the window." "Am I pressuring you?"

"No, I called the ad in yesterday morning. It runs for five days, including Sunday. And I found the sign for the window in Marge's office when I was sorting through stuff, which was difficult to do." "I didn't mean to push."

"I know. I'm just having a hard time looking for someone so soon after Marge's death."

"I understand." "I know you do.
You always do."

"I *usually* do."

"If things weren't so complex, they would be easier to understand."
"Can I quote you?"

Mitch laughed. "I guess I'm at my quotable best when I'm lying naked next to you."

"Who's going to buy the 'dollar jar'?"

"I will. In fact, I'll sneak one out of work." "Anything but a mayonnaise jar."

"Got something against mayonnaise jars?"

"I'm on a diet."

Mitch threw her clothes on and vacated the area so Rebecca could have the place to herself.

Across town, Lisa had no such problems. She had an entire house all to herself. She rose early, ate a big breakfast and showed up right on time for work. Mary ran fifteen minutes late, and was in no mood to enjoin in the slightest conversation about the subject. There was one more day of cleaning to be done. Some of it was exacting, like the washing of the light fixtures. Other tasks were mundane, such as the restocking of grocery items. They would be ready for clients tomorrow. At four, Mary called Lisa into her office and closed the door. It had to be serious. Lisa waited, hands folded in her lap.

"This wasn't my idea, you know," Mary began pointedly.

"I know. I'm being passed around like a squawking baby."

"Just so we're clear, I need to tell you a few things."

"Sure. What?"

"We do very important work here."

"I'm not one of your donors. You don't need to convince me."

"You don't let anybody get through two whole sentences, do you?"

"I'm not stupid. Don't explain things to me like I was two years old."

"Okay." Mary inhaled slowly, "Tomorrow, we'll have women and children here who feel unsafe. We need to calm them, care for them, clothe them, shelter them, and protect them. Is there any part of that you have questions about?" "How many women and children?"

"Usually, we fill up pretty fast. Maybe twenty? Twenty-five?"

"How long is the average stay?"

"Until we get them to a safer place. Many leave the state to live with other relatives. Some go through the court system to get divorces, separations, restraining orders, and/or child custody revisions."

"What's my number one priority?"

"Answer the phone."

"Answer the phone?" Lisa sounded doubtful. It didn't seem like a crucial duty with all the other issues pending.

"And help with the kids if you get time."

"Help how?"

"Help with meals, toys, stuff like that. Just don't change any diapers." Lisa couldn't help but look relieved.

"It's a legal thing. And don't give out any medical or legal advice. We have others who help with that."

"Good, great, anything else?"

"Not that I can think of."

"So let me buy you that drink you missed out on last night."

"I think we should get to bed early."

Lisa looked at Mary with as little expression as possible. She even kept her eyebrows from wiggling. It was really hard. "That's not what I meant," Mary hurriedly followed up.

"I know. Here's my plan. Let's go somewhere besides the U, have a nice, early drink and part company early enough to meet Doc's deadline."

Mary thought it over for a few seconds.

"You could take the opportunity to fill me in on any last minute details," Lisa continued the sales pitch. "It could be a business drink!" "One."

"One."

They drove in separate cars to a nearby Mexican restaurant, one where no one would think to look for them. It was like going out with a mistress. Talk about a Tequila Sunrise. After one apiece, they had talked over a few more logistics of running a rescue center. As Mary drank, she spoke more from her heart than Lisa had heard before and she listened intently. There was nothing quite like the sound of a woman in love with her work. Mary grew embarrassed at her realization that she had dominated the conversation for an entire hour.

"I should be heading home."

"Me, too."

"Hilary will be wondering about her dinner."

"I understand. If I don't eat dinner at least once a day, I wonder myself."

Mary smiled, checked her watch, put a twenty-dollar bill on the table and was out the door before Lisa could charm her into sharing a meal. After all, Hilary was waiting. And we didn't want to keep Hilary waiting.

Lisa headed home a few minutes later, cooked up a bowl of instant noodles and curled up in front of the fireplace. She pulled an afghan over herself and ate her dinner in five minutes. She should have showered to avoid rushing around in the morning, but the couch pulled her close and lulled her to sleep. She awoke at five, her mental alarm clock never failed. Coffee, shower, and breakfast followed each other closely and she was at the front door of the Center just as Mary was unlocking it. Within an hour, Lisa had answered the phone thirteen times, social service representatives had arrived and three women walked in off the street with children in tow. By ten, there was no time for tea and crumpets for the staff. Coffee had been brewed and served to visitors. The children were treated to juice and cookies. At some point, perhaps after the thirty-first phone call, a cook had arrived. Delicious aromas wafted through the hallways and guests gathered in the dining area. Lisa more or less stayed at her post, where Mary checked in with her a little after one.

"What about lunch?" Mary asked.

"I guess I wasn't very hungry."

Mary was careful to avoid making a wisecrack about Lisa's appetite. It wouldn't have been very charitable.

"How about I bring you a snack?"

"No thanks. I don't want you going to any trouble for me."

"It wouldn't be any trouble."

"No, thanks, anyway."

Mary shrugged and went back to her office. There were a dozen things to do and she spent the next couple of hours tending to crucial details. Every detail was important when abused women and children were involved. Everything from animal cracker inventory to security system upgrades were in the "in" basket. At three, Mary toured around, ostensibly to check on the status of overnight guests. In reality, she was keeping tabs on Lisa as well. She looked pale. Still. But she was the vanguard of the phone, and had done a thoroughly professional job.

"You should take a break."

"I went to the bathroom a few minutes ago."

"I mean a real break. A fifteen or twenty minute break."

"The phone might ring."

Mary was beginning to wonder if Lisa was doing some sort of ritualistic fast or something.

"The phone always rings. It's paid to do that." Not even this silly joke could make Lisa smile.

"I'm okay, really."

The phone rang.

Mary went to the kitchen and grabbed a sugar-loaded cola and a glass with some ice. She popped the top and decanted it quickly over the cubes. Bubbles rose and fell by the time Mary delivered it to Lisa's desk.

"Here you go. Drink this."

"Thanks," Lisa mouthed as she took a phone message. Then, she managed to take a long draw before needing to write something else down. Another crisis, another overnight guest, Mary read upside down and then went into her office for the call transfer. She took the call and then, after reflecting on the beleaguered, overwhelmed look in Lisa's eyes, placed a call of her own.

"Lucky U, this is Mitch."

"It's Mary."

"Hey Mary. How's … things?"

"Things are busy."

"Sorry to hear it."

"In particular, Lisa looks a little peaked around the edges."

"She's going into her three o'clock swoon. Did she eat anything?"

"I can't get her to."

"She won't eat?"

"Nope."

"Put food under her nose."

"I gave her a soft drink. She's trying so hard to be conscientious, she won't even take a break. I think things have really gotten to her."

"Things like?"

"Just the reality of the work around here."

Mitch nodded, even though Mary couldn't see the agreement.

"I see."

"Do me a favor?"

"I'll try."

"Take her to dinner."

For once, Mitch was glad that work had given her an ironclad excuse. "Gee, sorry, I can't. I'm doing job interviews for bartender. I'm booked until nine tonight." "Okay. Just thought I'd ask."

"What about you taking her out?"

"I'm due home."

"Well, she can come here if she wants. I just can't take time to talk to her."

"I understand. Let me see what else I can come up with." Mary hung up the phone and after thinking for a minute, placed another call. After being put through, she said, "Hi mom." "Hello dear!" Rebecca answered, happy as always to hear from her. "Are you busy for dinner?" Mary asked innocently.

"I'm free all evening. What a nice coincidence."

"Good, I need a favor."

"A favor?" Rebecca now sounded suspicious, and rightly so.

"I want you to invite Lisa to dinner." "Excuse me?"

"Which part didn't you hear?"

"This is a joke, right? I'm checking my calendar to see if it's April Fools' Day. Nope, it isn't!"

"Look, I can't do it and Mitch can't do it."

"You asked Mitch?"

"Yeah, but she's doing interviews. And Hilary has plans. I have to be home, soon. I just thought that you could help me out. I'd understand if you're busy…."

"Why dinner?"

"Because," Mary sounded like she was explaining this to kindergartners, "she hasn't eaten all day." Rebecca gave it about two seconds thought.

"Put her on the line."

Mary breathed a grateful, "Thanks," and then switched the call to ring at Lisa's desk. She picked up automatically.

"The Center, this is Lisa."

"It's Rebecca."

"Rebecca who?" Lisa asked, taking a message from habit.

"The governor!"

"Oh, just a minute, I'll patch you through to Mary." "No, wait, I want to talk to you first."

"Okay," Lisa replied cautiously.

"I want you to be a guest at the mansion this evening for dinner."

"Really! Why?" Lisa was always seeking truth, from others. It was easier to deal with life when you knew everyone's beliefs, motives and secret agendas.

"To thank you for working so hard at the Center."

"You don't have to do that."

Rebecca cut to the chase, not allowing herself the temptation of accepting the easy way out. "Should I send a car for you or do you want to drive?"

"Oh, I'll drive. No use frittering away the tax-payers money on little ole me." "Dinner is at six."

"Great. You want to talk to Mary now?"

"No, that's okay. We've talked enough."

"Whatever."

Two more lines lit up simultaneously.

"Gotta go. Bye," Lisa cut the call short.

Rebecca exhaled. Slowly. She walked from her office to the kitchen, delivering the news that there would be two for dinner. The menu sounded reasonable: French onion soup, spinach salad, grilled salmon, green beans, rolls, and blueberry cobbler. It was amazing that any governor stayed a reasonable weight.

Sensing that this was good enough for company, and knowing that there was nothing she could do to alter the menu at this late date anyway, Rebecca went upstairs to change into sweats. The last thing she wanted to do was give the impression that she was trying to impress Lisa. She collapsed on the bed and closed her eyes for a few minutes. A knock on the door startled her awake from her luscious nap.

"Company has arrived, Governor."

Rebecca checked her watch. She had slept for an hour. Six or seven more and she would feel human again.

"I'll be there in a minute."

Rebecca walked to the bathroom and splashed water on her face. She studied her reflection in the mirror. Not too bad, she thought, all things considered. Love agreed with her. She strolled downstairs and greeted Lisa, who was way overdressed. Dress and pantyhose and pumps overdressed.

"Welcome to the mansion."

"I've been here before, remember."

"Ah yes, upstairs."

"Right."

160

"You want something more comfortable to wear. I forgot to tell you over the phone that it's casual night around here. Actually, it's casual night a lot of nights around here. Don't get me wrong, of course. You look very nice. Would you prefer to change into something more comfortable?" Rebecca realized that she was rambling on and mercifully stopped before Lisa noticed.

"Yeah, why not."

"Come on upstairs."

Rebecca led the way as Lisa trailed behind. In spite of how she felt about Lisa, Rebecca could roll out the red carpet with the best of them. Making company feel at home was one of her more polished skills. They entered the master bedroom and Rebecca opened the closet.

"Let's see what we can riffle from Mitch."

Resisting the temptation to remark on Lisa's familiarity with this process, Rebecca instead pulled out a couple of sets of soft fleece for Lisa's approval. She selected cherry red. Rebecca left her to change and checked on the status of dinner. It was ready when they were. Lisa trotted downstairs looking red and pink and healthy in the outfit. She looked like she was back from a jog. Once she was in front of food, she realized she hadn't eaten since breakfast and made short work of the first course.

"How was your first day at the Center?" Rebecca asked when the soup dishes were cleared. "It's my third day."

"Okay," Rebecca nodded, noting for future reference Lisa's penchant for being accurate as well as abrupt.

"How was your third day?"

Lisa didn't answer and gave no indication of doing so anytime soon.

"Something wrong?" Rebecca followed up as the salads arrived.

"I just don't want to talk about it."

"Okay. That's fair." Rebecca pondered why they had to be so accurate if they weren't going to discuss it. "What do you want to talk about?"

"Mitch."

Ah yes, there was that abruptness again.

"You start," Rebecca invited.

"I know that you two are hopelessly in love."

"It shows?"

"Oh please. The two of you ooze bliss." Lisa made it sound like an infectious disease.

"I see."

"And I don't intend on causing trouble, although it's a little late for that already, I guess?"

"You guess?"

"But really, that kiss you saw?"

"Yes?"

"Mitch has really lost her touch, so to speak."

"She has?" Rebecca kept the conversation going by asking simple questions.

"I almost snoozed off. What a bore."

"That bad, huh?"

"Worse than kissing a guy!"

At least Lisa hadn't kissed Jeff, Rebecca mused to herself. Now, *that* was a bore.

The salmon arrived and Lisa dove in without further comment. She would have caught it going upstream if given the opportunity. Two helpings later, they had talked in sketchy, autobiographical terms, each taking a quick swing through the family tree at the polite behest of the other. Dessert would be taken in the parlor. Rebecca steered Lisa away from the couch. The kissing couch. Lisa asked about the couch evasion.

"It's uncomfortable," Rebecca fibbed. At least, it could have been.

"I'm not surprised. There's something under the cushion."

"There is?"

"Looks like silverware to me."

"So, that's where she hid it!"

"Who hid what?"

"Mitch hides silverware from the staff."

Lisa looked perplexed. Rebecca noted for the record, the unofficial record, how alluring this particular expression was on her.

"It's a 'millionaire eccentricity' kind of thing."

"The staff treats her like crap, she told me so herself."

"We're fixing that problem."

"I heard the mansion was torched, early on. Are you getting that problem fixed as well?" "Mitch and I have endured a lot."

"So, one little boring kiss from an ex-girlfriend shouldn't have been a big deal. I mean, Mitch took off and showed signs of never coming back."

"She needed a break."

"All the way to … where? New Mexico?"

"Santa Fe, to be exact."

"That's a pretty part of the world," Lisa nodded, looking like she knew the area well.

"You went there with the two million?" Rebecca inquired.

"Gosh, no! I went to Trenton, New Jersey."

"That's quite a long way."

"Over three days by bus, if you take the scenic route."

Rebecca tried to imagine such a thing while she served strong coffee and cobbler. She noshed on a tiny portion. Lisa scarfed down the rest with about a pint of ice cream. "And then you went to Santa Fe to find her?" Lisa picked up on the earlier thread of conversation.

"I tracked her down through phone records. Seems as though I really didn't need to."

"Why?"

"Well, you know Mitch. Everywhere she goes she becomes a celebrity of sorts. If anyone wants to find out where she lives, you just ask around." "It can't be that easy."

"I guess not. But the villa is close to town at the end of a winding street named Adobe."

"Sounds cool," Lisa arched an eyebrow.

Mitch wandered in about somewhere around the second cup of coffee. It was close to ten. "Hi there," Rebecca greeted.

"Hi there, yourself," Mitch pulled her close and kissed her intimately, like they were the only two people in the room. Which was Mitch's perception, not having seen Lisa. She gave Rebecca her usual 'inside the parlor' brand of kiss. The kind that could lure any fly into any spider's web. She tasted sweet, like blueberries. Yum.

163

"You taste good," Mitch said when she got to within nibbling distance of Rebecca's ear.

"That's all you get for now," Rebecca breathed back, explaining, "Lisa ate the rest."

Mitch looked just a tad bit puzzled. Then, she realized that they weren't alone. Lisa came into view.

"I meant the blueberries," Rebecca uttered quietly.

"I knew that," Mitch said, still a tiny bit confounded. Lisa stood to leave.

"Don't run off on my account," Mitch said, unconvincingly.

"Although you're dressed for it. I have a matching outfit upstairs."

"Not anymore. Well, I need to get up early for work."

"I understand."

Rebecca escorted Lisa to the door.

"I'll get your clothes." "That's okay. Just send them over with Mary one day. We'll do an exchange program."

"Okay, goodnight."

Rebecca walked back into the parlor where Mitch was examining the silverware.

"Lisa found the missing forks," Rebecca stated.

"Never could hide anything from her. How did she end up in your custody for the evening?" "Mary outsmarted me."

"That's hard to believe."

"It was in a moment of weakness."

"And you gave her my red sweat suit?"

"She was way overdressed."

"Okay, fine. She looked like one of Santa's elves." Mitch shrugged. "Are you jealous?"

"No, just surprised. I thought you hated Lisa?" "I'm trying to be more charitable. Mary was really concerned about Lisa. I guess that first day at the Center is tough."

"I don't know how Mary does it."

"She's tough, like her mother," Rebecca smiled.

"And tender, like her mother," Mitch added. "By the way, what was that about blueberries?"

"Lisa ate the entire cobbler except for the tiny piece that I got."

"And you tasted wonderful!"

"There's more where that came from," Rebecca pulled Mitch closer and proved her point.

Chapter 9

The phone was ringing even before Lisa got a chance to sit down at her desk. She answered the call, took a message and then went into the kitchen to get a cup of coffee. Three children and two mothers were huddled around the table. Lisa recognized them from the day before. Except that some of the purple in the bruises was turning a sickly shade of green. She smiled and then pretended to hear the phone so she could dash away without having to see any more. Mary was already in her office with a stack of papers and two new visitors. Prior to this week, Lisa had paid little attention to the various conversations Mary and Mitch had had about the Center. From what little she had actually paid attention to, she had imagined it being more like an orphanage. She hadn't realized how many abused mother and child combinations there were until now. Technically, this was more like a domestic violence ward. Lisa made a mental note to talk to Mary about it. Later. Much later. Mary worked nonstop through the morning and only had a chance to have a personal chat with Lisa over lunch.

"I appreciated your mom's invitation to dinner last night." "You had dinner with my mother?" Mary tried to look surprised.

"And I know you arranged it. Thanks." Mary didn't bother to look innocent anymore.

"Guilty as charged."

"She was actually very nice."

"She's a nice person."

"It runs in the family."

Was it Mark Twain who observed that only humans blush because they have reason to? If Mr. Twain wasn't dead, he would've gotten a piece of Mary's mind.

"Thank you."

"And then Mitch walked in."

"I thought she was busy."

"It was close to ten, and *why* did you think she was busy?"

"I talked to her earlier in the day."

"Calling in all your markers?"

"I knew you were having a rough day."

"I would have settled for an after-work drink with you."

"That just isn't going to work."

"Why not?"

"It just won't."

Signaling the end of the conversation, Mary picked up the lunch dishes. Lisa went back to her desk and sorted through the work. Several times, children, mere toddlers, would peek around the corner of the office door. Lisa had a small stash of toys that Mary had put in her drawer during cleaning time. One by one, Lisa would pull out a toy. The children resisted at first, and then slowly warmed up to the overture. It took hours. Abused children were cautious by habit as well as by nature. By the time Lisa gathered her stuff to go home for the night, the Center was filled to capacity. They were protected overnight by a staff of three. Two guards and a nurse. These kind people worked at non-premium wages just to be benevolent. One guard worked from five to midnight, the other from midnight to seven. The nurse altered her hours depending of the health of the residents. When flu season was in full swing, she worked early morning hours, which gave Mary a little leeway when fighting rush hour traffic in the mornings. Lisa caught on to the system and actually obeyed all speed limits and traffic laws the following morning. Not only was the nurse still on duty, but the guard was as well. Lisa had worn a skirt the previous day. Word traveled fast. The

a.m. guard, a handsome, strapping six foot five youngster was hanging out in the kitchen. Near the coffee pot. Real near. Couldn't miss him. Couldn't get to the coffee, in fact. It was being guarded really well. He poured a cup for her in a gracious manner that belied his enormous stature. Apparently, his mama taught him manners. Maybe she had to teach him from a step stool, but he was taught well. He knew all about cream and sugar; two lumps, you silly thing.

Lisa spent a polite minute chatting and then checked in at her desk. Mary wasn't in yet, so Lisa worked that phone and kept order until about nine. When Mary checked in, she was taciturn. They exchanged information briefly and then Mary busied herself on the phone for at least two hours. Lisa tracked the residents. Three were departing today, having found relatives in distant states who would take them in until they recovered from their life crisis. Two were arriving. Fleeing from crisis. Lunch was cooking. It must be barbecued chicken. What an unmistakable aroma.

When Mary gave no indication that she was hibernating on purpose, Lisa ventured in with a plate full of chicken, corn, and potato salad. Mary hardly bothered to look up. A brief, clouded glance and then a dismissive wave. Well, everyone was entitled to a bad day.

Perhaps it was just coincidence, but the swing shift guard showed up about four. Lisa drank a cup of coffee with him out of politeness and then did one more check of her message log. She took one more stack of notes to Mary, who seemed to be settling in for a siege. Lisa left at five, and headed home only to discover Mitch setting up a painting studio in the spare bedroom. Things were crowded before. This was going to be mayhem.

"Okay, van Gogh. What the hell is going on here?"

"I don't dare dribble paint at the mansion."

"Who's running the U?"

"I hired a new bartender."

"And now you think you can sit back and doodle!"

"I think it's legal to doodle in your own house. Besides, what are you doing home so early?"

"It's five thirty."

"Can't be!"

"Which means unless you get your ass in gear, you're gonna be late for dinner."

"I still have a couple of minutes," Mitch put up the unfinished painting of Tim on the easel.

"What's that?" Lisa asked, truly puzzled. Mitch peered at Lisa.

"What do you think it is?" Lisa peered back at Mitch.

"It's a woodpecker. I could tell from a mile away."

"A woodpecker!?" Mitch repeated with her new found wounded-artist attitude.

"A boy woodpecker?"

"It's a nude male."

"That's a really strange thing for a lesbian to be painting!"

"You want to try your hand?"

"Honey, I tried my hand. Believe me, it's not what they want!"

"Don't tell me anymore. I don't want to know!"

"This art studio concept is going to get crowded pretty quickly." "I know. The house I rented in Santa Fe had a room almost as big as this whole house just for painting. I could just have an addition built onto this house."

"You mean a major remodel."

"Sure, why not?"

"Why not?" Lisa repeated back, with just a tad of hesitancy in her voice.

"You're not crazy about the idea?"

"It's a lot of dust and mess and confusion."

"I'll make sure you're not inconvenienced. A hotel room. Room service. A cleaning crew. How's that sound so far?"

"It's your house."

"How about a say in the design? Would that make it more palatable?"

"Palatable is when you eat."

Mitch looked directly into Lisa's eyes. "I won't do it if it bothers you." "It's okay."

"Really?"

"Really! Really, really! Now go have dinner."

"Okay. After that, I'm checking things at the U."

"You don't need to report to me. But if you see Mary?"

"What?"

"She was just really edgy today."

"I'll keep an eye out for her."

"Not that that will help."

"What's that mean?"

"She has a hard time getting time to herself, it seems to me."

"The old ball and chain?"

"Exactly."

Mitch drove at moderate speed to the mansion. Since returning home from Santa Fe, Rebecca had convened what she referred to as a

"Come to Jesus Meeting" with the staff. Two were fired summarily before the meeting even took place after phone records and time schedules fingered them as the notorious losers-of-messages. The remaining staff was on heightened awareness, having heard the message loud and clear. They forged an agreement. Mitch would refrain from hiding the silverware. Staff would be cordial and helpful. So, now, if Mitch was a few minutes late, the firing squad used blanks. No, really, it was much better than that.

Mitch wandered through the kitchen and found Rebecca having a sherry at the table while she scanned through some paperwork. Ah, a Governor's work is never done.

"Sorry I'm late."

"It's okay. I had some last minute stuff to do."

"And then, I need to check the U after dinner," Mitch said as she bent down to kiss Rebecca. Was this a scene from a fifties TV show or what? Mitch almost started to whistle the "Leave it to Beaver" theme song.

"How's the new bartender?"

"Ever heard that termite joke?"

"Uh oh."

"You'll like this one. The first termite says to the second termite, 'Where's the bar tender?'"

Rebecca groaned, closed the file and dinner was served. God, this was great. A calm, quiet night at home.

"So, I can't expect you home 'til late?"

"I'll try to be home by midnight."

"Midnight, got it," Rebecca had it in memory.

Mitch reluctantly went back to the U. It was remarkable what being an owner of a bar did to you. It wore you out, mostly. Even with good help, there was so much to do. Marge, it was now clear, had nothing else to do when she was still living. No family close, no girlfriend, no budding art career. Mitch smiled at her private joke. Art career! That was a good one. When someone couldn't tell the difference between a woodpecker and a man, there was still much to learn.

The U was buzzing, but at a reasonable pace. Vickie, the new bartender, had things sparkling clean.

"Hi, Vickie, how are things?"

"Great. And you?"

"I'm doing okay. Any problems that need my immediate attention?"

"Check the beer tap?"

"Sure."

Vickie had been sexually harassed at her previous place of employment and was currently pursuing the matter in court, with Mitch's knowledge and support. Mitch promised her no such problems at the U. Even if she was a straight woman surrounded by lesbians, she was still going to be a lot safer than the situation she had just left. Mitch wouldn't put up with anything else.

However, checking the beer tap wasn't Mitch's strong suit, particularly with her arm damaged from a gunshot wound. She went in the kitchen to recruit help. Just Joe could wrestle a keg with the best of them. So while he performed this he-man task, she had a sample of his flan. Ohhh, yes, it was fabulous. She told him so and he was so flustered at the compliment that he nearly let her have a second helping. Nearly. He was running short. Maybe at closing time?

When Mitch wandered out of Flanville, she noticed that Trish had wandered in and was looking around for a familiar face.

"Hiya stranger," Mitch said, pulling her into a big bear hug. "Stranger than most!" Trish came back quickly and made herself at home in Mitch's arms for longer than their usual hug.

"I missed you."

"Buy me a drink."

"Sure."

They sat in Mitch's booth and split a bottle of Cabernet Sauvignon. It was strong and earthy, matching Trish's mood. "I want you to do me a favor," Trish said.

"I'll try. What do you need?"

"I need you to look at my nose."

"Your nose?"

"My nose."

Up until this moment, Mitch had been doing what she normally did, which was alternate her glance between Trish's mouth and eyes. She knew from previous experience that she tended to watch people's mouths when they talked and looked at their eyes when they were quiet. Now, as if unable to disobey Trish's request, she focused on her nose. It was beautiful. She said so.

"NO. I mean *really* look at it!" "I really did. It's *really* beautiful!"

Trish downed half a glass of wine, teetering on the verge of pouty.

"Fill me in, Trish."

"You like my nose?"

"Yes."

"Tell me the truth."

"I like your nose."

"Hmm." Trish almost carried a tune.

"Who doesn't like your nose?"

"Judy."

"Judy doesn't like your nose?" Mitch asked, truly lost now.

"Well, I don't know for sure," Trish explained, and then fell silent.

"Did she tell you that?"

"No."

"Then how do you know?"

"She looked at it a lot while we were still spending time together."

"How can you tell?"

"A woman knows these things."

Mitch accepted the gospel of the nose according to Trish. "Then doesn't it stand to reason that she likes it if she looks at it?" Trish drank down her wine. "Forget I said anything."

"You're really upset about this," Mitch tried to soothe.

"She won't be intimate with me. We haven't been in touch since she left Denver."

"Some people need a lot of time."

"Not even a phone call?"

"Did she go back to Aspen?"

"Yes."

"So, call her and ask!"

"About what?" "About

your nose!"

"You're kidding!"

"What could it hurt? She hasn't kissed, hasn't called. If I were you.
I'd force the issue. If she has a nose fetish, it's better to find out now.
I mean, it's nothing to sneeze at."

"Har de har har."

"Sorry. I know this is serious."

"You know, after talking to you, I agree. I'm taking this way too
seriously. I'm gonna call her and ask her and if it's a big deal to
her, she's blown the relationship!" Mitch grinned.

"You see," Trish teased, "You're not the queen of the puns."

"Right, just be sure you *pick* a good time to call."

"Oh geez, I'm leaving before this gets any more sophomoric!"

"I love you, too."

Mitch cleared the glasses and wiped the table. She carried the dishes
to the kitchen and helped out with the dinner rush. By ten, her
midnight exit looked entirely possible. Thoughts of Rebecca floated
through her mind. What did her nose look like? Why would anyone
care? Mitch gave Vickie the rest of the night off and served drinks to
the three customers remaining. Just Joe locked up the kitchen and
headed home. By eleven, Mitch was alone. She spent a few minutes
picking up trash and sweeping when the door opened. The last thing
Mitch wanted was one more customer, until she saw who it was.
Mary waved a hello to Mitch and settled into Mitch's booth.

"Want a root beer?"

"No, I think a glass of wine, instead."

"Sure thing," Mitch said and then asked, "What kind?"

"Whatever."

Mitch selected a Mosel Riesling as she searched mentally through her
earlier conversation with Lisa. What did she say about Mary?
Fatigue played terrible tricks on the mind. She took the glass over to
Mary and sat across from her. It was water time for Mitch, and she
poured water and wine like she was a priest and this was a sacrament.
Maybe it was?

"Thanks." Mary put a twenty on the table and then made short work of the drink. It was light and fruity and went down like punch. "You want another?" Mitch asked as she struggled to recall Lisa's comments. Lisa was never one to make a casual observation about human nature. Edgy? That was it. Mary was edgy. Perhaps Mitch had chalked it up to the very fact that the two of them had been working together in such close proximity. That alone would make most people act edgy. Working with Lisa was an experience unto itself. Now, however, as Mitch sat here with Mary, she knew it was something else.

Mitch brought the bottle with her this time. Another glass of wine went down. Mary never even had two root beers, let alone two glasses of wine. Something was up. Mitch switched sides of the booth and put her arm around Mary. It was eleven o'clock, and no one in the place except Mitch and Mary. No one to pry their nose into their business. Nothing to keep Mary from talking. When Mitch squeezed Mary's shoulder, there was little left to the mystery. She winced in pain and moved to avoid further contact. A reflex action that baffled Mitch, but only for a moment. Then the awful truth began to dawn like the searing hot sun.

"What's going on, Mary?" Mitch asked gently, knowing somewhere in her heart that Mary's greatest need right now was a confidant. "It's nothing."
"Let me see."
"No, I don't want to take off my shirt here."
"I'll take you home."
"I can't go to the mansion!"
"My other home."
"Lisa's there."
"She won't mind, although I will call and tell her we're coming."
"It really isn't that big a deal."
Mary was still in denial. What she could diagnose in children instantly she couldn't see in herself if she used three mirrors. "If it wasn't a big deal, you'd be home by now instead of here and drunk." "I'm not drunk."

174

"Okay, let's go anyway."

Mitch locked up without doing any prep work, knowing full well that meant a very early morning later today, and drove Mary to her home in the woods. On the way, she used the cell phone to warn Lisa and by the time they got there, she had made a pot of coffee and was sitting at the kitchen table drinking the first cup. Mary hadn't talked in the car and now, sitting at the table, didn't appear any closer to discussion.

"Maybe you two want to talk in private?" Lisa ventured, sensing the unease.

"No, it's okay," Mary nodded.

"You want something to eat?" Mitch asked.

"I'll get some cookies and ice cream," Lisa said without waiting for an answer. She needed to be up and doing something. This was making her nervous. For all she knew, it involved her work at the Center.

"I just want to sit here for a minute," Mary said, with a new quaver in her voice. She was mentally trying to find the way to confess. It seemed utterly ridiculous to Mitch that this should be like sin to Mary. She hadn't done anything wrong, and yet she felt so guilty. Mitch just nodded and patted her hand. The silence was somehow getting more comfortable between all of them.

Then, the phone rang. They all three jumped like it was a school bell and they were late for class. Lisa answered it, "Hello?"

She nodded, "Oh, hi governor."

More nodding.

"I'm fine, and you?"

"Uh huh,"

"Oh yes, she's here. I'll put her on."

Lisa gestured to Mitch and held the phone out to her. Mitch looked at Mary, who shook her head. Mitch took the phone and began to talk.

"Hi, Honey."

"Hi, Honey?" Rebecca echoed, a perturbed echo.

"I'm sorry I'm late."

"You said you'd be home by midnight."

"I'm sorry, things just sort of got busy at work."

"I called work. Things must have apparently been too busy to answer the phone?"

"I've been here for a little while."

"I'm not sure I even want to know why," Rebecca was beginning to get a full head of steam now. She had every right to be angry. Just not for this.

"I have a good reason," Mitch said. Her tone of voice must have sent a clear signal to Mary, who asked to speak to her mother. "I'm sure you do," Rebecca carried on her half of the conversation. "Are you sure?" Mitch asked Mary, and the question perplexed Rebecca, who didn't know what she should be sure about.

"I'm sure," Mary replied.

"Good, uh Rebecca?" Mitch said into the phone.

"What is going on there?"

"Mary is here and she needs to talk to you, okay?"

"Mary's there too?"

"Yeah, and she wants to talk to you."

"Okay?" Rebecca sounded very concerned.

"Okay," Mitch handed the phone to Mary.

"Hi, mom."

That's about all the dialogue that Mitch and Lisa heard. Mitch took Lisa for a walk so that they could give Mary some privacy. Lisa followed orders but as soon as they were out of the house, she began to grumble about having to take a midnight stroll.

"The fresh air will do you good," Mitch told her and they walked a way down the path. One of the more charming features of this otherwise bland acre was an old wooden gazebo that the previous owners had built and then immediately neglected. It was splintery if you didn't watch where and how you scooted, but otherwise it was a place to sit when none other was in sight. Mitch guided Lisa to a seat, and watched her shiver for a few seconds. The night was cooler than expected. She had two choices, she could set fire to the wood, which was practically kindling already, or she could hold Lisa closer and share her angry, burning warmth that had been smoldering in her since she watched Mary recoil at the lightest touch.

"Come closer to me. I'll keep you warm."

"I'm okay."

"You're so cold you're shivering."

"I know."

"May I please hold you?"

Lisa looked at Mitch and then acquiesced. They had struggled to find their way in this area. Touching, hugging, it was all so tied up in emotional pain that it had caused angry words, tender feelings and a general stand-offishness to date. Now, things were changing again.

"You're asking permission?"

"I guess I'm just really sorry for the way I've treated you since you came back."

"What are you talking about?" Lisa asked as she inched a little closer to Mitch. "And yes, I guess you can warm me up if it will help you assuage your guilt."

Mitch would have laughed, but she kept thinking about Mary inside, on the phone.

"I think that very soon we are going to have the governor at the house."

"We are? Good thing I cleaned the bathroom!"

"You've taken very good care of the place. Thank you for that."

"What did you mean a minute ago, about how you've been treating me?"

Ah, Lisa, always ready to talk about herself. Mitch smiled.

"I fear that I've been abusive to you."

"Really! How? Certainly not physically, hell, you wouldn't even come near me in that way!"

"There are other ways to abuse people."

Lisa took a long moment to think this over. "Is that what's going on, with Mary and Hilary?"

"You didn't hear it from me, but in about fifteen minutes, you'll know everything."

"I see. If and when I'm asked, I figured it all out by myself. So tell me," Lisa went back to her favorite subject, "how have you abused me otherwise?"

"I took advantage of you when I knew better."

"No you didn't."

"Yes, I did."

"I'm the one who offered the deal."

"And that's when I took advantage. I should have never agreed to your terms, even if you set them yourself. But I was weak, and it sounded like great fun, watching you work away, knowing that I had the power to make your life miserable. I indulged in some sort of perverse emotional abuse and I'm sorry if you at any time felt less than …" "Less than what?"
"Less than appreciated, I guess? I told Trish to warn me when this happened." "Warn you about me?"
"Oh, heck no. Nobody needs to warn me about you! I learned that the first time. What I'm talking about is that I told Trish to warn me when my money went to my head."
"I think Trish has been too preoccupied to keep tabs on you." "I guess I'll need to ask someone else to tell me when I'm being a jerk. Maybe you'll do the honors?"
"You know, Mitch, you're just one big puzzle that I don't think I'm ever going to figure out."
"Really?"
"I took your money, I offered to give it back, and as I'm doing so, you give me a job, a paycheck, you arrange for medical care, lend me a home to live in and new clothes to wear and a car to drive and you still think you're abusing me?"
"That's why domestic abuse goes unreported so often. It's so tied up in all the other issues that people don't see it when it happens."
"I guess I just don't believe that Mary and Hilary are in this situation."
"Why?"
"I've never associated gay people with domestic abuse."
"That's a common misconception. Domestic abuse happens with gay couples. I'm not sure that it happens with the same frequency or percentages as straight couples, but it still happens. I'm sure the situation really tweaks the noses of the right wing."
"What do you mean?"
"Well, you know how the right wing is always saying that gay people are together just for sex, and yet, there are so many domestic violence cases in the gay community that it's just like we're regular folks. And yet, the right wing can't very well use the gay DV statistics, what few there are, to talk about how violent gay people can be, because then it just proves the opposite point, which is that gay couples stay together

for love through thick and thin and abuse. It's a real 'catch 22' for them."

"I want you to know something," Lisa said with conviction.

"What?"

"You can think if you want to that you emotionally abused me, and I'm not going to argue about it with you but I really don't think that's the case at all. Furthermore, the time we spent together, the first time, you know, you were never anything but sweet and kind and gentle and as far as I'm concerned, you don't have an abusive bone in your body!"

Lisa had to stop just to breathe and then fell silent, all out of further insight. She just shivered again. Mitch held her tightly, and rubbed her shoulders to keep her warm.

"You'd better stop that," Lisa said.

"Okay, I know I'm overstepping my bounds."

"It isn't that at all."

"Then, what is it?"

"The governor's car just pulled into the driveway and she wouldn't want to see you doing that."

"Don't worry about what she does or doesn't want."

"Okay, but she's the one calling all over town at one or two in the morning to find you." "She worries about me."

"Somebody better do that. You need looking after."

"Do you think we should wander back?"

"I think so. They'll maybe need more coffee and besides…"

"Besides…?"

"I left the ice cream out. It's probably good and melted by now."

They walked back to the house slowly. It gave Rebecca enough time to go in and gather up her only precious daughter in her arms. They were in full flood of tears when Lisa and Mitch appeared and began their chores. More coffee, more food, more warmth. It was going to be a long night. Lisa took care of the food, Mitch set a fire in the fireplace. It was roaring within minutes and Rebecca and Mary sat together on the couch and held on to each other for what must have felt like survival. Mitch thought Lisa had been shaking until she saw Mary. She was trembling in spite of the blankets and fire, so strong was this emotional upheaval. It was as if her heart had caught the flu and was on the critical list. Since Mary wasn't even able to hold a cup of coffee without spilling it, Mitch held it steady as she drank. Even Rebecca wasn't steady enough to do this. When Mitch finally trusted herself enough to look into Rebecca's eyes, she saw everything she needed to see. Forgiveness, appreciation, and love. It was overwhelming and Mitch wandered away, not wanting to lose her reserve now. It took her a moment to realize how much the situation had shaken her to the core and she quietly but firmly packed that tidbit of information away. It could come out later, but right now, she needed to be there with strength and hot coffee and food and everything else for the truly affected. It must have been close to the business-like way some rescue workers felt at the scene of disasters. Pack up your feelings in an old kit bag and take care of business. Lisa, thank God for her, was changing the sheets on the bed, and defrosting food she pulled from the freezer.

"What is that?" Mitch asked when Lisa took the pan out of the microwave. It didn't look like anything store-bought.

"It's beef stroganoff."

"You made it yourself?"

"Well, the great chefs of Europe offered, but I told them I could handle it!"

At least Lisa was back to her old self, quick on the draw with a wiseass remark. She would be good therapy for Mitch, and she knew it. Mitch took a snifter of brandy to Rebecca, who had settled down enough to hold a glass, and asked Mary if she wanted some, also. Mary just nodded. Ah, yes, a brandy chaser to those two glasses of wine and don't forget the coffee...it would do the trick. She would maybe be able to sleep. Maybe. Besides, she had already cried out about a pint of tears, and more seeped out here and there as she talked to her mom. When Lisa was finished with her microwave magic, they ate. Mary, after getting a slow start, warmed up to the idea of food and ate a decent amount of dinner. Rebecca picked politely. Stroganoff at two-thirty in the morning wasn't on her diet. Mitch ate like she hadn't seen food in hours, which, come to think of it, was the truth. Lisa was her usual self. No explanations necessary.

Afterwards, Mary went in to lie down and Mitch sat next to Rebecca back on the couch.

"I'm sorry," were the first words out of Rebecca's mouth.

Mitch took her index finger and gently touched Rebecca's lips. "You don't need to apologize."

"Yes, I do," Rebecca took hold of Mitch's finger, and then her entire hand. "I was out of line on the phone."

"I'm glad you worry about me."

"I was jealous and angry. That's half a hemisphere away from being concerned."

"I'll take it anyway."

"You shouldn't have to."

"I assume you're going to spend the night here, since it's half over already."

"I think it would be a good idea, so I can be here if Mary wakes up from a nightmare or something."

"I agree. Why don't you sleep in the same room with her."

Mitch waited a full ten seconds for Rebecca to ask the pending question, which was, "And where will you sleep?"

"Here on the couch."

Lisa was cleaning the kitchen with finely tuned ears. Well, not literally. She popped into the conversation. "I can sleep on the couch!"

"You're not going to sleep on the couch," Mitch admonished.

"It would be no trouble. Really."

"Goodnight, Lisa."

Realizing that Mitch wasn't going to hand over custody of the couch anytime soon, Lisa acquiesced and went to bed. Mitch turned her attention back to Rebecca.

"How is Mary?"

"She's really shaken. This is terrible for her."

"And for you."

"Thank you so much for helping her out."

"She couldn't talk to me about whatever was going on. I'm so glad you called when you did." "And jumped all over you!"

"I'm glad you worry about me. And that's what it is. Really. Truly."

Rebecca didn't argue any further and allowed Mitch to hold her steady for a good half hour. When she seemed relaxed enough to sleep, Mitch walked her to the bed.

"Night."

"Love you."

"Love you back."

Mitch stretched out on the couch for about ten minutes and then went out and bedded down for the night in the RV. It had a much bigger bed, and was cool and quiet. She felt safe and snug, something she realized Mary hadn't felt much of until tonight. How frightening it would be to not be safe at home.

Chapter 10

Mitch woke up to a banging on the door. Of course, it was Lisa. Who else would it be, the tooth fairy? Still groggy, Mitch opened the door. "Well, geezuz, scare us all half to death and back!" was this morning's greeting.

"Have some respect for the sleeping, why don't you!" Mitch snapped back.

"We thought you had been taken away in the night."

"You obviously found me."

"Oh, don't appeal to my brilliant side and think you're not still in trouble. Get in the house and help me cook breakfast!"

With that, Queen Lisa headed back to Apronville. She looked so cute in frills.

Mitch, who hadn't even taken time to undress before she fell asleep, now found that fact rather convenient as she went into the main house.

"Good morning," Rebecca said, not even close to a hint of consternation or panic in *her* voice.

"Hi."

"Slept out in the North Forty, I see."

"It was more roomy than the couch."

"That was good thinking."

"I thought so," Mitch studied chef Lisa, who was mixing omelets or pancakes or something to the frothy stage. Whatever it was, it was going to float.

"How's Mary?"

"She slept through the night, and is still dozing on and off." "She can stay out here if she wants to. I don't think Hilary even knows about this place."

"I don't know, I think she might be safer at the mansion. We do have guards there."

"That's true. But I'm not sure that Hilary is the kind that will come after her."

"Do you want to take that chance?" Rebecca asked, sincerely.

"I could stay with her, but I don't own a gun."

"She can't hide out forever. What are we going to do?"

"Oh, don't worry. I have that all figured out. Nothing like a night out in the North Forty to clear your head."

"What are you going to do?"

"Just trust me on this one," Mitch said and then stubbornly refused to elaborate.

Instead, she helped out in the kitchen, which got her one step closer to forgiveness with the cook. Never hurts to get in good with whoever is fixin the vittles. The crepes, honestly, who could tell from the far end of the room, were magnificent. Mary had gotten up by the time the table was set, and all things considered, she looked better. Not great. Not terrific. But better. A little. She agreed to go back to the mansion with Rebecca, for at least a day or two. There was no discussion about how to get her things moved out of Hilary's house. Rebecca left Mitch to meditate on that as well. They hugged gently and then parted. Lisa was left to monitor the Center, with complete phone cooperation from Mary.

"So, how are you going to get rid of Hilary?" Lisa asked when Mary and Rebecca pulled away.

"I'm going to give her what she wants."

"You tried that with me and it didn't work."

Mitch couldn't honestly think of a good reply, so she commented instead, "Breakfast was superb."

"Go do the dishes!" Lisa ordered. God, what a woman!

By nine, Mitch had made one of the toughest phone calls since she found herself informing folks about Marge.

"Hello?" she had picked up on the third ring, sounding annoyed.

"Hilary, this is Mitch Tanner."

"Oh. Hi." She sounded caught off guard but made a smooth if not entirely believable rebound. "Have you seen Mary? I'm worried about her."

"I've seen Mary. And her bruises. I'm worried about her as well. As is her mother."

Mitch could visualize Hilary mulling this over in her mind.

"What happened to her? Was there a problem at work?"

184

At least she had the good sense to avoid the "rough sex" defense.
"I'm going to come by and pick up Mary's things. Do you want to
make a more formal appointment or would you prefer just setting her
things on the porch." "Mary's not moving out."
Inhaling and then counting to ten helped Mitch avoid screaming into
the phone.
"Do you want to set up an appointment with me or do you just want to
put her stuff on the porch?" Mitch calmly re-asked the question.
"You talked her into this, didn't you!" Hilary was heating up even
with Mitch's calm demeanor. "You and that slut Lisa." "Whatever
you say, Hilary," Mitch answered back quietly. "Well, if Mary
wants that slut instead of me, she can have her. Her stuff will be
on the porch by ten."
Hilary hung up without further conversation. Mitch called Rebecca.
"Hi, what's up?" Rebecca queried quickly.
"Do we still have Fido and Gruff on the payroll?"
Fido and Gruff were Mitch's nicknames for two of Rebecca's
bodyguards. What they lacked in charm they made up for in girth.
They were glowering, nasty and monosyllabic. And that was on their
best behavior.
"I sent them to one of those seminars on being more sensitive in the
workplace."
Oh great! Fido and Gruff were enrolled in charm school.
"Is there anybody down there who could escort me to Hilary's in
about a half hour?"
"I'll go with you."
"No!" Mitch practically jumped through the phone.
"Why not?"
"Because Mary needs you to stay with her.'
"You think I'll pick a fight?"
"I know you'll pick a fight!"
"I don't think it would be a good idea to send someone official,
anyway."
"I guess not, now that I think about it."
"And I don't want to call the police."
"That would be a lot of paperwork and embarrassment." "So,
I'll meet you there," Rebecca said just before hanging up.

Mitch, once again, had a dead phone in her hand. Twice in ten minutes. Damn.

She jumped in her car and made good time to Gaytown. Gaytown was the slang term for this gentrified suburb of downtown Denver. No one may admit to saying so, but whenever anyone mentioned gay people, Gaytown came to mind. When things were good for Mary and Hilary, a scant two months ago, they had happily set up housekeeping together in Hilary's two story brick home. The house remained solid, the relationship had long since crumbled. Rebecca was already there. She was out of her car and halfway up the walk when Mitch bounded out of her vehicle. Mitch could hear voices. Exactly what she had hoped to avoid. Hilary was on the porch with a bottle in one hand and a shotgun in the other. Mitch approached slowly at the sight of this. Didn't this only happen in the movies? She could hear the dare from Hilary loud and slurred.

"You want your slut daughter's stuff? Do ya!"

By now, Mitch was close enough to Rebecca to edge in front of her. "What are you doing?" Rebecca asked in a stage whisper. "I'm trying to get a matched set," she replied, pointing to her good elbow.

"Mary didn't say she'd have a gun." "Betcha a dollar it's not loaded."

Mitch had, by now, almost totally blocked Rebecca from harm.

"Hilary. You have Mary's stuff packed up?"

She talked like it was a bag of groceries and they were at 7-Eleven. "I want her to try and get it," Hilary gestured toward Rebecca with the bottle. It looked like bourbon. Very expensive bourbon. That's what you get for being a bartender. A useless grasp of trivial information where liquor was concerned.

"Should I call the police?" Rebecca muttered quietly.

"No, that won't be necessary."

"It won't?"

"If she hasn't shot us by now, chances are she never will."

"So, we just stand here all day?"

Nothing like having a type-A personality in back of you and a shotgun in front.

"I'm going up on the porch and get Mary's stuff."

"You're insane."

"No, just watch."

Mitch started to walk toward the porch. Hilary raised the gun, but Mitch kept on walking until she was on the first of four steps.

"Stop. I'll shoot."

"No, you won't. If you really wanted to shoot me, you would've already done it."

"How do you know?"

"Because I've already been shot twice this year. I know a thing or two about the process."

"Stay back."

"Is there a lot of stuff in the box you packed?"

"Just a buncha crap."

"Is there any of it that you'd like to keep?"

"Why would I want to?"

"So, why are you guarding it with a gun?"

Hilary thought about this for a brief second and then took a step back and gave the box one mighty shove with her foot. It fell end over end and thumped at the bottom of the steps. A few things spilled out, toothpaste, books, an alarm clock. This stuff wouldn't have brought a second glance at a garage sale. Mitch bent over and put the box upright, refilling it with the remains of a shattered relationship. "Get off my property," Hilary ordered.

"Sure, thanks, and stop by the U later and I'll buy you lunch. Okay?" Mitch picked up the box and walked without even a glance backward. She kept her eye on Rebecca's face. If Hilary decided to use her for target practice, something Mitch doubted seriously, then she still wanted Rebecca's face to be the last thing she saw.

They walked back to Rebecca's car and Mitch put the box on the passenger side seat. Then she got in her Subaru and followed Rebecca for five blocks. That was as good a time as any to pull over and regroup. "You okay?" Mitch asked Rebecca.

"I'm confused. You're buying Hilary lunch after what she did to Mary?"

"I thought it was the least I could do to thank her for not shooting me in the head."

"I don't think she was going to shoot you."

"Brave talk, coming from the person behind the bigger target." "I can't help it if you pushed your way to the front of the line," Rebecca retorted dryly. It was an odd conversation they were having. Rebecca was relieved but pissed. Mitch was experiencing the kind of rush you get when you cheat the hell out of death. She would have looked around for some water to walk on, but Rebecca interrupted.

"What's your plan from here?"

"I'm going to work. I'll be home for dinner. Business as usual."

"If you're not home by six. I' putting out an APB."

"And I love you, too." Mitch kissed her on the cheek. Eight blocks later they split up their two-car convoy. Rebecca went downtown. Mitch headed west.

Sandy was buffing up the glassware when Mitch arrived. It was a little before eleven. Hilary showed up at noon, and not nearly as drunk as she had been earlier. Still, her attitude was sour.

"You didn't think I'd come, did you?"

"I hope you took a cab."

"I want to see Mary."

"Let's eat, first."

Mitch ushered Hilary to her booth and beckoned Sandy to bring the menus. They ordered simple, greasy food. Nothing like a balanced diet of beef fat and corn liquor. Mitch refused to serve her anything stronger than coffee. But then again, their coffee was pretty strong. As they ate, Mitch kept quiet. She knew that the more Hilary ate, the better she would feel. By twelve-thirty, she was up for amateur counseling.

"Who beat who at home when you were a kid?" Mitch cut to the heart of the matter. Something about staring down the barrel of a shotgun made her feel omnipotent.

"My dad."

"Your dad beat up on your mom."

"He wasn't choosy. He beat anybody."

"I'm sorry to hear that."

"Yeah, whatever."

"Hilary, I'm not the best person to talk to, since I don't know anything about the subject, but would you take my advice and get some help."

"This is the first time! It isn't something I do all the time, okay?"

"Once is enough, don't you think?" Hilary considered the notion.

"I love her."

"I don't doubt that."

"It won't happen again." "Is that what your dad promised?"

"I want to tell Mary that I'm sorry."

"I'll pass along your request."

"Look, I'm gonna be late for work." Hilary stood to leave. "One more thing."

"What's that?" Mitch asked.

"Do you know how many resources there are for lesbians who batter?" "No."

"Try zero. If you're a man and you batter, you have support groups all over." "Drive safely."

"Yeah."

She was gone before Sandy could get dessert orders. "She sure is a pretty lady," Sandy remarked. Mitch looked up.

"She sure is."

Mitch wondered how ugly her x-rays were. Hilary had hidden it well. When Vickie showed up at four, raring to work, Mitch left for the mansion. She preferred a pre-dinner nap to an APB any old day.

Mary was asleep in her old room, probably under a doctor's care by now. Life made better through pharmaceuticals. Mitch went to the master bedroom with every intention of calling Lisa and checking her status. Instead, Mitch crashed like the 1929 stock market. She was awakened by a kiss.

"Are you going to sleep right through dinner?" Rebecca was leaning over her, looking more beautiful than a dream.

"I might sleep through breakfast."

"It's almost six."

"How's Mama Fairbanks?"

The term "Mama Fairbanks" was what Mitch used when she was referring to Rebecca's emotional state where Mary was concerned. Their code word worked well.

"Mama Fairbanks is still pretty shaky."

"That's understandable. Are you still angry at me?"

"I'm still in awe of you."

"Well, let's hope that never goes away. How's Mary?"

"She's remarkable, under the circumstances."

"And how's Lisa?"

"I don't know."

"Someone should call her and check on her. She's trying to keep the Center going," Mitch talked through a still somewhat sleepy brain, "and besides I wouldn't have caught on if it hadn't been for Lisa."

"Here's the phone," Rebecca gave the handset to Mitch. Mitch dialed and waited two rings for a pickup.

"Hello?"

"Hi, it's Mitch. You okay?"

"Sure, fine."

"Did you have dinner yet?"

"Are you kidding? I just got in the door. What a day!"

While Lisa went on and on, Mitch looked at Rebecca with such a pleading countenance that she nodded agreement without even hearing the question.

"Come here for dinner."

"You're serious!"

"Yeah, see you in fifteen minutes?"

"Ten."

"Don't speed!"

Mitch hung up. "She needs to stay all night."

"She does!"

"Well, either that, or I should go to the house and spend the night there to protect her."

"Because Hilary blames her?" the truth finally dawned on Rebecca.

"Exactly."

"She can sleep in Charlie's bedroom."

"Ah, yes, Charlie's bedroom."

Mitch had been in Charlie's bedroom once. Naked. Now, don't jump to conclusions. It happened during a migraine attack. She had shown up for a press conference, gotten very ill very fast, was carried upstairs and the rest was a blur until she awoke recovered and naked. Rebecca kissed her on a dare and the rest was history. The room was named so because Charles Lindbergh had slept there. And so had Mitch Tanner. Maybe other folks looked up to him for his aviation skills, but a Nazi was still a Nazi in Mitch's book. "I know what you're thinking," Rebecca cut through the reminiscences.

"I doubt it."

"Let's go eat."

Mitch allowed Rebecca to pull her off the bed. She stopped in the bathroom to take care of life's necessities and then met up with Mary on the stairs.

"I invited Lisa to dinner," Mitch informed her.

"That's nice."

"Hilary blames her for…to tell you the truth I don't know what she's thinking."

"I heard you were looking up the wrong end of a shotgun."

"Did you know Hilary owned a gun?"

"No."

They walked into the dining room. Rebecca was allowing a red wine to breathe. It gave them something trivial to discuss, how red wines needed time and space to improve. In the distance, they could hear Lisa's arrival.

"I hope she brought my sweat suit back," Mitch was always a sucker for wishful thinking. Lisa bounded into the room, getting more and more accustomed to being invited to dinner at the mansion. No sign of a sweat suit but no pantyhose either.

"Damn," Mitch muttered.

"What a day! Is that a Pinot Noir? *Good choice*," Lisa approved. Rebecca poured a generous glass for Lisa, who went through no predrinking ritual. No swirl and sniff for her. Instead, she downed about half the glass in one draw and nodded wisely. Mary passed on the wine, since she was on medication. Mitch and Rebecca started with half a glass apiece. Dinner was beefy. Roast with potatoes and carrots and biscuits so sinful that they would have been prohibited by an eleventh commandment if it addressed such things as baked goods.

191

Don't even go into the honey and butter that were within arm's reach. If the staff minded an extra guest, there was no outward sign. That part of life at the mansion was improving. Lisa hadn't heard about the confrontation with Hilary yet, so they filled her in over meat and gravy. Lisa only mildly resisted the suggestion of being an overnight guest in Charlie's room once the truth was out. Mildly was the operative word. By the time dessert was served, heaven forbid this coincidence, cherry pie, Lisa was malleable to almost any suggestion. She only had one question, which was, "Is Charlie going to be there?"

"He's dead," Mitch assured her.

"Oh, good. I guess?"

Mitch ushered Rebecca upstairs soon after dinner, telling her that Mary and Lisa could use the time alone to talk over Center issues, and could be trusted to find jammies on their own. Besides, didn't cuddling up naked sound like the perfect end to the day? Rebecca had remarked that why should tonight be any different, but still went along with the idea. So, there they were, cuddled up together. It was stunningly intimate despite the fact that Rebecca wasn't completely undressed yet and also that she still had more to say on the whole Hilary, Mary, Lisa subject.

"You talked to Hilary after the gun incident?"

"Yes."

"What did she say?"

"She said she's sorry."

"I won't let Mary go back to her!"

"Has Mary indicated that she will?" "No, not yet. But I'm worried that she will."

"Then I won't mention to anyone Hilary's professed act of contrition. Unless you think that would be manipulative of me."

"Give it a few days."

Mitch nodded and then sighed. The sigh of the ages.

"What?" Rebecca asked.

"What what?" Mitch asked back double.

"You sighed."

Mitch smiled. Here she was, lying on her back with Rebecca on her left side. Mitch was holding Rebecca's left arm close to the body. Their fingers were entwined and Rebecca's arm stretched from

Mitch's throat to just below her belly button. Mitch wasn't even sure of her zip code most days let alone her erogenous zones, but this was one thing that made her sigh with genuine contentment. She stroked Rebecca's arm softly, making the hair stand on end.

"Do you realize how lucky we are?"

"Yes."

"That was a succinct answer."

"It was an easy question," Rebecca stated.

"I know that I'm not a perfect partner."

"Perfection is neurotic."

"And I never will be."

"Good."

"And if my candle had three ends, I'd be burning every one," Mitch hoped the concept made sense.

"A candle with three ends?"

"A figure of speech, sort of."

"I've seen a candle with three wicks before."

"A candle with three wicks?"

"It was a really big candle."

Mitch nodded, knowing that somehow she had gotten her point across.

"So, that only leaves me with one question," Mitch followed up,

"Which is, of course, 'Why do you still have your clothes on?'"

"I don't have all my clothes on."

That was true, she was down to her underwear.

"I didn't say all."

"But you meant all."

This struck Mitch as nervous bantering. Maybe it was too soon after Mary's crisis.

"Are you okay?"

"It's just the timing."

"You mean about Mary."

"No, I mean monthly."

"Ah," the light dawned. Mitch understood. "You don't feel like making love."

"On the contrary, I'm horny as hell."

"I can fix that."

"I didn't know if it would bother you?"

"Does it bother you?"

"It bothered Jeff."

Mitch raised her head and looked around the room.

"What are you doing?"

"I'm looking around to see if Jeff's here. Jeff! Oh Jeff!!!" Mitch yoohooed.

"Would you stop it! Mary will wonder what in the hell is going on!" Rebecca giggled.

"If we can't hear them, they can't hear us!"

"What's *that* supposed to mean?" Rebecca asked pointedly.

"It means the walls are soundproof, aren't they?"

"I meant, what did you mean by 'they' and 'them'?"

"'They' and 'them' are pronouns." Mitch made an attempt to explain the obvious.

"You meant Mary and Lisa. Together? In one bedroom?"

Mitch finally got Rebecca's point.

"That's not what I meant."

"If it was, you'd tell me?"

"No."

"No?"

"That would be up to Mary to tell you."

Rebecca changed lines of questioning, like any good lawyer who was trying to catch the witness off guard.

"Why did you take that risk today?"

She avoided calling it a foolish risk. Or a stupid risk. God, she was good.

"You mean that stupid, foolish risk?" Mitch clarified.

"Only if you say so."

"I've been thinking about that all evening, when I wasn't thinking about making love to you."

"And?"

"I don't have any other risks in my life."

"Most people don't."

"On the contrary, most people do."

"I don't understand your point."

194

"Signing a mortgage with a balloon payment is a risk. Staying employed is a risk. Guessing which careers are going to be viable is a risk. I don't have any of those risks."

"That doesn't mean you need to step in the line of fire."

"What was your excuse? Hilary had the gun pointed at you first."

"I'm protecting my daughter."

"Mmmm," Mitch muttered noncommittally.

"You're saying I shouldn't have done it?"

"Not for a box of junk."

"I didn't see the gun until it was too late."

"I know. I forgive you."

"For what?"

"For taking such a risk."

"I guess we're even."

"What did you forgive me for?"

"For burning a three-wick candle."

Rebecca laughed in that sexy way that Mitch could've sworn tickled her ear drums. She reached for her more earnestly. "This really won't bother you?" Rebecca asked again.

"Do I look bothered?" Mitch replied and she held Rebecca's steady gaze.

"Not a bit."

Not only didn't it bother Mitch to touch Rebecca, she enjoyed the opportunity. Legend has it that achieving climax during menstruation can alleviate cramping. Mitch felt like she was giving aid and comfort to the very friendly. Once Rebecca had stopped thinking about Jeff, she closed her eyes and telegraphed her desires with murmurs of delight. Mitch already knew what to do, but the words from Rebecca inspired her to be even more gentle. Good thing about those soundproof walls!

Breakfast was awkward. Lisa was dressed in Mitch's blue sweat suit. If she wasn't careful, Mitch would need to go to the mall and raid the sweat suit store. She couldn't stay peeved, Lisa looked absolutely elfin and gorgeous. Mary looked drained. It must have been the medication. The sooner she was off it, the better. When Rebecca showed up, her chaste kiss of Mitch prompted awkwardly averted glances from both Lisa and Mary. On her next day off, Mitch was going to conduct an experiment on the alleged soundproof quality of the walls. She didn't know how she was going to accomplish this, but she felt it was necessary.

After breakfast and over everyone's objections, Mary went to work. "It's a shelter, for God's sake!" she explained crossly as she left with Lisa, who was still in Mitch's sweats. Damn.
"I guess she has a point," Mitch said as she watched the door close. "That doesn't mean I need to like the idea," Rebecca retorted.
"I know. I have to go take care of something. See you later?" "I have a jam-packed schedule today. You might be in bed before me."
"I'll consider that a dare!"
Mitch chuckled as she kissed Rebecca goodbye. Now that the 'kids' were gone, it was a little more intense. It would carry her through the day. Just barely.

Mitch jumped in her car and weaved through the busy downtown traffic, heading to her other house. It had a phone. That would work, for starters. The calls took about an hour. Those bankers and advisors and university presidents could talk, talk, talk! Mitch's ear felt like it had gone ten rounds with the Cauliflower Kid. But it was worth it. Then, she dragged herself back to work, even though the woodpecker nude male painting beckoned to be retouched. The U was quiet. Mitch did some boring bookwork and then chatted with Sandy. Things were good in Sandy's life. One person who had it under control. It was soothing to hear.

Remembering that Rebecca's schedule was full, Mitch decided to lunch at the Center. When Mitch had donated a substantial amount for the refurbishing of the Center, Mary had told her to stop by anytime. Now seemed like a good time to her. Lunch was hamburgers with mushroom gravy and French fries. Talk about comfort food! There had been no incidents involving, for instance, Hilary showing up, which gave Mitch and Lisa a chance to talk like sane people for about fifteen minutes. Mostly they talked about future sleeping arrangements. Lisa, understandably, didn't really care to

196

stay at the mansion every night. Enough was enough. Good thing she wasn't the governor. "It can be awkward, I know," Mitch nodded.

"I'll be fine at the other house. I'll lock the door."

"Maybe I could talk Trish into staying out there for a night?"

"No! Thanks!"

"Just a thought."

"I'm sure she has a lot of time on her hands, but hanging out with me can't be high on her list."

"Time on her hands?" Mitch went fishing.

"Judy's rejected her by now, of course!"

"What are you talking about?"

"I have to go back to work."

"You can take ten seconds to explain your point."

"Her nose," Lisa finished with eight seconds to spare.

"Are you psychic or something?" Mitch said irritably.

"No."

"Tell me more."

"I can't. I have work to do."

Lisa picked up her dishes and then went back to work. Well, the conversation had started out sane.

Mitch waved goodbye to Mary and once she got over the irritation and shock of Lisa's remark about noses, discovered that she had driven all the way back to work. At work, she devised a plan to ply the rest of the truth from Lisa. She took her to a steak dinner. It was thick, juicy and priced way over the top. Lisa selected an appropriate wine. She was getting good at this. Halfway through the meal, or bribe depending on your point of view, Mitch began the interrogation.

"So, what's with the nose?"

"Mine?"

"No, Trish's."

"You don't think a lesbian can be a bigot?"

Mitch turned the question over in her mind.

"You're saying that Judy's a bigot about noses?"

"You ever read any of her books?"

"She writes books?" Mitch was clueless and didn't mind it showing if it would give Lisa the impression that she could lord it over her.

"Really deadly boring crap about war."

"The War of the Noses?" Mitch said dryly.

"Wars have been fought over genetics."

"Of course, it's called ethnic cleansing."

"So, the next time you're at the library, check out her book about World War II."

"You're saying that Judy is anti-Semitic?"

"You said it, I didn't."

"But that's your contention."

"She's not that blatant in her book. I mean, it isn't Mein Kampf or anything like that, but it's what's between the lines. A derision thinly veiled."

"You've read the book?"

"I've read all of her books. I didn't need to take sleeping pills for a month!"

"So, Judy won't get involved with Trish because she thinks Trish is Jewish?" Mitch summarized, mostly for her own benefit.

"In a nutshell."

"That's ridiculous."

"It worked for Hitler."

"Not for long. What does Judy write about Hitler's persecution of gay people?"

"What the little boy shot at."

"According to the old saying, the little boy shot at nothing."

"That's right. Judy was trying to be real mainstream. How antiSemitism could be construed as mainstream is quite a stretch."

"Maybe it's good that Judy is dumping Trish," Mitch steered back to the practical issue at hand.

"I jumped at the chance to leave."

Mitch let that remark slide away. Other issues were of greater concern. Mitch remembered that she had encouraged Trish to confront Judy about the issue. Mitch was batting zero in the giving advice department, having already talked earnestly to Mary about moving across the country with Hilary. Now, she had advised Trish badly. Maybe it wasn't too late to reverse this. She punched Trish's phone number into her cell phone and actually got her instead of her answering machine. The good angels were working overtime.

"You talk to Judy yet?"

"Hello to you, too."

"Sorry, didn't mean to start in the middle."

"Well, now that you're there, in the middle, no I haven't. Yet."

"Don't!"

"Why not?"

"I want to talk to you about something."

"So, talk."

"Not over the phone."

"I'll come over."

"I'm not at the house, yet."

"When?"

"Thirty minutes?"

"Okay, thirty minutes."

Lisa heard this and stepped up her pace. She still had a baked potato to devour. With sour cream *and* butter. Her arteries might seize up and congeal any day now. Mitch paid for dinner and felt it was worth every penny. They got to the house just in time to perk coffee. It could be a long night. Trish breezed in, undaunted by the sight of Lisa. It couldn't be classified as a truce, but it was miles away from war.

"How about a cup of coffee?"

"Decaf?"

"Does it matter?"

"Not really. Sure."

"Let's sit down."

Room for three on the couch wasn't going to work. Lisa pulled up a chair.

"Are we *all* going to talk about my nose?" Trish asked, somewhat unnerved. Apparently between here and there, she had figured out the topic of the summit.

"Lisa is responsible for an important insight."

"About *my* nose?"

It was obvious that Mitch was in trouble for talking this over with Lisa.

"About Judy's viewpoints," Mitch split hairs.

"Tell me exactly what you mean," Trish encouraged.

"Judy's a bigot," Lisa jumped right in.

"A bigot?"

"She may be anti-Semitic," Mitch said.

"I'm not Jewish!" Trish remarked.

"But she thinks your nose is," Lisa explained.

"This is ridiculous."

"I thought so too, at first," Mitch nodded.

"Then I told her about the books."

"Her 'war' series?"

"Have you read them?"

"No."

"Well, I have," Lisa intoned, sounding just a tad superior. "I wanted to know who I was involved with."

"I see."

"Yeah, I took the money and ran and I'm not even Jewish!"

"Neither am I."

"You already said that," Mitch reassured Trish, who seemed to be agitated. Not about the idea of being Jewish. Just about the general disorganization of the conversation.

"This is unbelievable. I will definitely confront her about it!" "Just don't do it alone," Mitch pleaded.

"Use the phone," Lisa, the practical one, added.

"You're acting like she's going to go ballistic."

"It's been a tough week. We want you to stay safe."

"What's going on that I don't know about?"

You never could get anything past Trish. Mitch and Lisa exchanged glances. It was bound to come out sooner or later.

"Mary and Hilary are splitting up."

"And that's a safety issue?"

"Not for long, I hope."

"What's that supposed to mean?" Trish probed.

"Yeah, what are you talking about," Lisa added on, apparently happy to be teaming up with Trish on this fact-finding mission.

"Just trust me, I know what I'm doing."

"I'm calling about this Jewish nose issue," Trish stated.

"Just pick a good time," Lisa said wisely, not noticing the rolling of eyes. "And just so you know, I like your nose."

"Now I can die happy," Trish came back wryly. "I'm outa here."

"Goodnight," Lisa and Mitch chorused. Together.

"I need to go back to work," Mitch said and she headed out right behind Trish. "Drive safely!"

"Sure, and thanks for your help with Trish."

"Anytime."

Mitch took advantage of Rebecca's busy schedule to do a thorough inventory of the U. It helped her balance the books. By one, she was on the road home. She dragged in at two, exhausted and dispirited. No pun intended. Not even bothering to shower, she pulled her dusty clothes off, noting for the unwritten record that this dust was totally different from the nice, clean dust of Santa Fe. This dust had been indoors too long, and smelled musty like a dirty dishrag. She slid into bed, feeling grimy and not really giving a damn. For once, Rebecca didn't wake up. Good thing. Mitch was unhuggable. Things had to get better. The old silly poem came into her head. "And when they said roses, I thought they said noses." This was insane.

Chapter 11

Nobody bothered to wake Mitch up the next morning. Perhaps Rebecca had taken in the entire aura of Mitch's presence and decided to let her sleep. One of those, "Don't wake me up unless the bed's on fire" decisions. She allowed herself the luxury of falling back asleep about three times before finally coming to at ten. Everyone was long gone. Mitch rubbed her eyes. She didn't want to go to work, she didn't want to go to the Center, she didn't even want to paint. She wanted, instead, to keep a promise.

Of course, Rebecca was in a meeting. Running an entire state can do that to you. Mitch requested of the staff to have the governor call her at the first convenient moment. While she was waiting for the call, she phoned four limousine services before she found one available for the remainder of the day. It was rented at a premium and would be stocked and ready in an hour. It saved time to have it come directly to the capitol.

Ten minutes later, Rebecca got through.
"Good morning," Mitch said.
"Is everything okay?" Rebecca asked quickly.
"Sure, I guess so."
"I thought it was something about Mary."
"No, just me wanting to have lunch with you."
"I have a thirty-minute window."
"Good. There will be a limo waiting."
"You didn't!"
"I did."
"Thirty minutes isn't very long…."
"I rented it for the day."
"I don't get off work until seven."
"That's okay. Where do you want to eat a thirty-minute lunch?"
"I'll make a reservation downtown."
"Great. Thanks."
Mitch showered and dressed in decent clothes. She still had her

Republican blue blazer and slacks. She felt geeky wearing this, but Rebecca liked it. They picked up Rebecca at the side door of the capitol building. The one with the drive through driveway. For all the money she was spending, so far they had traveled about five blocks. But they did it in style. As they ate a quick lunch, they chatted.

"Why the limo?"

"I promised I'd rent one when you got back from Japan. Remember?"

"I remember. And I remember *why*."

"Well, don't feel pressured. I just wanted to give you a treat."

"You seem restless."

"Do I?"

"Yes, very much so. Instead of going to work, you're sitting around thinking up ways to surprise and delight me. Are you that bored?"

"I don't know what I am."

"Does this have anything to do with the shotgun incident?"

"You mean about taking risks?" "I mean, are you going to start jumping out of airplanes or driving race cars or anything like that?" "No. At least, not today."

"You know, Mitch, there are a lot of ways to be a quiet hero."

"As opposed to a reckless hero."

"Exactly. Your artwork is a great beginning. Just think how the children at the Center would enjoy an art room. It would be good therapy and enjoyable as well."

"I'm not sure there's room at the Center for an art room."

"I'm sure you could think of something."

Had Rebecca been talking to Lisa about the cramped art studio at the old house? Mitch had already decided to take out a wall or two and expand the place. Why not so this at the Center as well. It might be as simple as adding an enclosed porch. An atrium or solarium or whatever the hell they called them!

"You're a genius!" Mitch exclaimed.

"A beautiful genius," Rebecca added.

"Come on, let's eat up. I have things to do."

"What about tonight? Are you still going to squire me around?"

"Absolutely!"

Rebecca was delivered back to work forty-five minutes into her thirtyminute window. The republic survived the fifteen-minute delay.

Mitch and the driver, Steven, conferred for a moment on the best place to buy art supplies for kids. They prioritized a list of the top three destinations. By five o' clock, they were unloading at the mansion. It didn't make sense to deliver these supplies to the Center before there was room. Mitch invited Steven to relax for a while in the kitchen, where he could eat a whole plate of cookies all by himself. Mitch made reservations at the Briarpath for later and then saw to a real meal for Steven. They were chuckling at the dining room table when Rebecca arrived.

"I'll be back down in a few minutes," she asserted. "Don't mind the mess. I went crayon shopping today." "This ought to be good," she quipped back.

"I forged a path through the purchases."

Mitch gave Rebecca twenty minutes and then went upstairs. She was being incredibly nosy, picking through the boxes of goodies.

"Just can't keep you out of this stuff, can I?"

"You think you got enough?"

"It's all I could fit in the car."

"If I suggested that a therapy dog would've been a good idea, you would have one-hundred and one Dalmatians in this room!"

"Actually, I like beagles. They tend to nip when they are young, so you have to watch them every minute."

"A lot like you, in fact!" Rebecca observed with a lilt.

"Oh, Honey, you better get dressed or we're gonna miss our dinner reservation!"

Rebecca kissed Mitch long and slow and then held her at arm's length.

"Hold that thought," she said.

Mitch went downstairs to warn Steven of their impending departure. As much fun as the evening was, Mitch couldn't promise a repeat performance anytime soon. Rebecca understood, and frankly breathed a private sigh of relief. So what if the bedroom smelled like crayons for a month. They were both busy and content with work and projects.

A week zoomed by. Mitch had convinced Mary that the "Art Museum at the Center" was a good idea, as long as she threw in a new garbage disposal. What one had to do with the other was anyone's guess. Lisa called eight contractors before she found one who would consider donating part of the cost of construction. It had nothing to do with Lisa's physical beauty, but her phone charm didn't hurt. He was invited to give a bid the next day. Lisa went split-skirt shopping to see about getting even deeper discounts. Mary just shook her head. In the lull, Hilary had contacted Mitch to ask one more favor. She wanted to say good-bye to Mary and hoped Mitch would broker a meeting.
"I can only ask." "I'd appreciate the effort."
Rebecca went ballistic. Understandably.
"At least it's a good-bye meeting," Mitch soothed.
"Where is she going?"
"She didn't say," Mitch reported factually, if not candidly.
"I don't like the idea."
"Don't you think it should be Mary's decision?"
"Yes, of course, but it needs to be done safely."
"We could have Hilary check her gun at the door."
"I'm trying to be serious."
"Me, too. Don't we have a metal detector around here somewhere?"
"I'll talk it over with Mary."
"Good choice."

The meeting happened the next day. At the mansion. At three in the afternoon. Fido and Gruff were back from charm school and in attendance. Everybody agreed that the sooner this happened, the better. At least there would be closure. Lisa stayed at the Center, holding down the fort and serving coffee to her new best friend - the contractor. Mitch went to work at the U, although her heart wasn't in it anymore. Rebecca went to work reluctantly. All this was best because the meeting between Mary and Hilary only took about five minutes. Fido and Gruff were extremely disappointed at the overall civility. They hadn't done a decent frisk in a long time.

Mary didn't say much at dinner, and went to bed early. The few facts Mary did impart prompted Rebecca to steer Mitch to the parlor couch for a *talk*.
"You arranged this, didn't you?"
Rebecca had guessed correctly. Again. Why didn't she just go on one of those game shows and win a new refrigerator? Mitch cast about for a good noncommittal answer. One didn't pop immediately into her mind, so she chose evasion as her next best ploy.
"Depends on what you mean by 'this?'"
"Hilary's sudden departure for Maryland."
"The University of Maryland, to be exact."
"You spent thousands of dollars on the woman who beat my daughter?"
"I got rid of her, didn't I?"
"Yes," Rebecca acquiesced the point, "but when are you going to stop playing God?"
"When I get tired of it, I suppose. Besides, you're the one who told me to be a quiet hero." "I'm not sure I meant this."
"I understand your anger, but just ask yourself, how much fun will eight years of nonstop med school study be for Hilary?"
"I guess it's not like a Hawaiian vacation."
"And she might be able to get help for her problem." "When you die, we're putting you up for sainthood."
"Saint Mitch. I like the sound of it."
"You're going to have a busy two weeks."
"I'm excited about the Center."
"You're like a kid yourself."
"I'll set aside a box of crayons for you."
"I'd settle for an hour of quality time every day."
"Make it two hours and I'm yours for life."

Construction at the Center began in earnest the day Hilary left town. Lisa wore her most revealing skirt and Mitch settled for her blue sweat suit that had been laundered and returned all fluffy. Mary kept a ten o'clock appointment with an old friend who stopped by the Center to catch up on old times. The two of them went to lunch at eleven. Lisa watched them leave, and only tore her gaze away to answer the pesky phone. Mary came back alone at two. Lisa was crestfallen.

"Where's your friend whom I've never met before?"

"Back at work."

"Oh, I see."

"Why?" Mary was watching Lisa for a clue.

"I thought maybe she was going to stay here."

"She did once, with her child."

"She has a child?"

"Yes, you sound surprised."

"Well, she has such a beautiful figure."

"She said the same thing about you." "She did!" Lisa sounded thrilled. "Settle down, Romeo. She also has a husband." Lisa looked crushed. "Well, an ex-husband by now."

"That's better! What else!"

"I don't want to go into any more details."

"Confidential. I understand." Lisa nodded like she understood the wisdom of the ages. "So, introduce us and I'll ask her myself!" Mary shook her head and barricaded herself on her office to get through the rest of the day.

By the next morning, Lisa had it all figured out.

"You like her."

"Who?"

"Your friend!" "Of course I like my friend. Duh!" Mary sounded like she was in middle school.

"No! I *mean* you *really* like your friend. I understand. I'll step aside."

Who said chivalry was dead? If Lisa had a coat, she'd be tossing it over a mud puddle by now. Mary caught on. Finally!

"Well, that's very noble of you, Lisa, but you really don't have to do that. I don't love the woman."

"Why not?"

The question caught Mary off guard.

"Why would I?"

"Because she's gorgeous."

"Well, you're gorgeous as well... I need to get to work."

Mary went into her office and closed the door. Firmly.

Lisa stared at it for a moment and then tended to her own duties. One of which was checking on that construction crew from time to time, ensuring that they had coffee and doughnuts and whatever else their little ole hearts desired. Almost. After looking over five different plans, Mary, Mitch and Lisa had taken a vote. Who said great minds didn't think alike! They all had picked the same design. It was much bigger than the original "porch" idea, taking up an area the length of the back of the Center, but it would be magnificent. The walls would alternate between chalkboard, floor-to-ceiling marker boards, corkboard, and windows. The children would be able to draw, erase, create and display their works of art until they would be taken to permanent homes. The floor had to be linoleum, since Mitch fully intended to bring in everything from finger paints to oils. She agreed to start small. Crayons and paper and canvas and easels and pencils and chalk pastels. No one thought this sounded small. It sounded more like Mitch the art supply broker.

Like all constructions projects, this one had its delays. While everyone had their opinion about what caused these delays, they all should've known the truth. It was Lisa and her famous skirt collection. But even they were not entirely correct in their assumption that Lisa was wearing them for the benefit of the crew. Lisa was wearing the skirts just in case Mary's friend happened to drop by again. It happened the following week. Another lunch. This time, both Mary and her friend looked a little more distracted. A little more serious. And no one was more willing to offer comfort and coffee than Lisa. Mary finally introduced Lisa to Pam. Pam. What a beautiful name. It rolled off her tongue like it was a royal title. Pam. Pam, Pam, Pam. Pam who? Pam Foley. Then, Pam and Mary hid out in Mary's office for a chat.

"I like your friend Lisa," Pam admitted.

"She's a bit of a rotter."

"Really?"

"But she's trying to reform."

"What did she do?"

"She has a habit of stealing money that isn't nailed down."

"Sounds like my lawyer," Pam tried to joke, but then found herself choking on the sentence. "I know it's been hard," Mary said.

"It's been hell."

Mary knew about the custody battles, the abuse, her husband's criminal record. It had all been a nightmare for Pam. And now, it was returning for an encore.

"I appreciate your kindness and support." "Anytime," Mary nodded.

"So tell me more about Lisa."

"She'd be more than happy to do that herself."

"Would it be okay if I stole her away from work for a drink?"

"I think that in itself would speed up the construction process!"

"Maybe I should keep her for a week?"

"That would probably make her week."

They laughed the easy laugh of friendship. Pam went out and ran the idea past Lisa, who practically jumped out of her chair at the chance.

"You'll be okay, here alone, Mary?" Lisa asked three times.

"I'll be fine. You two kids run along."

Lisa offered to drive. She did have, after all, a brand new safe car. They decided that they would get to know each other over margaritas at the Cantina de Mexico. It was a bar for upwardly mobile professional people who could afford to spend five dollars per drink. Lisa knew the actual cost, but didn't mind the mark up. She would buy anything this woman asked for.

"So, Mary tells me that you are a bit of a thief," Pam preferred to get the good stuff out on the table.

"That's about ninety-nine percent correct," Lisa fessed up.

"What about the other one percent?"

"I'm a big thief. If it's just a bit, it isn't worth stealing, now is it?"
Pam looked over the rim of her glass at Lisa. This was going to be an interesting cocktail hour.
"So you steal from the rich and give to?"
"Myself. It's a twist on the Robin Hood thing."
"With your way with words, you could be a writer."
"I could be a lot of things," Lisa replied, "but right now, I'm with you. So tell me what Mary won't tell me about you."
The story came out sounding more like a court deposition than an actual life event. Obviously, Pam had been forced to tell it over and over to people. The bland retelling kept her from crying.
"That stinks!" was Lisa's first comment.
"It does, doesn't it," Pam agreed.
"Your husband beats you and your child, gets jail time and is now coming back for custody because you're a *lesbian*!" "And he stands a pretty good chance of winning." "That's not possible!" Lisa retorted.
"It's not supposed to be possible, but it is."
"What do you mean?"
"I mean that if you get a right-wing judge, the case can go either way. And you know how public sentiment is right now in Colorado."
"But the laws are supposed to be fair to everyone."
"Laws aren't always the final say in courtrooms. If laws were the final say, we wouldn't need judges. Judges tend to interpret the law where it is ambiguous. And nothing seems more ambiguous than gay parents."
"But your ex-husband was in jail, for goodness sake."
"And became a born-again Christian in the process. He looks very favorable in the eyes of the court right now."
"So, what are you going to do?"
"I'm going to take another close look at cases in other jurisdictions to see what is asked of lesbian parents in order to retain or maintain custody."
"Sounds exhausting."
"Where my child's involved, I will work myself to the point of exhaustion and beyond if necessary."

Lisa nodded. She had never met anyone quite like Pam before. The devotion to her child was palpable. Perhaps it was from habit, but Pam hadn't disclosed many facts about her child.

"Tell me about your child. Boy or girl?"

"Girl."

"How old?"

"Five, going on twelve."

"Oh, a prodigy?"

"Just a worldly kid. She's already reading a little bit."

"Smart like her mother!"

"Stop it," Pam blushed the blush of hearing compliments about her most precious daughter.

"I'm serious. She'll be adding and subtracting in no time."

"Actually, she already is."

"See, I'm right!"

"So you are."

"Are you ready for another drink?"

"I'd better not."

"I'm driving. I'll get you back safe and sound."

"But I'd still need to drive from the Center. Besides, I need to pick my daughter up soon."

"Maybe we can get together soon." "All three of us?" Pam tested the waters.

"Sure. I'm good with kids. Just look at where I work!"

"Maybe this weekend, then?"

"This weekend! Sounds lovely."

They drove back to the Center and exchanged phone numbers. Lisa walked in like she had wings on her feet.

"Nice drink?"

"A bit overpriced, and a little shy on the Tequila, but otherwise okay."

"Pam's a nice woman." "I can see that."

"And a nice mom."

"Right."

"And a good friend."

"What's your point?"

"If you hurt her in any way, I'm going to hold it against you for the rest of your life."

"Okay. Are you done with the lecture?"

"I think so."

"Good. I have work to do."

The weekend arrived like it had taken the express route. Lisa wasn't ready. She had gotten behind in her cleaning chores at Mitch's house when she took the job at the Center and felt most days like she'd never catch up. Nobody seemed worried but her. She had put in a call to Mitch to get her help in cleaning up "the mess", as Lisa stated, almost frantically.

"So, you're having company," Mitch said as she arrived very early in the morning to relocate her painting stuff to the closet. "Who is it, the Pope?"

"You may find this terribly amusing, but it's important to me!"

"I can help you clean."

"Just put your junk away for a while."

Mitch would have argued further, but she sensed an urgency in Lisa that she hadn't seen before. "Who's coming over?" "A friend of Mary's."

"A friend of Mary's?"

"A friend and her little girl."

"Okay. And you want to make a good impression."

"Of course I do. I want to make a good impression with everybody!"

"Everybody?"

"Are you gonna stand there all day and ask a bunch of pointless questions or are you going to help me!"

"I'll run the vacuum."

"It's in the closet."

"It must be the gay vacuum."

"Just get to work."

Mitch cleaned the floor and dusted after she put her 'junk' away. She had thought about relocating it to the mansion, and how that would have thrilled the staff. She had even thought up a great hiding place behind the crates of crayons, but had managed to talk Lisa into just having it stuffed away at the house.

"Maybe the little girl would like to play with the art supplies?"

"She couldn't do any worse than you."

"Gee, thanks."

Mitch finished her chores, drove across town, and was sneaking back into the bedroom at the mansion when Rebecca caught her.

"What are you up to?"

"Just cleaning things up a bit at the country house."

"It's the weekend."

"Got any better ideas?"

"I'm free for two whole days."

"I have an idea."

"You always do."

"We could take the RV up to the mountains, and camp out in the woods. Or we could drive it to Utah and see the Canyon Lands."

"You're serious?"

"I just think that we have the RV and we could make good use of it once in a while instead of it being a spare bedroom at the other house."

"We could take it to Santa Fe!"

"Why didn't I think of it first? We could be there tonight."

"In time for a gourmet meal."

"And we could eat out, too!"

Rebecca laughed and proceeded to alert the staff. Mitch called Bella to give her fair warning and then Mitch phoned Lisa to tell her that she would be back by to pick up the RV.

"Is that okay?"

"Sure. Just make it snappy."

"Yes, Ma'am!"

Mitch drove the RV across town, lumbering along. It handled nicely, but it was still a big hunk of metal on wheels. She pulled up in front of the mansion, no easy feat, and watched as the staff packed it nice and tidy. Rebecca had thought of everything. Even that sweet little almost nothing she claimed was a negligée that she had tucked away in her carry-on bag.

"Ah, the wilderness," Mitch exclaimed as she held it up. "Where angels fear to tread."

"You're no angel."

"You're right. Just Saint. Saint Mitch to you."

They drove slowly, enjoying the scenery. An entire weekend all to themselves. If this wasn't heaven, then it was the next best thing.

In the meantime, Lisa had an educational weekend. Pam and her daughter, Tracy, came over and after commenting on how sparkling clean everything was, took Lisa out for lunch. Then, they hit the law library to do research. Lisa thought that Tracy, being five years old, would have had enough of this in short order, but that wasn't the case at all. Pam had brought her daughter some books of her own to read, and she sat contentedly for a long time, engrossed in cats and hats and bears and dogs. Once in a while, she would wander around and look at one of the bigger books, reading through a sentence here and there, but then eventually would revert back to her books. Lisa got restless before Tracy did, and so after an hour, Pam claimed to have read enough to suit her for that day. It was painfully obvious that Pam had the kind of intellect that would have kept her glued to the law tomes all day. Her willingness to leave her studies for another day demonstrated either her compassion for the feelings of Lisa or her anticipation at spending more private time with her. It didn't take long to find out which it was.

"You were bored," Pam said after they had dinner at Lisa's place. Tracy was in the other room, watching TV.

"I guess I didn't realize how time consuming this could be. You must have looked up twenty or thirty cases."

"There actually isn't a lot on this particular subject. Compared to other situations, I was glad to find what I did."

"If you want to go in by yourself tomorrow or any evening, I'd be more than happy to watch Tracy."

"The library's only open from noon until four tomorrow." "So, go then. We can have breakfast and then Tracy and I will hang out here and do stuff."

"Have you ever done this sort of thing before?"

"Watch children? Not a lot. But I think Tracy and I will be fine."
"I know you will. I just don't want to put you out."
"It's my pleasure. You can even stay here tonight if you want.
There's room for both of you in the spare bedroom."
"It's tempting, but I think we'd better go home tonight. It isn't like
we packed for a slumber party."
"Well, don't rush off. You haven't even had dessert yet." When
Pam smiled at this comment, Lisa tingled with an excitement that
she hadn't felt in months.
"You have a nice smile," she said nervously, becoming more
tonguetied every second. "And you're blushing," Pam remarked,
arching her eyebrows.
Lisa just sat there, wordlessly. Her lips parted once or twice as if
sending a signal to her brain that it was okay to send another idea
down the pike to express. Meanwhile, Pam came up with a better
idea. She pulled Lisa closer and kissed her once. Very lightly. If
Lisa thought she was speechless before, she came down with absolute
reticence at this point. "Are you okay?" Pam asked when Lisa pulled
back without comment.
"I'll be fine. I've just never been kissed…" "Kissed
by a woman before?"
"No, just never been kissed by *you* before."
"Well, we've fixed that little problem, haven't we!" Pam laughed.
"We certainly have. Now, we should check out dessert before we get
any more distracted."
"Good idea."
Lisa went into the kitchen to fix plates of strawberry shortcake as Pam
called Tracy to the table. They went a little overboard on the whipped
cream, but no one was concerned with counting calories. Ah, the
good life.

Pam and Tracy left before dusk. No use driving around in the dark if
you didn't have to. Lisa didn't even try to kiss Pam goodnight in
front of Tracy. She knew the risk they were taking. One remark to
the judge could ruin everything. It was okay for now. One kiss was
more than memorable.

Chapter 12

Mitch and Rebecca pulled into Santa Fe late. Too late for Bella to be overjoyed about it.

"Jou late!" she declared from the door like she didn't care who else was listening as long as Mitch got the message loud and clear. "I'm sorry Bella. It just took a little longer than we expected." Mitch wasn't about to explain to Bella that Rebecca was so pesky about sightseeing that they had to pull off the road twice. And neither time did they even look out the window! But they were content. And happy. And starving.

"Jour dinners cold."

"Should I heat it up?" Mitch said.

Rebecca smiled. "That seems to be your specialty!'

"Jou learn to cook?" Bella asked with an askance look.

"Only in an RV!"

"RV smar-ve, jou sit down, I heat up dinner *again*."

"Thank you, Bella."

"I told you we'd get in trouble with Bella," Mitch whispered later as they lay in each other's arms.

"Wasn't it worth it?"

"Absolutely! I didn't know desert travel had this effect on you. If I'd known it sooner, I'd a bought a condo in the Sahara."

"Mitch of Arabia?"

"Only the camels would know for sure."

The weekend wasn't exactly turning up roses for everyone. Trish, after thinking things over way too long and skimming Judy's book, took a drive to Aspen. This time of the year was glorious. Spring may arrive late to this part of the world, but it elbows its way in with a breathtaking beauty that belies the usual white blanket of snow. She knew the way to Judy's house by heart, and the irony was not lost on her. Judy wasn't there. How many other places could she be? Oh, only about a hundred. There was a coffee shop/bookstore on the main street. That sounded like a logical place for an author. Trish walked in and found Judy drinking something that looked like it had about three thousand calories in it.

"Hi there," Trish said, sitting down without waiting for an engraved invitation.

"Well, hello. How are you?"

"I think I'm perfect. What about you?"

The tone wasn't lost on Judy. "I'm fine."

"Well, we all know that you think you're fine, but what about me? Don't you think I'm perfect?"

"Perfect?"

"Yeah, perfect as in faultless, unblemished, impeccable, exquisite. Which of those confuses you?"

"Have you been drinking?"

"No, but I have been reading."

"That's a good pastime."

"And educational. I read your books."

"I see. I didn't know war was something that interested you."

"And I didn't know prejudice was a specialty of yours until now." Trish had been a salesman too long to read anything but agreement into the heartbeat of silence that passed between them.

"I don't know what you're talking about?" Judy finally said. The remark was a little too late to be believable. Eye contact was gone. Heart contact was crushed beyond repair.

"You don't like Jews," Trish got to the point. She didn't want to spend any more time than absolutely necessary in this woman's presence.

"I don't mind Jews. Is *that* what this is all about?"

"You don't *mind* Jews? You think I'm Jewish? I'm not Jewish. I'm Irish."

"I've done enough research to come to the conclusion that you are Jewish. And I'm just not that interested in dating outside of my race."

"You didn't seem to feel that way when we first met."

"People change."

"They most certainly do!" Trish was struggling to contain her annoyance.

People were beginning to look at them. The attention bothered Judy.

"I'm not a prejudiced person. I just have my concepts."

"And those concepts are?"

217

"I write for the mainstream. And from what I've seen over the years, the mainstream believes that races need to stick together."

"That's a lie that you tell yourself to rationalize your greed. You write so that conservative universities will buy your textbooks. You never even mentioned the fact that gay people were persecuted by the Nazis. You're one step away from being a Holocaust denier from what little of your book I could stomach."

"Condos in Aspen don't come cheap."

"So you sold out. It's all just about the money, isn't it?"

"Do you seriously believe that people want to read about the Holocaust? People want to forget about the Holocaust. Don't be so naïve."

Trish hated to admit it, but Judy was right about one thing. She had been naïve. Trish had the mistaken impression that just because someone was gay, that they logically eschewed all other forms of prejudice and discrimination. She could only shake her head in disbelief and leave Judy sitting alone at the table. Leaving never felt so good.

Lisa cooked pancakes for breakfast. Tracy ate three. It was wonderful to see another female that wasn't concerned about her eating habits. They were pretty healthy pancakes, actually. Lisa had mixed in nuts and grains and served a preservative-free syrup. All this she had gotten at the grocery store after company had left last night. Nothing like a midnight shopping spree to get you in the mood to cook. Pam left a little after eleven and Lisa immediately took Tracy to one of those pizza places where kids could run around all they wanted, spending every token they could afford on games and rides. Usually, the pizza in these places was not top drawer, but Lisa had done her homework. She knew the best place to go after talking to Sandy at the U. In fact, they had made a double date of sorts, and Sandy and her boy joined Lisa and Tracy for lunch. They felt like two soccer moms on an eating spree. In fact, it was a great place for lesbians to bring kids. Seeing two moms at one table didn't bring a lot of down-the-nose stares like at some other places. It was a blast. Lisa won a teddy bear and a lion at the basketball toss, gave one each to the kids, and still managed to have Tracy and a box full of leftover pizza back at the house by four. Pam was waiting outside.

"Where have you been?" she asked. Tracy didn't hear the concern, but Lisa did.

"We ran late. We had pizza. Come on in and you can have the rest." Pam went in and told Tracy that she wanted to talk to Lisa for a minute. Tracy went into the bedroom to watch TV. "Are you okay?" Lisa asked.

"I just didn't know you were going out. I was worried."

"I didn't think it would be a problem. I'm sorry if I worried you."

"I came back at three and when no one was around, I panicked."

"I didn't stop to think. I see why you're upset with me."

"It's okay. It's just that when your ex-husband is suing for custody, well, you never feel safe."

"I understand," Lisa said, trying to figure out if it would be manipulative to try and hold Pam to reassure her, to kiss her worries away, to try to rekindle her faith in people.

"What are you thinking?" Pam asked, noticing the dilemma in Lisa's eyes.

"Really? Truly?"

"Really, truly."

"I want to make things good for you."

"I want that too."

"But I don't want to take advantage of you in your vulnerable state."

"Take advantage how?"

"Oh, I guess by hugging you?"

"You took my daughter to a pizza fun house. You're the one who probably needs a hug."

"She was an angel. Just like her mom."

"I bet you say that to all the angels."

"Just the ones I know personally."

Pam hugged Lisa quickly and then Tracy asked if they could go for a walk on the ranch.

"The ranch?" Lisa asked.

"She calls this place The Ranch."

219

"I like that name. I'm going to call it The Ranch from now on, too."

The phone rang, rousing Mitch out of a sound sleep. It was early. Must have been Rebecca's staff calling to check on her.

"Hello?" Mitch answered.

"It's Trish."

"Hiya."

"Did you run away from home again?"

"Well, yes and no. Rebecca's here too."

"Oh, maybe I should call back later."

"Hi Trish," Rebecca said from Mitch's side. "Go ahead and talk."

"Mitch, I called to tell you something important."

"Okay, what is it?"

"I was adopted!"

"When did that happen," Mitch asked after she found her voice.

"When I was a kid, you stoop!"

"I figured that much. When did you find out?"

"Last night."

"I'm going to make a pot of coffee," Rebecca said.

"Yum."

"Yum?" Trish echoed. "Are you sure this is a good time to talk?"

"I'm sure. How did you find out?"

"I called my parents and asked them."

"You asked your parents if you were adopted?"

"No!" Trish corrected impatiently. "You must not be all the way awake, yet! I asked them if there was a family tree I could get hold of."

"Why did you want that?"

"Because of my conversation with Judy."

"You called her."

"I went to see her."

"You did?"

"Sure, I'm not afraid of her! But here's the big news – not only am I adopted, but my grandmother survived the Holocaust! I mean, she had a tattoo and everything."

"My God, Trish. What a day you've had. Are you okay?"

"You mean, am I okay with being Jewish?"

"No, not necessarily. I just mean you've had a lot to think about. Where are you?"

"I'm back in Denver."

"You want to come down here to Santa Fe? It's quiet and peaceful."

"I'm tempted. Everybody here is busy. Mary is watching the Center like a hawk. Lisa has a new girlfriend."

"I thought she was just a friend."

"Whatever. Sure, I'll come down there."

"Okay, call me when you get to town. This place is a maze. I'll escort you personally."

"Does that mean you'll be by the phone?" "Only if Rebecca has her way!"

Rebecca came in on the tail end of the conversation and was happy to know she would have her way. She thought. Mitch hung up.

"I invited Trish for a visit."

"How long are you staying?"

"How long can you stay?"

"I should go home today."

"You can't stay another day?"

"Meetings."

"I understand."

"You have a job, too."

"Don't remind me."

"Well, you do."

"I don't want to talk about it."

"Why not?"

"Because I don't."

"You always make me talk about stuff that's bothering me."

"This isn't bothering me."

"Then why don't you want to talk about it?"

"You're not going to let this go, are you?"

"It's been more than obvious that you haven't been terribly enthusiastic about running the U lately."

"How can you say that? I just spent half the night there the other day doing inventory and bookkeeping."

"And thoroughly enjoying it?"

"Somebody has to do it."

"Well, okay. You can tell yourself all you want that you really enjoy your work, but please, next time, tell your face."

"It's that obvious?"

"If you had that expression when you talked about me, we wouldn't be together anymore."

"It just isn't the same since Marge died."

"What are you going to do about it?"

"What can I do? People depend on me for a paycheck. I can't let them down."

"That's one of the things I love about you, your strong sense of responsibility."

"And that thing I do with avocados."

"What thing you do with avocados?"

"You'll know before you leave today!"

When Trish arrived, Rebecca left. She looked extremely happy. They decided to switch the transportation around so that Mitch and Trish could use the RV if they wanted to. It didn't take a lot of convincing to talk Rebecca into driving Trish's BMW. It would be waiting for them at the mansion whenever they decided to come back. It didn't work out quite that way. After an afternoon of discussion, Trish had decided to head out to Illinois the next morning to visit her parents. Her adoptive parents. It was hard to get used to saying it. So, Mitch volunteered to lend the RV to Trish in exchange for a quick stop back in Denver to drop her off at the mansion. From there, it was a quick trip into work, where things were humming right along. No need to panic or worry. Running a lesbian/upscale restaurant wasn't exactly torture. It wasn't as if fistfights broke out every night. In fact, Mitch had never seen one fistfight in all her years here. Just jovial people out to have a good time.

Speaking of humming, Lisa had done so much of it on Monday morning that Mary was convinced she had swallowed a songbird.

"You're in a good mood."

"I had a nice weekend."

"You and Pam and Tracy?"

"We went to the law library. Boy, that Pam is one smart lady. She looked up divorce cases for two days."

"Hmmm," was Mary's total response. Lisa picked up on the tone. "What are you thinking?"

"Nothing."

"Oh please, you're always thinking about something."

"I know that Pam is doing research and that the more research she does, the more nervous she gets."

"She did seem a little agitated on Sunday, but that was because Tracy and I were running late."

"You just need to realize that Pam is really shaky on the custody battle that's looming."

"I understand that. I'd be shaky too if I thought I was going to lose a kid as sweet as Tracy."

Mary studied Lisa's face for a moment.

"What?" Lisa said, uncomfortable under the scrutiny.

"Just give Pam a lot of room, okay?"

"Okay."

Lisa gave Pam so much room that they only had dinner together four nights instead of five. Tracy loved visiting The Ranch and Lisa loved to cook. The supermarket was becoming her home away from home on the drive home from work. On the weekend, Lisa wanted to have a barbecue for everyone. The list was growing longer by the minute. Mitch, of course, and Rebecca, Trish, who was back from Illinois, Mary, the boss, always good to invite the boss to a cookout. Pam, Tracy and Sandy and her boy and Vickie and Just Joe and anybody else from the U and all other pedestrians passing by. Lisa bought twenty pounds of filet mignon just for starters, and the chicken industry might have considered sending her a thank-you card for her patronage. Hot dogs, mustard, ketchup, potato salad, from scratch, mind you, not that processed goo you find in so many stores. Beans cooked for two days in a sauce that made your mouth water in ecstasy. It was going to be fun.

Just Joe and Mitch offered to help with the gas barbecue, since they knew that if Lisa was in charge of the fire, she could easily burn down ten percent of the trees standing on the property. The crowd gathered at noon, and helped set up tables and chairs and coolers full of pop and beer. Trish was beaming.

"Come and see these pictures," she hearkened to Mitch.

"What are they?"

"My family. I try not to say 'real' family because if I got into that habit, I think it would crush my mom and dad. But they had some things stored away in a safety deposit box. It was to be opened at their death and bequeathed to me along with the estate."

Mitch sat down next to Trish and marveled at the photos. They were black and white and creased with age, but the people in them were young and plump and vibrant with youth. It was a stunning contrast.

"That's my grandmother, before the Camps."

"What a beautiful woman."

"And her parents! Would you look at them!"

"I've never seen more handsome people in my life," Mitch nodded.

"And even their noses are beautiful," Trish said with a quaver in her voice that arrived without introduction.

"Just like yours," Mitch said.

Before she could say anything more, Trish was holding on to her and shaking with tears. Sensing that this was going to be a long story, one of Mitch's more brilliant deductions, she just held on until the shaking slowed to an erratic hiccup now and again. Good thing the couch was earthquake proof.

"I'm so proud of these people and I never even knew them." "Why was this such a big secret?"

"It was one of the stipulations of the adoption. My mother had this shame about being Jewish. She thought it would be easier if I could pass as a non-Jew. A little like how some gay people pass themselves off as straight, I guess?"

"I guess so."

"Not that I blame her, or anybody for that matter for wanting an easier path for their children."

"I'm amazed they kept the photographic evidence."

"I was told that if I ever asked about it, that they could tell me."

"Then, in a really strange way, Judy did you a favor. Otherwise, you would've never thought to ask." "I'm not ready to give Judy any credit."

"Okay, well, then, Lisa helped."

"I'd give her some credit if I could find her."

It wasn't a big house. There weren't that many places to hide. After admiring Trish's collection of photos, Mitch wrestled free to go snooping. She only had to check two places before stumbling across, well, not literally, Lisa and Pam pretending to clean the kitchen. How they were ever going to accomplish that while lip-locked was worth watching. They might have never even noticed Mitch except that she sort of "ah, hummed" her presence.

"Oh, hi there," Lisa said.

"We're cleaning the kitchen," Pam added.

"Yeah, I know. Rebecca and I clean the kitchen at the mansion exactly like that. It's sparkling clean."

They both had the good grace to laugh. Rebecca came peeling around the corner at that moment.

"Well, *now* we know where everyone is."

"We're cleaning," Mitch explained lamely.

"*You* don't look like you're cleaning anything."

"I'm not into that sort of thing," Mitch couldn't stifle a chuckle.

"You certainly keep things clean at home," Rebecca assured them with an expression on her face that Mitch couldn't tell if she had caught on to the gist of the conversation. Such are the problems of living with a poker-faced politician. They were all giggling by now. "Lisa, when you get a minute, could you go in and talk with Trish." Mitch requested.

"Okay," Lisa nodded, sensing the importance of the request. Mitch then turned to Rebecca. "Let's take a walk." Arm in arm, they sauntered to the splintery gazebo.

"One of these days, when I have a lot of free time on my hands, I'm going to get some sandpaper and fix this thing." "Why don't you just tear it down and start over?"

"Lisa and Pam are in love."

"I gathered," Rebecca followed the conversational leap.

"I mean, 'kissing in the kitchen' in love."

"Is there any other?"

225

"Have we ever kissed in the kitchen?"

"Does what we did on the pull out sofa in the RV count?"

"Gee, let me think about it…."

"Kitchenette sex?"

"Sounds kinky."

Mitch leaned into Rebecca, needing to be close.

"What's wrong?"

"I don't know."

"I think I do. It's never easy when the old girlfriend gets a new girlfriend."

"Everything changes."

"Change happens."

"I don't want us to change."

"At all. Ever?"

"I don't want to lose you because of change."

"I hope that doesn't happen, but nobody ever gets a guarantee."

"Then I'll settle for a lifetime warranty." "You drive a hard bargain," Rebecca pulled away to see Mitch's face. She looked serene and happy.

"And if you get reincarnated as a tarantula, I'll still love you."

Rebecca sighed, "A tarantula, how romantic."

"Well, you do have the legs for it."

Rebecca looked askance at Mitch. They laughed as the sun began to set on The Ranch. In a while, the moon would be hanging over them, guarding them from harm. Mitch fell silent. For too long. This had happened several times now, and Rebecca finally got up the nerve to ask. "What are you thinking about when you go a million miles away like that?"

"Like what?"

"Like you are right now."

"I'm just thinking."

"About what?"

"About us. About how we have so much to offer."

Rebecca drew back a little so she could watch Mitch as she spoke. The drawing away made Mitch grow even quieter.

"Go on."

"It's nothing, really."

"And this 'nothing really' had been on your mind for weeks. Why can't you talk about it?"

"Because it's a difficult subject to talk about."

"I don't want to guess. I'm bad at it. Just tell me. Please." "I watch how amazing Pam is with Tracy and how you are with Mary and I think I'm missing a big part of life."

When Mitch dared to meet Rebecca's eyes, she didn't appear to be quite as shell shocked as Mitch had expected her to look. Maybe it was the moonlight.

"Are you saying what I think you're saying?" Rebecca asked the most maddening question on earth. Maybe in the universe?

"See! It isn't as easy as it sounds."

"You want to have a baby."

"I don't know. It's a big decision that I hadn't given much thought to until I met you."

"Me?"

"Yes, you. I see what a great mother you've been to Mary. And I see Lisa being transformed before my eyes into a responsible, caring person when she's around Tracy. It's like a miracle. If you saw a miracle walking down the street, you'd want to join the parade, wouldn't you?"

"I guess I already did."

"I think I hear my biological clock clanging in my ears, and it's saying I'd better either do something pretty soon or forget about it."

"I understand that. I'm old as the hills myself."

"Gee, thanks for empathizing."

"You know what I mean. You're a bit younger than creaky old me, but if you truly want to give this serious consideration, remember that if we have a baby now, I'll be sixty-five when our offspring is twenty."

"I know. You could have grandkids the same age as our child. That would be an interesting time at the family reunion!"

"Well, men do it all the time. Have generational families, I mean. In fact, it's in style."

"So, you wouldn't be totally opposed to the idea?"

"I'll tell you what. Let's give us a little more time. We haven't been together very long, and although we are madly in love right this instant, you never know what life will bring. Give me a few months to think about it. In the meantime, you should think about getting yourself to a doctor and getting a physical, and building up your strength, because as much as I enjoyed my last pregnancy, back in the dark ages, I really can't go through another one."

"You really mean it?"

"Mean it?"

"You're not opposed to the idea?"

"If this is something that's important to you, how could I stand in the way?"

It was all Mitch could do to keep from howling at the moon.

Construction was completed on the "Art Museum at the Center" the next week. It was a sight to see. Finally, Mitch had the chance to relocate all the art supplies from the bedroom that Rebecca had been stubbing her toes on. This was a good thing.

Too bad there couldn't have been press coverage. Cameras weren't allowed at the Center for security reasons. That was okay with Mitch. She hadn't done this for the notoriety. She could get plenty of that on her own. She wasn't about to use abused mothers and children for that purpose. Some of the children took to the concept like they were Titian, making masterpieces in reds and blues with brilliant, inspired brush strokes. And that was just on the windows.

One little boy, named Miguel, was a little less enthusiastic about the situation. Mitch noticed, and waited until all the hoopla died down to investigate further. Seems that Miguel had been subjected to verbal abuse as well as physical abuse. Sometimes, verbal abuse left deeper, more lasting scars. Mitch took a day off work to be with Miguel in the art room. For a while, they were surrounded by a few of the other children, as Mitch busied herself with crayons, drawing a huge landscape of a house with trees and horses and a barn. It was pretty lame as drawings go, but the boys and girls didn't seem to mind. They enjoyed her company and took turns helping her to improve her painting. Everyone had a turn but Miguel, who was in self-exile. Mitch beckoned him over a time or two, but he pulled a disapproving face and stood his ground. Then, lunch and nap time approached. Everyone else took off for the feast. Miguel hung back. Mitch held out a crayon and he walked over with the gait of a boy with a mission. He took the crayon, which just happened to be blue, and broke it in half. Then he threw it on the floor in front of Mitch.

Somewhere earlier in their friendship, Mary had counseled Mitch that if she ever wanted to hang out at the Center, she needed to know that many of these abused children were very angry. Of course they were, Mitch remembered nodding. "But the anger comes out in all sorts of ways." The voice still echoed in her mind. "So many ways."

Well, Miguel had found his outlet, thank the Lord. He let off steam by breaking crayons. So, undaunted, Mitch gave him another. This one was red. She was doing research to see if the color mattered. Gee, it didn't. He broke it as well, and then looked at Mitch with a blank expression. And so they went through an entire tub of crayons. When Mitch had discovered the gold mine of warehouse shopping, she had purchased dozens of buckets of two-hundred crayons along with a case or two of the deluxe 96 color box with the sharpener on the back. So they had approximately 150,000 crayons on the premises. Miguel would be a very busy boy. Mitch handed him a green. Snap. Yellow. Snap. Periwinkle. Snap. They had gone through about three hundred before his mother discovered them.
"What are you doing, Miguel?" she asked, taken somewhat aback at the sight before her.
"Miguel is helping me," Mitch grinned at her.
"He's what?"
"He is helping me to break all of these crayons because I need them that way to work with."
"You do?"
"Sure, watch."
Mitch took one of the crayon halves and peeled the paper off. Then, she used the side of the crayon to do some shading of the landscape. It added dimension. At least Mitch had learned two things in art class. Point of view and light. Tim the male model had helped a lot.

Miguel had to go eat lunch, but Mitch shaded for a few more minutes before taking a break herself. She had a bite with Lisa and Mary and then relaxed in a chair until nap time was over. After nap time, art class was subdued. Less screaming, more insight. Miguel set about to be helpful and before the afternoon was over, he had gone through several more tubs of crayons. Mitch peeled and drew, peeled and drew, until her arm was too tired to go on. Then, Miguel picked up where she had left off and drew a stunning image of a rainbow. He was a natural. No doubt about it. He should have been in Santa Fe with all the other artists! Mitch took off for home before rush hour traffic and rested her arm for the next day's work. Miguel needed honest-to-goodness art lessons someday. She hoped it could happen, but with he and his mom on the run from abuse, what chance did he have? And what chance did she have?

The next time Mitch got by to visit the Center, he was gone. Relatives in Nebraska promised help and protection. Well, it was a long way from Santa Fe, but it was better than what they had left behind. "I made sure he took some crayons when he left," Mary reassured. "Good," Mitch replied in a voice she couldn't trust to say more.

Chapter 13

Trish stopped in at the U early the next afternoon. Mitch was back behind the bar, taking her mind off Miguel. Now she remembered why she didn't visit the Center more often. The good-byes were too hard to handle, even when you didn't get to say them. When she got a five minute break, Mitch went over and sat with Trish.

"What's new?"

"I'm going up to Aspen again. Want to go with me?"

"What are you going to do in Aspen?"

"I'm going to have another talk with Judy."

"Why?"

"To clear up a misconception or two, for starters."

"For instance?"

"Well, when I last talked to her, I told her that I wasn't Jewish. Now that I know the truth, I want to correct myself."

"So, you can do that over the phone."

"It just wouldn't be the same. I want to tell her to her face that I'm Jewish and proud."

"Why does it matter if you don't respect Judy anymore?" "Because it would make it all the more personal to her. It's pretty easy to sit behind a typewriter and make all sorts of generalizations. It's another to actually have to face up to them in real life." "There's just one thing I don't get about this. Wasn't Judy actually attracted to you at first? I mean really attracted?"

"I'm sure she was, I'm pretty damn irresistible. But I think that once she got over the initial attraction, she started looking a little deeper. I know I kid around a lot, but I don't consider myself a paragon of beauty." "I just feel that this whole issue is about something other than your nose."

"I'm sure I resemble being Jewish in other respects. She probably picked up on that before I did."

"I doubt it. I think she was looking for an easy way out of a relationship and this just happened to be convenient." "Do you think Lisa and Judy would still be together if we hadn't interfered?"

"I don't know. I don't think Lisa loved Judy all that much."

"Speaking of Lisa, what's going on with Pam and the court case?"

"Lisa and Pam are nervously awaiting the custody hearing." "Sounds like a good time to leave town."

"You go. I need to stay and hold down the fort. But call me if you need support."

Trish took off right after lunch, never one to put off a task. If she hurried, she would make it there before too late. She had reserved the company condo in advance, and could easily spend a night or two in glorious mountain seclusion. Except of course, it was tourist season. Streets that were designed for horse traffic years ago were now expected to accommodate the crush of traffic that would have clogged a city. Bumper to bumper was not exactly Trish's idea of getting away from it all. When she arrived, it was time for a good, stiff drink and an early night in bed. The next morning, she called Judy at home.

"Oh hello," Judy said, sounding somewhat surprised.

"I want to talk to you."

"If you must."

"Let's meet."

"Are you in town?"

Trish took a deep breath. "Yes."

"Well, then, come over."

"To your house?"

"You can ambush me here just as effectively as in the coffee shop."

"I'm not here to ambush you."

"Whatever." Whatever worked just fine for Trish. She was on Judy's doorstep in ten minutes.

"Come in."

"Thanks."

It sounded strained even through the polite words.

"I have a confession to make," Trish began and then corrected herself. "It's not a confession. I take that back. I just want to tell you something."

"Do you want some coffee first?" Judy asked with an expression that was a cross between bemusement and confusion.

"What kind?"

"Strong."

"Okay."

Judy poured like she was the queen and then sat back to hear Trish's non-confession. "I'm Jewish."

"I know that."

"I didn't even know it until a few days ago."

"Well, then, I'm glad you discovered the truth."

"So, now, you're perfectly justified in your suspicions about my nose."

"You have a fine nose, for a Jew."

"I know that. You don't need to tell me that."

"Okay. Is there anything else you want to tell me?" "Why did you have to turn out to be a prejudiced person?"

"Everyone turns out to be a prejudiced person, Trish."

"Not everyone."

"Everyone."

Trish felt that this discussion was going nowhere.

"So, how did you become so anti-Semitic?"

"I was raised Catholic."

"And that's your entire explanation."

"Trish, when I was young, growing up in my neighborhood, we didn't call them Jews, we called them dirty Jews. I heard the phrase dirty Jew before I ever heard the word dyke or fag."

"And so you're using the excuse that you were raised that way." "I'm telling you that it was part of my childhood experiences. It's a reason, not an excuse. Jews were the antithesis of Christianity. I was raised to believe that my religion, Catholicism, was the only true religion and that anyone who claimed otherwise was going to hell."

"So it was the Catholics against the world?"

"I guess you could look at it that way."

"And you still feel that way?"

"I have struggled to get my balance where my childhood beliefs are concerned. I don't go around calling Jewish people dirty Jews anymore."

"Big improvement," Trish muttered sarcastically.

"From where I started, it is. Believe me, if you think that's a big deal, imagine how much of a struggle it's been about my sexuality. I was taught to hate myself as well."

"That's the trouble with most religions. Gay people don't belong."

"And you'll find that to be true in Judaism as well. Go on, check it out for yourself. If Hitler had persecuted only gay people, how many Jewish people do you think would have clamored to their rescue?"

The question stymied Trish. It wasn't something she had stayed awake at night thinking about.

"I still don't agree with you about how everyone is prejudiced."

"Okay, so then tell me, Trish, how many fat girls have you ever dated?"

"Excuse me?"

"You heard me. How many fat women have you slept with?"

"I don't think that's any of your business."

"So, that's your prejudice. You don't date fat girls."

"It's just a coincidence."

"No, it isn't. You don't think fat girls are good enough for you. Oh, sure they can own a house and vote and pay taxes. Just keep them away from you. They're just not quite good enough for you. You have this mental, subconscious block where they are concerned. A fat girl doesn't even get a second glance from you. Did your parents tell you to stay away from fat girls, or did you come up with that one all by yourself?"

"My attitude toward fat people is worlds away from how you feel about Jewish people."

"I don't think so, Trish. But you go on telling yourself that."

"I have to go."

Trish stood to leave, glad at last to be free of this woman. She didn't have anything to prove to her.

It might just as well have been Kansas. Trish didn't even bother glancing at the scenery on the drive back home. She stopped in at the U, a place where she hoped to find solace, a sounding board and a good glass of wine. Mitch was there. Oh good, all three.

"Hiya, stranger," Mitch intoned as she pointed to her booth.

"Got any good wine?"

"Nah, just this old stuff," Mitch held up a bottle of Beaujolais.

"Perfect."

They both took a long drink before Trish started in.

"Do you think I'm a prejudiced person?"

"This is about your trip up to see Judy, right?"

"Right. So am I?"

"Well, I don't think so."

"But you're not one-hundred percent sure, are you?"

"Why don't you just tell me what's on your mind."

"Judy says I'm prejudiced because I don't have a fat girlfriend."

"And what does that have to do with anything?"

"Have you ever dated a fat girl?"

"Trish, you've known me practically my entire adult life. You know who I've dated."

"Oh yeah. But you never even thought about a fat girl, right?" "Hey, I'm already doing my part for diversity in dating. I'm sleeping with a Republican!"

"But she's not a fat Republican."

"Well, not yet, but I figure that if I'm lucky enough to grow old with her, she'll put on a few pounds." "And that wouldn't bother you?"

"I don't imagine so."

"But you can't say for sure."

"I'm really pretty sure."

"But not one-hundred percent sure?"

"I'm trying to answer your question, but I don't understand your point."

"Okay. I guess I just always figured that fat people could change, you know, get thinner."

"People say the same about you and me."

"You mean about reparative therapy."

"Right. Attempts to change gay people into straight people have been going on for years. In some respects, fat people and gay people have a lot of the same issues. Fat people are told they are unhealthy and must change their behavior. Gay people are told they are unhealthy and must change their behavior. You might have a lot more in common with a fat person than you realize." "I think I'm going to broaden my dating horizons a little this year. You know, try to look at people for who they are rather than how they measure up on a scale or any other mindless criteria." "You might even find yourself a nice, plump Jewish girl."

"I just might."

Chapter 14

Tracy's custody hearing was the next day. Tomorrow. Lisa had done everything she could think of to help, but Pam had shut her out of the process a few days earlier. The judge assigned to the case was hopelessly conservative and had ruled harshly against lesbian mothers in similar cases. They were either denied custody, given limited supervised custody or forced to give up any and all contact with anyone gay in their life, including gay and lesbian community support groups, in order to retain custody. Pam was literally being forced to choose between Tracy and Lisa. Lisa knew who was going to win. There wasn't even a doubt.

Mitch gave Vickie the night off and was busy polishing glasses at nine when Lisa showed up. She looked like hell, understandably. "Have a seat at my booth and I'll get you something. What do you want?"
"A bribable judge."
"Never heard of it," Mitch bantered, just in case someone from the town of jurisprudence was eavesdropping.
"Then just give me the antidote for exposure to sanctimonious assholes." "How about a beer?"
"Sure."
Mitch selected a honey amber ale and poured it for her. She sat down opposite Lisa and waited for her to begin talking. It was quite a delay for Lisa, all of thirteen seconds.
"Pam's going to announce her engagement in court tomorrow."
Now, Mitch fully understood the thirteen second pause.
"To who?"
"Isn't it 'to whom'?"
"You want to talk about grammar or Pam?"
"Some guy."
"That narrows it down."
"Some guy she knows."
"Is she serious?"
"Can you believe she found some guy who wants to marry her?"
"Yes. In fact, that's very believable."
"I can't believe she'd do it."

Mitch fell silent. Her heart was breaking for Lisa and her predicament. Mitch had waited for years for Lisa to fall in love and then be rejected so that Mitch could stand there and gloat. She felt hotly ashamed at this fantasy and struggled to bury it deep. "What are you thinking about?" Lisa asked suddenly. "You're as red as a beet."

"Maybe it's menopause making an early appearance."

"Tell me what you're thinking about."

"I just was thinking that you've finally fallen in love."

"I loved you."

"Not the way you love Pam. It's different and I can tell. And I know it's breaking your heart to lose her to circumstances beyond your control. And I guess that makes me angry on your behalf."

"It's going to be really hard to stand around and watch from the sidelines as Pam marries this guy, but I know she'd do it to protect Tracy."

"She's a devoted mother."

"That's one of the things I love about her. She's a great mother. The best. The court should be able to see that without her needing to do something like…this!"

"The court is short sighted."

"Yeah. Well, there's nothing I can do about it now. Pam has shut me clear out of the process. I can't see her, talk to her, go to court."

"Want another beer?"

"I haven't even got a good start on this one yet, or aren't you paying attention anymore to how much your patrons drink."

"I guess it's just habit."

Lisa studied Mitch and remarked, "You look tired."

"I am tired. I'm perennially tired."

"Why don't you go home. I'll close up for you tonight."

"I think you're the one who needs the rest."

"I need a distraction. I need a good excuse to not go home and look at four walls."

Mitch thought it over. It couldn't hurt. The place had been missing her spark since she left. Rebecca wouldn't mind, either way.

"Sure. You can close up if you want."

"Great, thanks."

Lisa picked up her glass and poured the rest of the drink down the sink. She was ready for work. Mitch gathered up her stuff and was headed out the door when Lisa asked for one more favor.

"Can I have a hug?"

"Sure."

Lisa held on for a long time. Mitch didn't fuss. If this is what Lisa needed, then she was happy to give. Then, as Lisa was pulling out of the embrace, she caught Mitch's face with both hands and gave her a quick kiss.

"For luck," she said. "For luck," Mitch agreed.

When Mitch strolled into the bedroom at home, Rebecca was only mildly surprised.

"You're home early."

"Yeah."

"What's up?"

"I don't know."

"You don't know?"

"What am I supposed to know?"

"Why are you home so early?"

"Lisa is watching the U. She said she needs the distraction."

"Uh huh."

"What does 'uh huh' mean?"

"How distracting were you?"

Mitch's index finger traveled to her lips. Of course, the lipstick was still there.

"She kissed me. For luck."

"With the court case?"

"I don't know. She told me that Pam was going to get married to retain custody of Tracy. To prove to the court that she's capable of walking the straight and narrow."

"It's a good thing I didn't get involved in the court system over Mary," Rebecca said ominously.

"What would you have done?"

239

"I would have fought tooth and toenail for my rights. And I wouldn't have led a sham life to cover anything up."

"There has to be a better way out of this."

"That's not your concern."

"That's what has me worried."

"Are you going to the hearing tomorrow?"

"If they'll let me in. I'll be there for support no matter what."

"Who's going to watch the U?"

"I haven't planned that far ahead."

Mitch got ready for bed and fell asleep without further conversation.

The phone rang at seven the next morning. Mitch groped for the phone after she realized that Rebecca was already out and about. It was Just Joe.

"Mitch, when did you leave last night?"

"Early, why?"

"Did you close up?"

"No."

"Vickie said it was her night off, too."

"Joe, what's going on."

"When I got here this morning, the door was unlocked."

"Is there anything missing?"

"Not that I can see, but you better come down anyway."

"Did you call the police?"

"No."

"Well, don't yet. Wait until I get there."

Mitch pulled on some sweats and bounded down the stairs. It was probably nothing, but so goes the life of the landlord. She fought rush hour traffic all the way across town and arrived by eight. Joe was working. No surprise there. He told her that it was the back door that was unlocked, the front door was still locked and closed. Mitch studied the door for signs of forced entry and found none. "What about fingerprints?" Joe said. He loved crime drama. "Yours are all over it. So are mine. Let's arrest each other and declare the case solved."

He didn't laugh. Instead, he went back to work. Mitch opened the cash register and found everything in order. Next, she checked the liquor inventory. Good thing she kept a close eye on these things. If anyone stole a bottle of booze, they had been very surreptitious about it. Nothing behind the bar was missing either. Chairs and tables and stereo equipment and the TV sets were still in place. Mitch shrugged her shoulders and told Joe that she would be back later, after the hearing. She was halfway out the door before she turned on her toes and walked back in. One more place. She walked into Marge's office and opened the previously locked file cabinet drawer. It was empty. Empty as Al Capone's safe.

Mitch's mind, somewhat slow on the uptake, still grasped the obvious. She thought for a moment about Joe's earlier concern about fingerprints. Only two or three people's fingerprints were bound to be on this cabinet. One was dead, one was gone and one was in big damn trouble. Rather than wipe it clean and end up with an even more suspicious set of circumstances. She could hear the courtroom drama unfolding in her imagination. "Now, tell the court again why only one of these drawers was wiped clean and the others were filthy with dust? Uh, selective housekeeping?" Mitch went to the storeroom and gathered up as many rolls of toilet paper as she could carry. Three trips filled the drawer entirely. If anyone asked, the answer was obvious. Lisa was in charge of toilet paper and here was the stash. Hey, it was only a question of replacing one kind of paper with another.

Mitch hurried back to the mansion and dressed in something nice. That meant blue serge. The hearing was at ten. Mary had to stay at the Center, since Lisa had asked for time off to at least keep track of the events. Of course, she was nowhere in sight, that was the strategy. Trish was busy as well, so it was just Mitch there to witness the calamity. At two minutes past ten, the hearing doors opened and Pam's lawyer came out in the hall to summon Mitch into the hallowed room.

The room was nice, but not at all like how it looked on all those lawyer TV shows. There were mostly tables and chairs and a bench for the judge. He didn't look too unreasonable. But then again, it was only five past ten.

"Where's Pam?" the lawyer whispered to Mitch.

"I don't know! Don't you know?"

"She hasn't shown up yet. The judge is absolutely livid."

Mitch scanned the room. Tea parties were more raucous than this. The jailbird dad looked shaved, showered and holy. His counsel was poured into a tight-fitting blue suit that showed off a paunchy physique. Pam's lawyer looked ashen.

"The judge will issue a bench warrant in a few minutes if she doesn't show."

"I don't know what to tell you."

With that news, the judge crashed his gavel on the bench, hurting Mitch eardrums. He meant business.

"Counsel, approach the bench."

Both went up to have a side conference with the judge as Mitch sat in one of the chairs just behind where Pam's lawyer had set up shop. Mitch stole a glance at the father. You could never tell by looking at him that he was an abuser. But then again, you couldn't tell by looking at Hilary. Whatever was going on at the bench was growing more intense by the minute. Suddenly, the judge shooed them away and pointed a finger at Mitch.

"You! Approach the bench!"

Mitch looked over her shoulder. Both ways. There was no one behind her. Pam's lawyer had gone ever paler, if that was possible.

"You're acquainted with the missing party?" the judge asked when Mitch got up to the bench.

"I met her once."

"What's your name?"

"Mitch Tanner."

This registered with the Judge. He had finally made the mental leap as to who she really was now that they were formally introduced. Mitch felt a sudden drop in her stomach. This wasn't going to be good. No wonder Pam's lawyer looked like a corpse.

"You will tell the court where the missing party is."

"I don't know anything about this matter."

Even as Mitch spoke the words, she knew she was lying. Well, lying was such a strong word. She was finally putting two and two together. The unlocked door, the missing money, the missing party. Oh jeez.

"You will tell the court where the missing party is or you will be held in contempt of court."

"That's only fitting, your honor."

"And why is that?" the judge asked with much curiosity. "Because any court that would side with an abusive father over a lesbian mother is contemptible."

Things happened so quickly that they were a blur. Bailiffs approached her and had her handcuffed before she could say anything more to damage herself. Perhaps that was best. She walked as fast as the deputies to avoid even the hint of resistance. Being held in contempt of court was a little different than actually being arrested. But she still found herself sitting in a jail cell about half the size of the bathroom in her old apartment, handcuffed to the metal seat she was forced to sit on. Actually, it wasn't a real cell. It was a holding cell. No toilet, no sink, no bed. Just a metal seat and a handcuff that gave her about six inches of freedom of movement. Who could ask for anything more. Actually, Mitch did, after about an hour. She needed a bathroom break. Damn coffee. She was switching to water the minute her sentence was up. She hollered out for the guard. No one answered. Oh great.

Mitch daydreamed. Anything to take her mind off of her predicament. She whistled, hummed, tapped her foot and then started yelling again. She could hear them. Why couldn't they hear her? Okay, two choices. One, yell yourself hoarse and give them the satisfaction of your impending laryngitis, or two, well, let's not talk about number two. Number one was being pesky enough. Two more yells to the empty, giggling hallway. That would do it.

Mary picked up the phone call. It was Pam's lawyer with the news.

"The judge what?"

"He put Mitch in jail."

"In jail?"

"She's in the holding cell at the county courthouse right now. I can't get her out until she tells him where Pam is."

"Where is Pam?" "I don't know."

"Does Mitch know?"

"I don't know that either. Everything happened so fast that I don't know who knows what."

"Okay. Don't worry. I'll contact my mom."

"Good. Just don't make this judge any angrier."

Rebecca took the call in her meeting after her secretary insisted that it was from Mary and urgent. If this was another ploy to get her to take Lisa in for a dinner date, Mary would have some explaining to do.

"Mitch is in jail."

Okay, so it wasn't a trick.

"You're kidding."

"Nope."

"How did that happen?"

"It happened at Pam's hearing."

"What did Pam do that got Mitch thrown in jail?"

"Pam didn't show up."

"So why does that matter."

"The judge put Mitch in jail until she reveals the location of Pam."

"But Mitch doesn't know where Pam is."

"I'm not the one to convince. The judge is certain she knows."

"Okay. I'll take care of it."

Rebecca cut the meeting short. She hated doing this, it was a meeting with the Advocates for the Homeless in Colorado people about the homeless situation. They were happy to reschedule. When they left, Rebecca sat back to think for a few minutes. Where the holes were in the story, she began to fill in the missing pieces. Pam, Tracy, Lisa, custody, disappearance. It was beginning to make sense. She called the courthouse and talked to the judge presiding over the case. Although he accepted the invitation to come to the capitol and discuss the matter, he would make no promises.

He walked in right before noon.

"Don't even bother to sit down," Rebecca told him. He was stone-faced at the tone of her voice.

"You will release Ms. Tanner from jail. Immediately."

"She is in contempt of my court."

"No she's not."

"She knows the whereabouts of the mother and refuses to reveal the information."

"She doesn't know the whereabouts, but I do. So, are you going to put me in jail as well, or are you going to listen to reason." He considered his options for about two seconds.

"You know where the mother has fled?"

"I have a better idea than Ms. Tanner. I was privy to a discussion that Ms. Tanner was not involved in. You release her and I'll give you the information I know."

Rebecca pushed the phone set close to the edge of the desk. He stared at it for a moment and then said, "If you're lying to me, I'll make you pay."

"If you don't release Ms. Tanner, I'll make you pay in ways that haven't even been invented yet."

He made the phone call and was informed that Ms. Tanner would need new clothes if anyone wanted to know.

"Why is she going to need new clothes?" Rebecca asked, calm on the surface, furious underneath.

"I guess she's all wet. And now, I believe, you have some information for me."

"I do, but before I tell you, you should be aware that you shouldn't count on being elected to office the next time you run."

"I'd say we're both in that same boat." When he smiled, it looked like he had gas.

Mitch was soaked alright. Every time she shifted, she trickled. Damn them anyway. She could still hear them giggling. What a bunch of morons. Rebecca had required that she be present before Mitch was released so that she could assist. Mitch wouldn't even look at her as she came to the door of the cell.

"Don't even look at me!" Mitch pleaded as Rebecca stood back.

"I won't. I brought you some clothes."

245

"Thanks, but I need a shower."

"I brought that as well."

Mitch looked up and saw Rebecca's back. At least she wasn't watching.

"I have the RV just outside the door. You can step right in and shower and then change clothes. How's that sound?"

"Sounds like you're thinking every minute."

Rebecca walked ahead as Mitch squished behind. She didn't bother to wave farewell to her guards. Apparently, they were wondering about future employment. How many people make the Governor's girlfriend pee her pants and then get to keep their jobs?

Rebecca had things pretty well laid out. There was a plastic bag for the wet clothes, enough water in the reserve to take a halfway decent shower and then several outfits from which to choose laid out on the bed. Mitch was warm and dry and in the front passenger side seat within twenty minutes.

"How did you get me out?"

"I told the judge what he wanted to know."

By now, Mitch knew what had happened. Peeing your pants in prison gave you plenty of opportunity to try and keep your mind occupied with other things. Lisa had taken the money last night when she took over at the U. In her haste, or perhaps to make it seem like a robbery, she left the door unlocked. Then, she picked up Pam and Tracy and they left for Mitch's place in Santa Fe. No one was looking for them last night, so it was a safe place. By today, they would know it wasn't safe to stay for long. Maybe one more day to regroup, buy a new car, get some fake ID. Who knew what lengths they would go to hide?

"You told the judge where they went?" Mitch quizzed.

"Sure. It's obvious. They went to Trenton."

"Trenton?"

"New Jersey."

"Trenton, New Jersey?"

"Well, isn't that where you'd go?"

"Not in about a million years."

"Well, that's where Lisa went the second time she took the money."

"How the hell do you know that?"

"She told me. So I told the authorities that they needed to go to Trenton to find her. Makes perfect sense to me."

Mitch looked over at Rebecca. God, the woman could be devilish. "You lied."

"My sweet ass off."

"You lied to a judge."

"Well, don't make it sound like a federal offense!"

"Well, what do we do now?"

"Let's go home. I have a surprise for you."

"I've heard this line before."

"It's not that kind of surprise!"

"Oh darn."

They drove back to the mansion and were halfway up the stairs when Mitch heard the commotion.

"You didn't!"

"I did!"

Mitch opened the bedroom door to find the cutest little beagle puppy in the world. It was in a very roomy cage with about a dozen play toys, but it practically wiggled itself apart knowing that it could be free soon. It barked and growled like that would make a difference. It did. Mitch closed the bedroom door and then opened the cage. It scampered out and nosed around faster than a detective on vitamins.

"She's a real nose on feet." "A

what?" Rebecca asked.

"A nose on feet. A hound dog. Born to smell. Where did you get her?"

"From a licensed breeder. I've been working on the deal for about a week."

Mitch scooped up the pup and let her lick her hands and face for a second or two. She seemed disinclined to biting. Her teeth looked razor sharp but healthy.

"You're so cute!"

"She is, isn't she. What are you going to name her?"

"I'm sure she already has a name if she's from a breeder." "Oh sure, but what are you going to call her. I mean, if you use her real name, dinner will be cold by the time you get it out!"

"How about Doozie?"

"Doozie?"

"She looks like a real Doozie to me."

"She sure does."

"I'm sure the staff is overjoyed at this turn of events."

"We had a talk. Things will work out, but you know, you do have property."

"I could build a fence at The Ranch, couldn't I. She could go out there and run a lot, but she can't stay there at night. Alone."

"We will work something out. This place has a backyard, too."

"And a bed."

"And a cage!"

"Please, I've had it up to here with cages today. Don't make me think about it."

"Okay, how about a nice, luxurious doggie bed."

"I'll think about it."

By now, Doozie had wrestled free and was sniffing at the door.

"I also bought a leash."

"Oh, good. Let's go for a walk. Prison has atrophied my muscles."

"Heaven forbid you'd ever have to serve real time."

"Heaven forbid."

They put the leash on Doozie and went for a long walk. The summer was becoming intense in its heat, and that alone worked its way through Mitch's muscles. It had always been true that while Mitch had the legs, Rebecca had the arms and shoulders. They were a study in contrast even though they were both female. It was a match made in heaven. Mitch could do squats, Rebecca could open the pickle jar. They had all the bases covered.

The next morning, Mitch took Doozie out for a very early walk and then, reluctantly, left her in the cage while she went to work. That would change soon. She would call the fence people today, this morning. She breezed into work, determined to get things done early so that she could make that call. Not even Just Joe was here yet.

With the place to herself, Mitch checked the inventory and then set about to pay the bills. She heard the door open about ten minutes later. It must be Joe. She looked up. Whoever they were, there was two of them.

"Ms. Tanner?" said the taller one.

Why was it that the taller one always speaks first?

"Yes," Mitch said, sensing that this wasn't just another pair of confused customers who couldn't read the "closed" sign on the door.

"We're with the Liquor Licensing Authority."

With that, they both simultaneously pulled out some sort of flashy badge. They must practice this, like synchronized swimming.

"Okay."

"I'm afraid we're going to have to shut you down."

The news wasn't a complete surprise to her. In fact, it made perfect sense. She had felt early on in the deal that Marge had done something to speed up the process. Now, if it were true, it would come to light. Did someone have a reason to start nosing through records? Let's see if she could get it on one guess. How about the judge in Pam's hearing. He would have some pull somewhere. His fingerprints were all over this.

"Did you hear what I said?" Mr. Tall asked.

Mitch nodded. He seemed puzzled. It must have been that big smile that was spreading across Mitch's face. She didn't look unhappy. Most people look unhappy when you close up their business. Why didn't she look unhappy? This guy was most disappointed. Mitch stood up and took Mr. Short's face in her hands and gave him a big kiss. When she turned her attention to Mr. Tall, he held his hands up to block her. "I'm a married man!" he objected.

"Whatever. So, now what happens?"

"You'll need to leave the premises."

"And you get to inform the employees that they are losing their jobs?" Mitch asked.

"There will be an investigation. Of course, you'll want to call your lawyer."

"What should I call him?" Mitch started to giggle.

They both didn't get it. Mitch didn't give a damn. She hadn't done anything wrong. She knew better. If a bribe had been paid, Marge had done it without knowledge of Mitch. Of course, she could still end up in jail, peeing her pants again. But at least this time, there had to be due process. The judge who had secretly prompted this investigation couldn't abuse his Napoleon-like power everywhere. There had to actually be evidence. And if Marge was guilty, they could gather up her ashes and throw them in jail. Mitch checked to be sure she had her wallet in her pocket and came across the keys in her other.

"You'll want my key, won't you?"

"Yes, Ma'am."

Fine. Now, she was Ma'am.

Mitch turned it over and then walked out the back door. The sun was up, portending another hot day. She stretched long and slow. God, it felt good to be out here in the parking lot. She got in the car and drove back to the mansion to see if anything was new there. Doozie was asleep. She woke up when Mitch peeked in, so Mitch took her, cage and all, over to The Ranch. From there, she called a few fence companies until she found one who understood the needs of a beagle. They could come out today and give an estimate. Perfect.

Next, Mitch called Rebecca at work. Surprise of surprises, she wasn't in a meeting. "What's new?" Rebecca asked as she shuffled papers. "I just thought I'd tell you I'm at The Ranch and in bed with a cute little female with auburn hair."

"Sacking out with Doozie? Why aren't you at work? I thought that's where you were headed this morning?"

"I was. I did. I got tossed out." It sounded like Latin conjugation run amok.

"What are you talking about? I have a meeting in ten minutes." "The boys with the badges showed up. I'm suspended or something."

"Did you break the law?"

"Not that I'm aware of."

"Was there a problem with the change of ownership?"

"I think this is just a continuation of the deal yesterday. Revenge."

"If that's true, I'll find out about it."

"But then again, it may have been something that Marge did that wasn't on the level. She was in a hurry, remember. She may have paid a bribe."

"Did you ever see anything like that?"

"No."

"So, you're in the clear?"

"You're asking me. I'm not a lawyer."

"Do you have one?"

"Not really."

"Let's talk about this later. Don't say anything to anybody until we've talked again."

"Okay. In the meantime, Doozie and I are getting a fence."

"I hope you'll be very happy!"

"I love you, too."

"You never got me a fence."

"I'll make it up to you."

Mitch hung up the phone, and about ten seconds later it rang. It was Just Joe. He was locked out as well.

"Joe, see who you can gather up and then come over to The Ranch. We'll have something to eat and make a plan."

By noon, The Ranch was full. Between Joe, Sandy, Vickie, and all the various waitstaff, there was standing room only. Mitch saw this as the only downside to the closing of the U. She would secretly be happy if it never re-opened. But these folks needed a paycheck. They set about to work on plans for future employment. By afternoon, when the fence builder arrived, half of the staff were out on job interviews. The other half had gone home to work on their resumes. Mitch walked around with the fence engineer, who took into account the vastness of the property and the breed of dog. Mitch wanted more than a 'run'. She wanted a blissful 'wander'. A 'sniff around until you flopped down for a nap' opportunity for Doozie. Of course, it could be done, but in stages. They could enclose a small area quickly so she could be let out for necessities and a little frolic, and then they could work on expanding the area as she grew. It would be expensive, but it was for a good cause. Mitch signed the contract and then packed up Doozie for their trip back to the mansion. On the way, they talked. Well, Mitch talked and Doozie listened. Politely. "Rebecca's put out because you're getting a fence and she isn't." Doozie yawned her agreement.

"Sounds like a good time for something chocolate, doesn't it?" Doozie was snoring softly by now, her paws working even in her sleep. Talking to Doozie kept Mitch from worrying about Lisa. It worked for about a minute. If they ever caught up to Lisa, there would be hell to pay. Not even Mitch could get her out of this one. Hell, Mitch couldn't keep herself out of trouble most days anymore, but if one day in jail and one white lie by the governor could keep mother and child together, then it was worth it.

She stopped by a bakery that she had found by accident a couple of weeks ago and came out with chocolate eclairs. It was one of the few places she felt safe leaving Doozie alone in the car since she could watch her every minute. She trusted Doozie, it was everyone else she kept a close eye on. Then, they beat a path back to the mansion in time for dinner.

By now, Rebecca had conferred with counsel over the Lucky U transaction. He required a retainer, of course.

"Make a check out to this guy's law firm and make an appointment with him."

"I don't feel like getting into a long, drawn out legal battle over the bar. I've been looking for a way to get out from under it as it is. Even you've noticed that."

"I know that you've been tired lately."

"But I don't want to end up in jail again. I've had enough of that kind of fun this year."

"I'm sure this guy, his name is Patrick Williams, will do what he can."

"There's one more thing to consider."

"What's that?"

"I remember that I promised a long time ago to let the Advocates for the Homeless in Colorado host the Thanksgiving Dinner for the homeless there. I guess I'll need to make other arrangements?"

"We could always open up the mansion."

"That's a great idea. How many people could we fit in here if we scooted back the furniture?"

"At least as many as the U would have held."

The next day, Mitch touched base with Just Joe. He was looking seriously into relocating to Santa Fe. This would work out great. If Pam, Tracy and Lisa had gone to Mitch's villa for just a night, they had to be already gone. So Joe could borrow Mitch's villa for a few weeks. Mitch could just imagine Bella and Just Joe under the same roof. Two cooks sharing a kitchen. Wasn't that, like, against the law?

Sandy took over where Lisa left off at the Center. She was already great with kids, having one of her own, and the hours worked well into her schedule. Vickie was offered a position at the university where she was studying law. Keep her on the list of friends! Never know when you need a lawyer who owes you a favor.

The rest of the staff had already found new jobs, with the shortage of restaurant help in the city being at epidemic proportions. Mitch still gave them all a one-month bonus check for their inconvenience.

In her spare time, Mitch made an appointment for the physical that Rebecca had discussed. It was about as much fun as poking yourself in the eye with a popsicle stick, but she managed.

Trish decided to put her real estate career on hold for a while and write a book. She came over to The Ranch one afternoon to talk it over with Mitch.

"I'm going to write a book!"

"What's the book going to be about?"

"I want to find people who had relatives in the concentrations camps and write about their stories and lives."

"That sounds very ambitious. And very important."

"But I'm already finding out that there's so much to do. So many places to find information. I wanted to ask your advice."

"*My* advice?"

"You always have such clarity of insight."

"You want to borrow my brand new computer, don't you?" Mitch offered. She had purchased a computer when she realized that she no longer would have access to the old, outdated one at the U.

"Oh please, I have one myself, although this one is nice and fast and brand new."

"You can use it all you want."

"Thanks. But tell me how am I going to be able to find families of the gay people who died in the camps?"

"Oh, I see what you mean. So many of them probably never went on to have children."

"It will be very difficult to find sources."

"Well, there are still brothers and sisters, maybe?"

"And maybe lovers?"

"And maybe lovers!" Mitch repeated. "And you think I have the bright ideas?"

"But how many people are left? I mean, we're talking about people who were in their twenties back in 1945. I would need to find 75 year-old gay survivors."

"Trish, if they're out there, my bet is that you will find them."

"Someone had better find them fast. We're running out of time."

"We'll start an Internet search tomorrow."

"Thanks. Why not today?"

"I have plans with the two women in my life."

"Two women?"

"Yeah, Rebecca and Doozie."

Doozie and Mitch held a private celebration in honor of their new fence. Okay, so they invited Rebecca. It was Doozie's idea. There was champagne and hot dogs, and Mitch and Rebecca ate well, too! No, really, Doozie shared nicely. Mitch would've probably sold The Ranch by now if it wasn't for Doozie. Having Lisa here for a while and then gone again would have made the place so incredibly full of memories that Mitch wouldn't have stayed under normal circumstances. But there was Doozie and her fence to consider. And the faint scent of shampoo. It was as if even the walls of the house had wanted to be near Lisa and absorbed what little they could of her. Right after Lisa left town, Mitch had done what she considered a fairly thorough search of the premises. Fearing, perhaps, that the custody police would swoop down, she had checked the drawers and closets for forgotten items or clues. Lisa had packed completely. Nothing was left to bag and tag. It never had come to that. Pam's husband had only wanted custody as long as it was easy. He didn't have the budget or inclination to fight the flight. At least Pam and Lisa had guessed correctly on that point.

But leave it to the nose on feet to find a treasure. Mitch and Rebecca were into their second bottle of champagne in the fenced in patio when Doozie pranced outside with a prize. It looked like an envelope, and smelled like Lisa.

"Come here, Doozie, what have you got?"
Doozie wasn't about to give this one up. It was hers. She held it softly in her teeth and shook her head from side to side.
"Come on, girl. I'll trade you."
Doozie sat with her prize, awaiting terms.
"I'll give you a dog biscuit?"
Oh, gee, like we don't have enough of those in the diet, Doozie communicated with another shake of her head and a renewed grip on the envelope.
"How about a slipper?"
Depends on the color. Doozie was holding out for something fashionable. Mitch had a box of slippers to choose from. She had picked up about ten pairs at the store one day, trying to introduce Doozie to as many bad habits as possible.
"If that dog-" Rebecca began in earnest.
"She *has* a name," Mitch interrupted.
"If Doozie ever chews up one of my slippers, you are in big trouble!"
"Why would she ever chew up one of your slippers when she could have *this*!"
With that, Mitch pulled out a big, fluffy purple slipper bootie that looked like a stupid dinosaur. Doozie wasn't having any of it. Purple dinosaurs, harumph! Mitch checked the other inventory.
"Here we go. How about a blue doggie slipper?"
This didn't go over so well either. Maybe Doozie had a sensitivity about chewing slippers that looked like her long lost uncle.

255

"Picky dog, if you ask me," Rebecca remarked, with mock snootiness.
"Did you hear what she called you, Doozie!"
"I called her picky."
"You called her *dog!*"
"Oh geez!"
"Okay, let's see what else I have in the slipper box. Here's one just like what Aunt Rebecca wears at the mansion!"
Doozie immediately dropped the envelope and waggled her tail. Doozie got the slipper. Mitch got the letter. Rebecca got the bright idea to lock up all her slippers the minute she got back home. Mitch sat for a moment with the envelope in her hand. Part of her wanted to throw it out now. The other part of her had to know for sure. She tore open the envelope like she was at the Academy Awards and it was "Best Picture".

The letter began, "Dear Mitch and Mary and Rebecca" and then a generic "and everybody else" was added like the note had been written hastily.

I just want you to know how much I appreciate all your help. I'm gone by now, as you know. I had to leave this where you would find it one day. I did what you said and it feels good. Maybe not lawful. Maybe not right. Maybe not ethical. But it was a good thing. I hope I didn't get anybody in trouble. From time to time I will stay in contact. Keep an eye out.

The letter was unsigned.

Mitch knew she couldn't give it back to Doozie and risk its eventual discovery. Not that it would have survived a bath in slobber and still be readable, but still, it was just not a chance Mitch was willing to take. After showing it to Rebecca and allowing her one last read through, Mitch took it into the house and burned it in the fireplace.

"You're going to miss her, aren't you?" Rebecca said from behind Mitch.
"I used to think I'd miss her like a case of the chicken pox. Now, I know differently."

"You never forget your first."

"Maybe, but my second is the best thing that ever happened to me."
Mitch pulled Rebecca into her arms.

"I need to talk to you about something."

"Serious?"

"Yeah, kinda."

They sat together on the couch. Rebecca waited with her heart in her throat.

"I went to the doctor."

"I remember you mentioned it."

"And I'm fine, so stop looking at me like you're going to need to pick out funeral dirges and pallbearers!"

Rebecca exhaled. God, what a nut she lived with, she thought to herself!

"But there was a downside to the news."

"What's wrong?"

"Nothing's wrong, per se, but the doctor advised against having a baby. Something about my physical build. She thought it could be a difficult pregnancy. And of course, you never get a guarantee with these things anyway."

"I see."

"Yeah. I didn't know whether you'd be relieved or...whatever."

"We could adopt."

"We could, but that has an awful lot of legal complications." "There are a lot of kids in the world who need a lot of love. If this is something that you want to think about, I'm right there with you. If you think about it, there would have been an awful lot of legal complications even if you carried the baby yourself."

"You never cease to amaze me."

"Thank you. But, do me one favor."

"Sure. What."

"I remember asking for a few months-worth of consideration about this. Let's still do that before we jump headlong into the adoption mode."

"That's more than fair. I'll agree to that and anything else that would make you feel good about the decision."

"Okay. I mean, we already have the famous slipper-eating Doozie. Let's see how we do raising a puppy together."

Mitch laughed. "If I didn't know better, I'd think you were jealous of the dog."

"Indeed! Did you hear what she called you?" Rebecca directed the comment toward Doozie. "She called you a dog! Come here, Doozie."

Doozie, upon hearing her name, jumped up on the couch with her new slipper toy and snuggled between them.

Lucky her.

LIZZIE

A Life Lived

Samantha
McKeating